'A rich, gut-punch of a crime thriller that delivers a confronting examination of maternal love and the expectations that weigh so heavily on women, even in their most unthinkably dark moments. In both pace and prose, *Breaking* is a hugely satisfying debut.' Ashley Audrain, *Sunday Times* bestselling author of *The Push*

'Amanda Cassidy captures a mother's guilt perfectly. A compelling, intriguing and thoroughly engaging read. Amanda is a very talented new voice in Irish writing.' Liz Nugent, author of *Our Little Cruelties*

'Expert plotting and great characters. It had me guessing throughout and kept me turning the pages at speed... I really loved the twists and turns!' Patricia Gibney, author of *The Guilty Girl*

'Wonderfully compelling and at times, painfully sharp. This is a beautifully constructed and beguiling debut novel.' Andrea Mara, author of *All Her Fault*

'This had me gripped from the very first page and I whizzed through it in a couple of days. A great debut and definitely an author to watch.' *Prima*

'Outstanding debut... What a brilliant novel.' Sheila Bugler, author of *You Were Always Mine*

'This dark, disturbing story of a child's sudden disappearance from a beach in Florida is a contender for thriller of the year. *Breaking* dazzles from the opening line. Powerful, sharp and moving, with an ending that flabbergasts.' Glenn Meade, author of *Unquiet Ghosts*

'Masterful story-telling, breakneck pacing and compelling characters kept me glued all the way to the explosive final pages. Addictive, unnerving and utterly unmissable.' Sophie White, author of *The Snag List* and *Sunday Independent* columnist

'Amanda Cassidy's debut is utterly brilliant and pacy. A roller-coaster of a read that I guarantee you won't be able to put down.' Sophia Spiers, author of *The Call of Cassandra Rose*

BREAKING

Amanda Cassidy

San Diego, California

CANELO US

Canelo US
An imprint of Printers Row Publishing Group
9717 Pacific Heights Blvd, San Diego, CA 92121
www.canelobooksus.com

Printers Row Publishing Group is a division of Readerlink Distribution
Services, LLC. Canelo US is a registered trademark of Readerlink
Distribution Services, LLC.

This edition originally published in the United Kingdom in 2022 by
Canelo.

Published in partnership with Canelo.

Correspondence regarding the content of this book should be sent to Canelo
US, Editorial Department, at the above address. Author inquiries should be
sent to Canelo, Unit 9, 5th Floor, Cargo Works, 1–2 Hatfields, London SE1
9PG, United Kingdom, www.canelo.co.

Publisher: Peter Norton • Associate Publisher: Ana Parker
Art Director: Charles McStravick
Senior Developmental Editor: April Graham
Editor: Angela Garcia
Production Team: Beno Chan, Julie Greene

Design: Brianna Lewis

Library of Congress Control Number: 2022947664

ISBN: 978-1-6672-0528-1

Printed in India

27 26 25 24 23   1 2 3 4 5

For Eva Valentina, hero of my real story.

To and fro we leap
And chase the frothy bubbles,
While the world is full of troubles
And is anxious in its sleep.
Come away, O human child!
To the waters and the wild
With a faery, hand in hand,
For the world's more full of weeping than you
can understand.

The Stolen Child, William Butler Yeats

Prologue

Sun worshippers unfurl sandy limbs, oblivious to the imminent horror.

Nearby, a child dances in the surf, the way only children do, her sequined sundress moving in the breeze. Around her neck, a gold chain glints in the sunlight. She's thinking of her red fishing net and those curious darting fish she spied from the spindly boardwalk when they arrived on the island.

The heart-stopping scream, when it comes, catches everyone off guard. On the horizon, a speedboat cuts viciously through the waves. Foamy entrails bubble in its wake. Above the beach, a glass-fronted hotel looms. The sharp angles of the Coral Beach Hotel slice through feathery palms.

Two honeymooners sit up simultaneously when they hear the commotion, knocking over half-drunk piña coladas in their haste. Later they'll report seeing a woman walking quietly away with a small child. Towards the rocks, they'll say, remembering the twin shadows they made, long and narrow against the fading light. Past the resort's velvet rope dividers, on the public beach, a group of teens lie on their backs vaping. They've joined their beach towels side by side like a colourful patchwork quilt.

Later, the youngest will describe to an officer with a scruffy notepad, the speedboat that caught his eye. The boat's engine roared to life, he'll say, an ugly sound above the stillness of the day. The spine-tingling wail, when it comes, is heard as far back as the public pathway that snakes up beyond the sand. A teen girl lies on a sarong beside two men who've been admiring her fledgling curves. Headphones in, she wiggles her newly painted toes to the beat. The men, two of them brothers, survey the beach from where they sit. A distraction like this is exactly what they need. At the other end of the smirk-shaped shore, a woman has been sitting alone among the cheap plastic chairs of a scruffy beach bar. Her book closed on the table; her face turned towards the sun. The waiter will tell island police that she'd been crying – that she had six drinks.

Nearly everyone on the beach that day is enchanted by the sea's endless blue beauty. The horizon, muddling the sky with the ocean, creates a confusing fog of blues. There's a sensation of change, a ripple in the air, as if a shadow passes silently overhead. The pulled-silk sky puckers into milky clouds. Waves whip up. Above the hollow boing of beach ball on sand and slosh-slop of waves, comes the mother's scream.

The woman from the bar shouts her child's name over and over so many times it feels theatrical. People turn towards the noise, unsure at first, then afraid. They watch as she runs up and down the beach screaming, her head whipping every which way. Until she trips and falls down, anguished, into the silent sand.

1

Mirren Fitzpatrick

One week before

I'm completely mad, I admit to my therapist. Booking a holiday back to the place Nick and I got married when things are so bad between us, was one of the worst ideas I've had. But she thinks it could set us on a healing path. There are nine minutes remaining on our remote therapy session. Reflective work, she calls it. I've to stand in front of the bedroom mirror and go back to the start.

'What do you see, Mirren?' the therapist asks, solemnly.

Pulling my dark hair back, I let it cascade forward across the soft lines of my face. It swishes comfortingly across my eyelashes. My sharp features stare back at me from the mirror, unrepentant.

Bitch, I mouth.

This will be the first time I say these words out loud. To confess something no mother should ever admit.

'When I look in the mirror, I only see one daughter.' I hesitate. 'The one that shares my face.' I tuck a strand of my hair behind my ear, its darkness emphasising the delicate gold piercings dotted up one lobe.

'Go on, Mirren,' my latest therapist, Judy, coaxes.

Judy coaches me from the speaker on my mobile which lies propped up on top of my chest of drawers, video off. But I can hear the strain in her voice – her words now sodden with the same distaste I feel about what I'm admitting about my own child.

I know it's time to face my deepest shame, even if I haven't had the words until now. I take a deep breath and clarify, more for myself than for the person on the other end of the speaker.

'I favour my biological daughter over my adopted one.' I fiddle with the catch on the thin gold bracelet on my wrist and force myself to finally speak the truth.

'I always have.'

I look at my reflection, noticing gratefully no trace of my mother across my softly ageing face. Outside, past the mirror, it's bright and cold – my favourite Connemara weather. The mix of light and wet softly blurs the landscape around our cottage. I drag myself back to the session and rearrange my face into doctor mode, using the neutral smile I've learnt to give to my small patients at the hospital – the one that belies my heartache at seeing wispy pink heads and tightly stretched skin over bones.

'Alannah is amazing.' I glance sideways as if she might be in the room, attempting to keep my voice as steady as possible. 'But I can't deny there is a tiny fracture in my love for her.'

I hesitate – prepared for the judgement.

'I'm a mother to two girls, but I can't pretend anymore that I don't see a difference in how I treat my daughters. And I don't know how to change that.'

I brush away the tears that begin to trickle down my cheeks.

'But I want to try.'

It's a deeply uncomfortable realisation, one I've spent a long time avoiding. These words don't come easy. Downstairs Nick is clanking plates into the dishwasher. Somewhere nearby, the radio lolls and pitches. Everyday sounds.

I pull the satin kimono tighter around my waist, shivering, and flip an elastic bobbin up and over my hair to hold it in place. Scraggly hairs need plucking under my eyebrows. Judy is talking again, her voice smooth with manufactured sympathy. I imagine her in front of her own mirror at home – trying to get that perfect tone, that sweet spot between pity and concealed horror.

I glance at my phone screen. It's almost time to collect Alannah from ballet. Now a pretty eight-year-old, my youngest daughter is tall for her age; future ballerina, champion eye-roller. She has strawberry-gold hair her big sister calls dirty blonde.

The day I set eyes on her I wanted to love her. But immediately, the protective element, that which a mother *should* feel, was overshadowed.

By grief. But by something else too.

The story of the changeling is ridiculous, but when you had a childhood like mine, everything means something. One bird for sorrow, two for joy, a pinch of salt thrown over your shoulder for luck, count the stars a hundred times if you've lost something. Old wives' tales, superstition, religion – call it what you like. As someone who now works in science, that is hard to reconcile. But the duplicity of our beliefs is an unavoidable part of human nature – the endless conundrum of being two things at once. How ridiculous that as I held our newly adopted baby in my arms all those years ago, I was haunted by a fairy tale which foretold nothing but misfortune – a changeling, swapped by evil, out of malice or revenge.

Facing the full-length mirror of my bedroom, I let my robe slide down and crease into a satin puddle on the carpet. I view my naked body with the usual pang of regret. Only one child escaped alive from that jagged half-smile scar. The miscarriages had represented a rejection of sorts – that somewhere in my core was a misalignment of my cells, a refusal to let a small thing thrive. Alannah was supposed to be my hard fought-for prize. But when I finally placed her in the cot, the one that had been too-long empty, uneasiness descended. Of course, everyone thought my tears were gratitude, the awe of new life. In reality, I was reliving death – her face the reminder of all that could have been. There was no locking-in moment, no love at first sight. I felt overwhelmed, resentful and something else. Disconnected.

The voice from my mobile phone repeats reassurances that what I'm feeling is understandable. But the weight of my ineptitude as a parent is too heavy for platitudes. Because, as I see it, mothers are picture-perfect, angelic. They are not angry mothers, or resentful mothers or sad ones like me. Nobody in the mother and toddler groups chat over coffee about how they sometimes handle their small charges more roughly than they should, or cry for days. Hyper-aware that Alannah and I met as strangers, I'd pressed her to my chest and tried to cut through the grief that bubbled just beneath the surface. I tried so hard.

Through the square of my bedroom window, I see the Clare Hills. They lie like sleeping giants against the water, purple and still. I could throw a stone and it would hit the beach, miles of uninterrupted sand and a slick of blue. We used to laugh about that, Nick and I, our stones-throw beach. I pull on the faded blue underwear I find folded among a pile of fresh laundry on the bed. The material neatly obscures my c-section scar.

The truth is that when I look in the mirror, I can still only see Réa in my face. My flesh-and-blood eldest daughter. I named her *Réaltín* – the Irish for little star. Everyone told us that we looked like twins. As a child, my own father admired that combination of dark hair and blue eyes. 'Mirren's a true Celt,' he'd say proudly in the rare times he was home. My mother was a lot less complimentary with her words – especially after an evening drinking. Having to raise her own two daughters alone was tough for her but being raised by a drinker in rural Ireland made me even tougher. She sharpened my sea-wild edges. Because my childhood has ripples around it, like rocks just below the shallows. That's the reason what I say and what I mean have never really aligned.

I think of Réa, who at sixteen, is deliciously unaffected by the chaos that surrounds me. She is a free spirit like I once was, porcelain-skinned and artistic. I keep her close. I see a familiarity in her – a sameness of self that I enjoy. We are each other's whole world. My last therapist called that narcissism, but I prefer to think of it as just being in awe of my own creation. As a child, back when it was just the two of us, I'd catch her in a corner of our one-bedroom apartment in Dublin city drawing the world around her. That was before I met Nick and he catapulted into our lives.

I glance at the phone.

Three minutes until I have to leave.

Judy's voice floats around me. Réa's face fades in the mirror and I see my own. I'm drained and pale without make-up, my shoulder-length hair emphasises dark pools under my eyes. I surrendered to Botox once I reached my forties. My sister Tara says I do a lot with what I have. But beneath the well-cared for skin and twice-straightened teeth, I know who I really am, and I'm starting to fear for her. They say the apple never falls far from the tree. But they don't tell you that its shadow slowly rots it. Lately, Nick looks at me with a new expression too. Ever since my mother's funeral two weeks ago. I glance quickly over at my handbag with the vodka-filled Lucozade bottle tucked inside. A crutch some call it, but the complicated emotions accompanying my mother's death pushed me back to a place I promised Nick I'd never go. It's also what made me confront the truth about Alannah.

'Alannah entered our lives after a very difficult time,' I tell the therapist instead, not yet ready to dwell on my own childhood. 'I didn't have the capacity to give her all she needed. I'm not sure Nick has ever forgiven me for that. I'm not sure I've ever forgiven her for it either.'

'How so?'

These open-ended questions again. Does she think I don't know what she's doing?

I hear Nick calling up the stairs that I'm going to be late. His resentment has begun bleeding into every aspect of our lives. He's bent so far for me, that he's bound to break.

Two minutes.

I hold up a sundress against my body and smooth the silk across the curve of my midriff, turning slightly so the light from the window catches the mirror. Something flickers. In the corner of the glass frame, a small butterfly trapped against the glass bangs dizzily. I undo the latch and feel the salty whoosh of air in the room. Scooping it to freedom, it flits away, bouncing erratically with the joy of release.

I add the dress to the heaped suitcase that lies open on the bed. It contains a blend of cotton dresses, an oversized sunhat, expensive swimwear. In a week's time, we are going back to the place where we got married a decade ago – the Coral Beach Hotel in Florida. I want everything to be perfect, to try to capture some of that impossible happiness. To remind myself it existed once.

'How does Nick deal with this?' Judy insists.

'Nick still struggles to understand everything that happened,' I try to explain, turning my wedding ring slowly on my finger. 'I don't feel his love as strongly anymore. I don't know if it's me or if his feelings have changed, but there's a distance, and I can't catch up.'

My voice cracks. I clear my throat quickly to hide the true emotion that wells. I need to do better for all of us. My mother's passing showed me that. I need to try harder to love both my daughters the same.

I hear Nick's voice calling me again. I'm properly late.

Stuffing my feet into my black Converse, I grab a soft hoodie dress from the back of the bedroom chair and wriggle it over my head.

Then I'm racing down the stairs, grabbing the car keys off the hall table. The vodka tingles, warm in my belly, as I say goodbye to the therapist. Bye, bye, bye, we take turns saying.

I realise I've run out of time. I've left it too late.

We found Alannah eight years ago.

But then I lost her.

2

Detective Antonio Rolle

Dawn splits the sky in two as Detective Antonio Rolle manoeuvres his Audi up the pristine driveway of the Coral Beach Hotel. Yellow police tape flickers across one side of the resort. The building is at least ten storeys high, with glass balconies reaching over the aquamarine sea. He'd only ever seen this place on TV before, in the background when it hosted some golf tournament. Swanky, his buddy Sam would call it. Flashing his badge at the officer blocking the road, Detective Rolle pulls up beside the neatly trimmed grass and kills the engine. The car may be an old crock, but it was his old crock, and Antonio Rolle refused to give it up in favour of the sensible SUV that came with the job. Being sent here to Kite Island in disgrace was one thing, but he'd damn well drive whatever the hell he wanted.

Frowning, he checks his slicked-back hair in the car door reflection and turns towards the hotel. His wife teases him that with his light Latino colouring and slightly protruding forehead, he looks like a younger Benicio del Toro.

'See… brooding like him too,' she'd laugh when he objected. Rolle didn't tend to spend too much time thinking about his appearance, nor watching movies, but lately he'd noticed a disturbing curve that hung heavily over his belt. He presumed this new arrival was the announcement of mid-life. It didn't stop Alice pinching it and called him a softie. In fact, it was Detective Rolle's mean streak which had landed them here on Kite Island in the first place.

His wife says bedlam usually follows him, but today Antonio Rolle feels as if he's walking right towards it. The hotel entrance, framed with impossibly skinny palm trees and a polished forecourt is guarded by two sleepy-looking uniforms. The air around him smells of freshly turned dirt, piney and new. The beach, Detective Rolle was told, has been sealed off already. Although it's early, local reporters gather by the steps, alerted initially by the missing child activation that had been sent to phones within the surrounding area. Adjusting earpieces, a TV crew gears up for a live broadcast.

Jesus, this is going to be huge. And it's only sixteen hours since the child vanished.

A tourist disappearing from a high-end resort is news editors' gold – the fact that the tourist is a child makes it an even bigger story. The child of an internationally renowned cancer doctor gives added weight. But Rolle knows that missing child cases are never glory-makers. Dead kids haunt you in a way no other part of the job did. He could deal with shot-up skank-heads every day of the week and still go home and eat a full dinner. But unless this kid is hiding from its parents under a bed somewhere, he knows it isn't going to be pretty.

Inappropriately jazzy music plays as the detective enters the reception area. The hotel is open for remaining guests, despite everything. According to its customer relations person, Candy, whom he'd spoken to on the phone that morning, they are trying to 'contain the situation'. Whatever that meant.

Rolle's leather shoes gently thwack as he crosses the glossy-floored reception to the elevator. LED candles flicker on mirrored display tables. Coral Beach was the talk of the island when it rose majestically from the sands fifteen years ago. Developed by a chain of US resorts, there were two Coral Beach Hotels in his hometown Miami, an hour's boat-ride away. American golfers flock to Kite Island for its Nick Faldo-designed golf courses, but it's popular internationally too – for its snorkelling excursions and Keys day trips. A haunt of the well-known and the powerful who come here to do whatever else rich people do, he supposes.

With a quick flick of his wrist, Detective Rolle flashes his badge to an officer he doesn't recognise. Lovell's already upstairs. He's been up all night dealing with the family since the call first came in. The lift pings to announce the second floor and Rolle steps out onto the low-ceilinged corridor towards the conference room which has been designated search HQ. Rolle wonders if the hotel is in any way prepared for the spotlight that is hurtling towards them. Most aren't. He'd learnt that on the last case, before he was booted out of Miami; the warped attraction people have for tragedy. Can't get enough of it. Misfortune porn they call it, back at the station.

The music has stopped by the time he enters the large, air-conditioned room. A boardroom-style table with twenty or so chairs takes up most of the room which overlooks the sea. His eye is immediately drawn towards the view – a dizzyingly perfect setting belying the horror he knows lies below. A lone computer sits in the corner next to a printer and phone, relics of a time before Wi-Fi. A pile of paperwork is spread out across the window-end of the table, and more than a few coffee cups lie scattered. Spotting Rolle, Lovell Logan finishes his call and strides towards him, slipping his phone into the breast pocket of his suit.

There's a pause while they both weigh up what this new switch in dynamics is going to look like. Everyone knows it should have been Antonio Rolle who got the promotion. If the Miami incident hadn't happened. Open and shut.

'Didn't get to say it before, congratulations, Lieutenant.' Rolle extends his hand and pulls Logan towards him with a semi-violent handshake.

'I guess this is my baptism of fire,' Logan responds, in the distinctive nasal voice the guys back at the station loved to mimic. Rolle always thought Lovell Logan looked more like a movie star than a police detective. His hair was cut short, and he typically wore a tie. His aviator glasses gave him the appearance of a man much younger than forty-five. Not pretty, but confident, like his grandfather who'd moved here from Zimbabwe forty years before, always told him to be. Lovell Logan was universally disliked by colleagues. But even more so now that he'd been promoted. Rolle worked with him a few times back in Miami before they'd both been banished to Kite Island. Logan was here to claw his way up, that part was obvious. By being a big dumb fish in a small pond – in Rolle's opinion. All style over substance. But then again, Lovell Logan rolled with the high-fliers around these parts. There were rumours his hot-shot daddy got him his first gig. Not surprising that he'd made it this far. Down these parts, it's all about who you know. Rolle also knew that Lovell needed a few more easy wins to climb the greasy ladder left out by his father. Rolle's own transfer here to Kite Island from Miami was more of an enforced penance.

When big cases like this cropped up, it was all hands on deck. But Rolle didn't really do teamwork. Not now, anyway.

'Sorry to hear about your father,' Rolle scrambles, keen to fill the silence.

Rolle knew all about Logan's father, Assistant Chief Floyd Logan from the Criminal Investigations Division of Miami Police Department. A formidable man – unpleasant. One to be avoided at all costs. Right now, he was holed up in Miami General after a stroke. Rolle figured you couldn't have a father like Floyd Logan and not have Daddy issues. But still, he understood the pull of fathers.

Lovell Logan nods curtly.

Surveying the weather from the window, Rolle blows out his cheeks slowly.

'Not great for it, is it?'

'It's made the search a lot harder. Chopper had to come down.'

Rolle slumps into the nearest boardroom chair and pulls a page towards him. He's exhausted already and the day is just starting. The thing with Logan is that he wears you out simply by his need to act smarter than everyone else.

'You sure this kid didn't just run off somewhere to scare the parents?' That'd give that frenzied mob down there something to report, thinks Rolle.

Logan's features tense. For the first time this morning, he seems sincere.

'Unlikely.'

The air in the room feels colder suddenly. They both know how this is bound to end.

But Rolle never liked to underestimate the power of hope. That and good police work.

The pressure from above to find a swift resolution – come what may – suited Rolle. 'Like a pit-bull when it comes to an investigation,' he heard Alice say about him once to someone. 'He can't let anything go.'

An exhausted Logan runs a hand over his face.

'The mother's been drinking. The husband said she was in a beach bar a few minutes' walk from the resort when the kid disappeared. We have witnesses confirming she was alone and polished off six drinks while she was there.'

'The fucking press will love this,' Rolle mutters, more to himself than his new superior.

'Eight-year-old kid wandering off while its mother is off downing shots.' Logan's tone is surprisingly vehement, but Rolle's instinct is to hold off on any judgement and see where the evidence takes them instead. He surveys the incident report: NCIC entry done, BOLO issued. No immediate evidence of any concerning medical or mental status, no history of running away or school issues, according to the family. But they'd eek that out. There's a full description of the kid, long blonde hair, blue eyes, slight, 4 ft 3 inches. The picture is a hastily printed out image from a phone of the child grinning by a pool. He presumes better ones are in circulation already.

Logan checks an update from his phone.

'Coastguard has nothing within fifteen miles of here in both directions yet. Roads and ports are closed, and we've requested assistance from Miami. We're in touch with the mayor's office but we don't have enough evidence to push an Amber Alert.'

Rolle gets up to look out the window. The criteria for alerting the public to a missing child were strict – otherwise they risked desensitising the most serious of cases. They couldn't prove the child was in imminent danger. Not yet anyway. He can see activity going on below – cars and volunteers milling around, not fast enough for his liking. He sees a lone figure standing on the beach. The mother, perhaps. That's where he'd be – searching the waves.

'George has the witness statements from those on the beach at the time.' Logan interrupts his thoughts. 'Not much to go on. One saw a boat moving suspiciously close to the shore.'

'Go on.'

'A guest from the hotel says she saw a woman walking away with a young girl.'

Rolle turns sharply to look at Logan.

'Surveillance cameras?'

'George is working on it.'

Rolle rolls his eyes.

'I'll speak to those witnesses myself too if you don't mind.'

Logan looks up, annoyed.

'I've spoken to most already.'

'No harm doubling up.'

Rolle holds eye contact for a moment, until Logan looks down at his files again, shaking his head slightly.

'We're searching the immediate area, and the public beach has been cordoned off, as has the private Coral Beach area, but the manager is keen to wrap this up and open for business. She's worried about the other guests.'

Rolle mutters something about priorities as Logan continues.

'We've a few looking into the family. You know she's adopted. The child?'

Rolle shrugs. So what? It was usual for the parents to be put under the spotlight. To uncover any red flags; financial issues, drug problems, neglect, abuse – the litany of potential horrors he came across too many times in this job.

Turns out the people you love don't always have your best interests at heart. He notes that Candy from the hotel has been named as the victim advocate; the front-facing coordinator on behalf of the Fitzpatrick family. Logan hands Rolle another page – one with a list of names and addresses.

'We asked a few who were on the beach to hang around for another day, even those who planned to leave,' he explains, keeping his eyes on the page. 'Okay?'

Rolle nods, but in his experience, the cameras are their best bet to see what really went on.

'We'll need any pertinent surveillance footage. When will George have it?'

Logan hesitates.

'Candy says there's only one camera that's pointed towards the beach. I don't believe they've found anything yet.'

'Oh, so they've found nothing, have they?' Rolle repeats, trying to hide his annoyance. An uncomfortable moment of silence lingers, dense like fog. He remembers his father's advice when he started in his first job – upwards management, he told him. You may be someone's employee but that doesn't mean you don't have the power to change things from beneath. What Pops never explained was the trouble you get in when that gets clocked.

Logan speaks again. His voice cooler now than before.

'Do you have a problem with this, Detective?'

He sounds like the only kid in a fight with a stick – overly confident that he has the upper hand. Rolle grunts a no and runs his hands through his hair.

'Like I said,' Logan says sharply. 'George took statements and a couple of contact details.'

He gestures to the pages.

'We'll go over any CCTV that's available. But we told most of those on the beach yesterday that they were free to go. It's not like we could keep everyone there indefinitely.' He was annoyed. Good, Rolle thinks. It might light a fire under that neatly ironed butt of his. Rolle sits into the leather conference chair and spins as he thinks. From somewhere nearby comes the sound of a vacuum cleaner. As well as the foot and vehicle search, the canine unit has been notified, and once that wind calms, they'll get the drones up too.

'We need a list of the hotel staff. Look into every employee. Think George can handle that?'

Logan's phone buzzes. Rolle picks up Logan's glasses from where they are lying on the table and tries them on. Prescription. The world blurs.

Logan listens to the call, nodding every now and then. 'Uh huh. Yeah, okay.'

Then, sliding his finger across the screen, he finally looks up. He snatches his glasses out of Rolle's hands.

'They've found tyre marks by the cove next to Wilkes Beach,' he says slowly, considering this new information.

'The problem is that there's no vehicular access – no road at all that side,' he tells Rolle.

Logan stacks the early witness statements into a thick plastic folder and snaps the elastic across it.

If the poor kid was swept out, we'll find her soon enough, Rolle thinks suddenly, looking beyond the windows into the distant blue. He watches as the lone figure below on Wilkes Beach walks slowly towards the shore. Dr Mirren Fitzpatrick, he imagines. Alannah's mother.

But they aren't there yet. Far from it.

Besides, if there's one thing Rolle abhors, it's laziness. There's a lot of it going around these parts. Maybe it isn't their fault, maybe none of them have ever been shown how to investigate a case properly. In Rolle's experience anything's possible. You had to walk into a case knowing that. You had to look, to really see, what was going on, because sometimes it was hiding in plain sight. A child out there alone is a whole different priority – one that Rolle's afraid newly appointed Lieutenant Lovell Logan doesn't seem to share.

'You coming?' They make their way out of the conference room and take the lift in silence.

A press conference is necessary, Rolle guesses, to take the pressure off a little. He's sure any CCTV will yield something. Or the witnesses. Kids don't just vanish into thin air in the middle of a crowded beach without anybody seeing a thing. That's why he'll have to push the mother for more information. They have to move fast.

A golf buggy is waiting, motor running, to take them down the steep path towards the main beach. The driver, in pristine whites, turns the wheels away from the hotel, pointing the buggy towards the hotel's beach club – the area where the child was last seen. As they jolt over the pebble pathway, Rolle continues to replay Lovell Logan's words about the tyre tracks in the sand. There's something familiar about all of it. The boat, the tracks, a child vanished. A tiny alarm suddenly sounds in Antonio Rolle's head. He knows he won't be able to let it go. He can never let things go.

He remembers reading about a different investigation on the island – one just a few weeks before he first arrived here with his messed-up head. A mother, local woman, pleading with officers to find her twelve-year-old daughter. One less fatherless brat, he heard one of the guys at the station say dismissively when Rolle asked about the case. 'Ran off to join some strip joint in Miami most likely.' The officer smirked, slapping Rolle on the back. 'You'll get to know what really goes on around here.' He'd winked. Rolle had shrugged him off, disgusted. She was just a kid. But why hadn't *he* done anything about it at the time? So much for his vow after Miami to never let another child down. Rolle screws up his face to help him remember the local girl's name. Mariah, that's what her mother said she was called. Like the singer.

Funny how that kind of missing persons case would never have interested the local press and certainty not international media. As far as many around here were concerned, it simply didn't matter. Who makes up the rules, Rolle wonders. Who decides which crimes to solve just because of the status of the parents, or the nationality, or the circumstances? Why are some babies considered more precious than others? He realises too that that child's mother lived close to this side of the island. Despite the warm morning breeze whipping his hair, Antonio Rolle shivers. The buggy's wheels crunch onto the sand, announcing their arrival.

3

Mirren

The sickening jolt plays on a loop as I swallow hot coffee somebody's placed into my hands. It tastes bitter and scalds my throat, but I welcome the pain. My eyes sweep the horizon as strange voices continue to swarm. Somebody pulls my cardigan up around me. It's chilly sitting at the hotel's deserted beach club in the dawn breeze. There are no other guests this early – just a handful of staff from the hotel, police officers and the woman from the hotel, Candy, whose voice grates. With the first shards of daylight, I see the length of beach has been cordoned off with yellow police tape. Volunteers have gathered again to help search for Alannah. I spot the Dutch waiter from the bar yesterday among them. The wind caught everyone off guard, he told me, as we slid over the rocks late last night with torches, searching for any sign of my daughter. Twenty-four hours ago, me, Nick and the girls were waking up to another glorious breakfast overlooking the bay. Twenty-four hours ago, I had no idea about what would lead me to that tiny beach bar. The pang of guilt bends me double. I know that this is my penance – for not loving her enough.

People stare, uncomfortable perhaps, by my display of emotion. I get up and move away from them, unable to stay still for more than a few seconds at a time.

Wilkes Beach is dismal this time of the morning – like it's been turned inside out. Far from the throbbing blue beauty that dazzled yesterday. The water is murky-grey against the half-light and the sand soggy underfoot. I glance down and realise I'm not wearing shoes. My thoughts are muddled – the lack of sleep catching up on me. I try not to think of Réa's white face, back in the room with Nick, crying hysterically.

An officer beckons me towards the marine-themed beach club of the Coral Beach resort, where the chairbacks are woven to look like fishing nets and ropes hang from the walls. Light pink shells and plastic starfish are dotted along them, strangled by their raggedy edges. Beside one gnarled lump is a framed picture of different types of boat knots. I recognise the clove hitch – one my father taught me as a child, a lifetime ago. 'Nothing can escape it,' I remember him telling me, his hands salt-rough as he looped and stretched the chords, capturing my hand teasingly inside. I remember the coil of rope tight against skin and shiver. A lone lobster sits miserably in a tank, awaiting its saucepan fate. We sit at a table, and the officer folds his lips over his teeth as he asks the same questions his colleague asked just minutes before.

'Yes,' I repeat, feeling nauseous. 'Around four p.m. yesterday is the last time I saw her. She was playing on the sand. Yes, near her sister… I was just a few metres away.' I gulp. 'Yes, I was at one of the local beach bars. Over there.' I gesture towards the public beach side of the Coral Beach Hotel.

I have nothing else to say to those eyes that seem reluctant to ask the biggest question of all: *what kind of mother goes drinking and leaves her kid alone unsupervised?*

I answer a few more of his questions, but probably sensing he'll get no further, he finally leaves me be. The lines of reality jump and blur while those saviour sips of alcohol slowly saturate. Sunbeds scatter like empty stretchers as I leave the resort beach club and move closer to the shore. The seagulls screech manically overhead. If there is a hell, this is it, I decide, stealing a glance back at the hotel before I sip from the small plastic bottle in my hand – my coffee now abandoned. Police officers, around five of them, walk its length, as far as the black rocks at the other end. Their eyes are cast downwards towards the fine grains. From here they look like sleepwalkers. It's the fourth time they've done this sweep, and it's only just getting light. Dogs bark in the distance. They've a team searching the hotel, and all the areas that surround it. I hear Alannah's name being called over and over and wonder for a moment if it's just in my head.

Candy from the hotel appears next to me and grips my shoulder. She is wearing too much perfume and it catches in my throat, scratchy and floral. In the distance, the silvery outline of the Coast Guard boat churns against the white-tipped waves. I strain my eyes, searching the wild vastness for any sign of life. A few hours ago, the wind forced the search helicopter down. I could hear its desperate whir most of the night from the hotel room where I clawed and screamed and finally collapsed onto the neatly made bed. I lay in the dark, drawing short, panicky breaths as the moon inched her way across the sky. I kept Alannah's security blanket pushed tightly into the creases of my neck – its milky smell mingling with my warm vodka breath.

The scene from the day before plays over again in my head. Flashes of moments, like a dizzying mosaic; the brutality of that fight with Nick, the things he said.

Then, marching to the beach with the girls, trying to hide my fury and hurt. I picture Alannah asking if she could use her new net to catch fish. Me, refusing – too consumed with my own private devastation.

'Keep an eye on her,' I remember saying distractedly to Réa, as I eyed the scruffy beach bar sign just outside the hotel resort. 'Don't let her into the water.'

'Will you swim with me, Mummy?'

Alannah's tiny pleading voice followed me as I walked away from her. An irritation. I still hear it now floating on the breeze, just past my shoulder. Her last words to me. And mine snapping back.

'Just leave me alone for a bit, would you?'

I close my eyes and suddenly picture her terrified face under water, eyes wide in surprise and something else… horror. I shake my head violently to remove the image and Candy grips me tighter.

'They'll find her, honey. Don't you worry,' she croons. But nobody understands; I did this.

Leaning forward, I vomit violently. Wet rivulets of sand splatter back against my bare toes. 'Oh,' she says, trying to hide her disgust. 'Let me just…' She strides quickly away, and I drag the back of my hand across my lips. I tuck my bleeding and dirty feet beneath me and sit heavily down.

Another piece of the day before crashes back to me. I knew I needed a drink – to think about that conversation with Nick. I see in my mind's eye the red plastic chair, a drink in front of me. The slope of the beach bar where the shoreline's slightly dipped, Alannah's blonde hair bobbing up and down. She's just a few metres away. Réa is sunbathing nearby.

Another drink.

One more.

Another.

Same again, please.

Then secret sips.

I was trying to rewrite my future when I eventually felt the jolt, the one I can't escape from now – that sudden, inescapable importance – standing up to catch a glimpse of her. And then seeing just empty beach in the space where Alannah had been playing. The red chair tipped over behind me. Straight lines of sand and sea replaced the childish curl of her. Then my hand to my throat as if trying to stop the scream that will eventually haunt everyone on Wilkes Beach.

I force myself to remember those torturous moments; Réa's newly painted toes tapping, her face to the sky as I loomed over her demanding, then begging. Where is she? Where is Alannah? I can still feel the scrunch of coral fragments against the soles of my feet as I raced up and down, shouting her name, banging open public toilet cubicles that dotted this stretch of beach. I pictured her sitting in one, visualising a happier truth – that she had just disappeared momentarily. I imagined our reunion as I started screaming for help. I'd be angry with her, of course, then grateful. A tight hug and an ice cream. We'd be laughing about it by dinner. This couldn't be happening. Not to me. Not to her.

But there was Réa's desperate face trapped in my endless loop. Her frightened eyes. The realisation that Alannah was gone. On her watch.

No, worse. On my watch.

Despite my panic, I will never forget that change in Réa's sweet face. I see again and again the slow motion of my words coming out of my mouth and flowing through the air, hitting her brain, her ears, both our hearts – a dawning of a whole new reality.

The Before and The After, right there in a sinew of a second on my teenage daughter's face. Her headphones fall softly into the sand as she jumps up to face me.

-

Deeper voices, probably volunteers, approach behind me, interrupting my jagged thoughts. I breathe out to try and stop the shaking, but it comes out as a series of gasps. Their voices float over on the wind before they do, and I focus on not falling off the side of the world. Nick is with them. Pale and angry, he's leading two official-looking men towards me, and he is talking loudly. I rearrange my face into what a grieving mother should look like and then wonder why it matters.

The well-built man with stern eyes and slicked-back hair puts out his hand to help me stand. 'Dr Fitzpatrick,' he says respectfully, and I tell him please call me Mirren.

'I'm Detective Antonio Rolle. And this is Lieutenant Lovell Logan.'

I brush the sand off my black leggings, more to feel the world around me than anything else. I nod a muted greeting but avoid their gaze. I want to stay stuck inside my thoughts, because as long as I don't know anything, Alannah is safe in my mind. I float back into my head and change the ending. I decide to catch fish with Alannah instead of going to the bar. I'm looking at these people before me who are here to help – but I'm not on the beach anymore. I'm swimming through liquid sky pointing out clownfish, a tiny hand held tight in my own.

The intimidation of men leads me back towards the Coral Beach club. Trying to escape the other stranger's hand on my lower back, I squirm away and sit heavily into one of the wicker lounge chairs. Candy appears with tissues and a glass of water. Her lipstick looks freshly applied.

The men stand around me, vibrating with the need for action. Even though I'm busy catching fish in my head, I notice that the one dressed in a cream-coloured suit, seems to look down on me. It's the way he stands, an awkward shift of his feet. Someone should tell him to remove his sunglasses, I think absently. It's obvious he's already preparing to find a small blue body under the waves. But I'm just suspended in time. I'm a fish swimming under the silvery sun with my little mermaid. The world stopped at four p.m. yesterday. I'll stay back there.

If I wasn't occupied finding shells with Alannah on the other side of this moment, I'd question why this suited man is making me feel like I'm wasting his time. Then, the other person, the man who'd pulled me up from the ground, Antonio Rolle, opens his mouth to speak. Somehow his words pierce my thoughts. He brings me back. His lightly accented voice cuts through my dreams like glass cuts through skin, commanding and smooth. What he says is the blood-let – it is the deliciously awful moment that the red liquid escapes onto skin, streaking it crimson. His words introduce a different ending – one that is horrible and hopeful all at once. It's a disgusting possibility that I'd not even considered until now: that our daughter wasn't just lost, that there was a chance she'd been taken from us. And all my glass thoughts shatter, the frightened fish of my dreams bolt, and those warm fingers entwined neatly around mine slip away.

4

Mirren

The Past

Our wedding on Kite Island was joy-filled and carefree. We ate salty-sweet
lobster and drank cocktails with elaborate fruit displays at the rooftop reception
at the Coral Beach Hotel. We spoke about our future – of all the happiness that
lay ahead. It was a small party of eight, with a maid of honour in a small white
dress. Réa loved it. I have a photo of that day on my bedside locker at home in
our cottage in Galway – a silver-framed image of Nick and I laughing. My head
is thrown back and he is looking at me admiringly. In front of us is a wedding
cake of white icing with frangipanis trailing up the sides. If only I could tell that
smiling girl what would happen. I'd warn her of the complications weaving their
way towards her as she bit into cake, destroying all the carefully made flowers I
found out were weeds.

A few years later, we marked another precious day. We'd received the call
to say that we had been successful in our journey towards adopting a child.
We wanted to mark the occasion with something equally precious. We bought
Alannah's gold chain in the same jewellery shop in Galway that we'd picked
our rings. Nick, Réa and I spent an hour looking at displays of bracelets and
rings we hoped to give this child someday. Of course, Réa begged for one too but
we were firm. This was about the new baby. I was so torn, even back then. As
far as I was concerned, my babies grew inside me and then stopped. They were
our stars in the sky and I mourned the life they never had. I wanted a child,
yes, but I wanted *my* child.

We picked out the perfect gold chain, with a heart dangling at its centre. The
salesperson suggested engraving it. Nick and I looked at each other, remembering

the name we were going to give our first baby – the one that stopped growing inside me. And so 'Alannah' was written in tiny script across the thin golden surface.

A leanbh – meaning 'my child'.

Three weeks later, she was placed in my arms – a mewling beauty with a halo of golden fuzz and fiercely clenched fists. I breathed her in deeply. Réa stroked her soft skin curiously.

That's when I felt the first tug of bitterness that soured the creaminess of motherhood. Nick's wet face dampened her miniature cheeks and they gazed at each other mesmerised. A love story began. A complicated love story.

A leanbh. My child.

My poor foundling child.

5

Mirren

The boardroom on the second floor of the Coral Beach Hotel is too formal for these most violent of emotions. The first person I see when I walk into the room is Lieutenant Lovell Logan. He takes my hand, but there is no warmth to his skin. His eyes are bloodshot and he smells of smoke.

I don't let go.

'Please tell me what's going on?' I demand, unashamed of my rising desperation, pulling him towards me. 'Who has taken her? Who has Alannah?' It comes out louder than I intended – almost a shout – but I need answers. Logan looks panicked for a moment, then pulls his hand from mine sharply.

'Can you get Detective Rolle up here please, George?'

The officer standing by the door is young but clearly experienced enough to understand when a crisis is unfolding. He lifts his radio to his mouth and murmurs quickly into it.

'Please take a seat, Mrs Fitzpatrick,' he says, uncomfortable with my outburst.

'It's Dr Fitzpatrick.' I pace the room instead, raking my hair back in frustration. Lovell Logan slips into one of the chairs. He piles the folders in front of him and hits them off the table to align the stack.

'I just need you to—' I start saying, but the door opens, and another man appears; the kinder one. He's muscular but his movements seem quick, deft. Those brown eyes look straight into mine and he reminds me that his name is Detective Antonio Rolle.

'You need to be out searching for her,' I beg, unable to stay still, even for a moment. I walk to the window, look out at the mocking blues, the pretend paradise below. The sea is calmer now than before. The wind blew itself out, I heard somebody say earlier.

The kind detective explains that he understands it's a very hard time for us, but they just have a few questions, if I'll sit down for a moment. Nick is in a similar room being asked similar questions. Or was that earlier? I'm suddenly confused, my memories colliding, breaking and reforming. I run my coffee-sour tongue over my teeth, my legs suddenly weak. I collapse into the leather chair at the head of the table – the seat furthest from them.

'Would you like your daughter to be here with you?' Lovell Logan asks, looking at me over the rim of his glasses. I start violently, almost knocking over the plastic cup of water Candy has placed on the table for me. It takes a moment for me to realise he's referring to Réa. I think of her in the hotel room, lying on the bed, unable to eat or move, and shake my head.

'We've retrieved some relevant footage from a surveillance camera at the hotel,' Detective Antonio Rolle says gently, as if anticipating my panic at this bombshell.

I force my body not to move, to stay perfectly still while he continues talking.

'It's very early yet, and we are still examining it, as well as locating other CCTV, but we think there is a possibility it could show your daughter being led away by another person.'

'Where?' I whisper.

Who?

'On the beach,' he replies, his brown eyes kind. 'The only camera that captured any action on the beach was the hotel's beach club. It's pretty grainy, but we are trying to clean up the images right now.'

Detective Rolle goes to say something else but the other guy, his boss, cuts across him.

But I'm not listening. I don't know how to accept the horror of what they are saying. I close my eyes instead and remember returning to the room last night without Alannah.

-

I had to walk into that hotel room alone, everyone understood that. I didn't mean to glance over at Alannah's bed, her princess nightdress folded neatly on the pillow by the housekeeping, her rainbow flip-flops kicked off untidily by the door. But I looked nonetheless, I made myself. I remember how I sank to my knees, the pain in my stomach intense, like someone was carving me out. Nick lingered in the door for a moment watching, then turned and walked away. I needed to feel all of this – to face it alone. My hand, pressed flat against the hotel carpet, supported my body as I slowly leaned my head down towards the rough fibres. Everything blurred. I stayed there for a while, curled up, a strange sound gurgling in my lungs. Vowels ploughing together to form a low animalistic hum I couldn't control. Then I remembered her blankie. Scrambling to my feet, I searched the room, rushing from our adjoining room into her and Réa's.

'Help me,' I called out desperately to Réa, who was perched on the corner of her bed with her arms wrapped around herself, petrified. 'Please Réa, please. Help me find Blankie.' A few moments later, I saw the scrap of pink material poking out of the locker by the bed. I pulled open the drawer and saw Alannah's homemade bed for her miniature teddies. Her comfort blanket was wrapped around them. Réa still hadn't moved.

I sat down next to her. My weight on the bed toppled her slightly towards me and she let herself lean against me. Thick, soundless tears rolled down my face, but they gave no relief.

That's when I turned towards the minibar again.

-

I look up and realise that I'm in the boardroom. Lieutenant Logan is still talking. I blink, disorientated. I have no idea what time it is, or when I last ate or slept. He studies me – seems to be reading something into me that I'm not sure is even there.

'I asked you to tell me about yesterday,' Lovell Logan says again.

'Who could have taken her?' I burst out, standing up to pace again. Alannah could be out there injured somewhere, calling for me…

'Why aren't you out there?' I shout now, desperate. It's bad enough that I've caused this, but now they're wasting time asking me about what I had for my fucking lunch.

'Take a moment, Dr Fitzpatrick, if you need to,' Detective Rolle interrupts gently, and despite everything I'm grateful for his soothing presence.

'I know this is hard, but we need you to tell us what you know so we can target our search in the best way to find your daughter.'

'Sorry, it's all…' I put my hands over my face, trying to remember anything that could possibly help. But I'm not sure which parts are real and which I've imagined. I feel my wedding ring press into the crease of my cheek.

'The girls were playing on the beach… I went to read my book at the bar beside them.'

'What time was that?' Antonio Rolle asks quickly.

I shake my head impatiently. 'I don't know. Around three?'

The sooner we get this over with the sooner they can get out there and start properly looking for her.

'It was four p.m.,' Lovell Logan cuts in. 'And you could see Alannah the whole time?' he asks stiffly. He looks up before he asks the next part of the question – the one I should have known was coming.

'From the bar, I mean.'

There it is. The judgement I knew would be hurtling towards me.

Nobody tells you that when you become a mother, you have to sacrifice all your everythings. No matter what you become, how impressive your achievements, you are judged ultimately on your performance as somebody's mother first. If you don't measure up to how a mother should be – saintly, angelic, flawless – then you are left with absolutely nothing at all.

Except a torn scrap of blanket, a lifetime of regret, stomach-punching guilt.

Then it dawns on me, that no matter what I tell them, no matter what really happened to Alannah, I'll always just be the mother who was drinking when her child vanished. I'll always be the one who lost her.

Detective Rolle fills the horrible silence.

'What Lieutenant Logan means, I imagine, is that, at any stage, did you notice Alannah leaving, or anyone talking to her?'

I shake my head. My legs won't stop trembling, so I lean against the window. The glass is cool against my back.

'Even in the days before she went missing?'

I think back to the last few days. Alannah had enjoyed the kids club. She was practising for the show. *Cinderella*, her favourite. She had been so excited about the make-up and costumes they'd planned for her too. Réa made a face and called her a baby. 'You'll take pictures, Mummy?' Alannah asked anxiously, ignoring her big sister's usual taunts.

'Dr Fitzpatrick, did you see Alannah go into the water that day?'

I'm back in the room.

'No.' I shake my head again, as I return to the table and take a sip of water. This feels more like an interrogation. Rolle seems to agree. I see him hold up a 'take it easy' gesture to his superior and immediately understand there's conflict there. Interesting.

Then, a glimmer of something – a fragment of a memory floats on the periphery of my mind, I try to catch it, drag it back to where I can make sense of it, but it's gone.

'Did Réa?' Logan sounds annoyed by my answer.

'Réa was sunbathing, further back from the shore. Her headphones were on, I think.'

'And where was Nick?'

I look up, surprised. I want him to have no part in this.

'Nick was up at the pool. We'd been there with him a while before, but we left to go to the beach.'

Then, frustrated, 'Can you please tell me what you think happened?'

Logan leans forward.

'Where exactly was Alannah the last time you saw her?'

'I've been through this already fifty fucking times. You are not listening,' I shout. 'Alannah was standing by the edge of the water.

Playing.' I picture her again, my beautiful daughter – her brown legs, the sparkly sundress, the salty nothingness beyond.

'The waiter at this local bar you were at says he served you a few drinks. How many do you think you had?' Logan's lips press together, as if he wants to say more. I clutch my hands, trying to stop the trembling. My voice lowers in shame.

'Maybe three?' It's torturous. 'But that has nothing to do with her going missing.' I look Detective Rolle in the eye. 'Tell me who took my daughter, please Detective. Tell me what you know.'

I picture Alannah calling me and hearing only silence. Guilt turns to fury. Why are they acting like I've done something criminal?

Logan opens his mouth and then glances at Rolle who takes over. Raising a hand to his jaw, he rubs it, his face tense.

'Mirren, I know this is hard. The waiter says you had six drinks. We are trying to establish if you are a reliable witness to what happened.'

'Was I drunk you mean?' I push my hair back from my face, press my hands to the glass of the boardroom window. I remember the butterfly in my bedroom in Galway the week before we left. A dizzying trap. The inviting glass that blocks escape.

'We are all just trying to find Alannah,' Rolle says, clearly uncomfortable now. I almost feel sorry for him – he seems genuinely distraught. But enough now.

I turn and bang the table violently with my fist. All the men in the room jump. The plastic cups shift a fraction forward. Mine tips over.

'Then find her,' I say loudly. 'Stop wasting time and find my fucking daughter.'

They stare at me for a moment in silence.

Don't underestimate what I will do for my daughter, I want to scream.

Lieutenant Logan lowers his head, his mouth scrunched and sour. Detective Rolle casts his eyes towards the polished table. A slick of spilt water spreads thinly across its surface.

They should be giving me the answers – not the other way round. I close my eyes for a moment, but I can sense Logan's disapproval. Outside the sea birds shriek and swoop headfirst into the depths. We all listen to the slow tap-tap of water running off the side of the table onto the carpet.

That's when they find the blood.

6

Rolle

The room is silenced in a second. The bustle of sound-checks, clicking tripods and whispered chatter quietens immediately as the Fitzpatrick family files into the events room of the Coral Beach Hotel. Candy, the self-appointed family advocate with the badly bleached hair, walks first. She leans forward to carefully adjust the microphone, knowing all eyes are on her. Lovell Logan follows next, his chest puffed out importantly. He glances nervously at the five or so television cameras trained onto him – all the local stations – and at least two international feeds. To one side of the room, billowy drapes have been dragged across the windows to shield against sunlight. It gives the room a pale, twilight atmosphere. The camera lights shine directly onto the group, like spotlights on a stage. There must be fifty people crammed into the small area, most holding notepads and recording devices. Cameras click intrusively, snatching every moment of the Fitzpatricks' nightmare. Nick, ignoring the media scrum, sits down heavily next to Lovell. His eyes face downwards towards a piece of paper clutched between both hands. It shakes a little as he unfolds and refolds it.

Antonio Rolle takes his seat near the back of the room to observe. He watches Mirren trail in last. Her arms are wrapped around herself and she's staring straight ahead. Her gait seems unsteady, loose. There's no sign at all of the anger Mirren had displayed in the boardroom interview. There's an emptiness to her face he hasn't noticed until now. Candy guides her gently into the last seat behind the table and stands back to the side. Rolle sees that Mirren is holding her daughter's soft

35

night-blanket – a square of raggy pink material clutched between her fingers. Every breath looks like a struggle, for the woman who seems to have grown even thinner overnight. Grief does strange things to a person, he guesses, picturing his wife Alice suddenly. This is the moment every news outlet has been waiting for; the devastated mother, the frantic father, the heartbreaking appeal they know is coming. The snappers snap furiously in a collective wave, clacking quickly, desperate not to miss a single facial expression. Photographers push the cameras as close to the couple as they can get away with.

Lovell speaks first. Clearing his throat loudly, he reaches for his water glass and swigs nervously. He gestures to the photographers to give them some space. Then he begins, outlining the current situation. Even from his perch at the back, Rolle can see Lovell's hesitation, how careful he is with his words. He comes across as stiff, unfeeling. But this is once-in-a-career stuff. Everyone at the station understands the magnitude of an investigation like this. Global news. And Lovell, the face of the case, can't be seen to put a foot wrong. Maybe that's why he's sweating. The other, more pragmatic concern is that this incident could be detrimental to the island. Tourists had shunned destinations like theirs for far less tragedy. Pretty beaches or not, bad things are hard to shake. Already the negative media coverage was upsetting those at the top. Everyone agreed, a swift resolution was needed.

Today would be about two truths – what the media would be told initially, and what the investigation had also uncovered so far. Rolle knows there's always more than one story. Holding back is part of their job too. To protect the family, but also as leverage when it comes to leads. He sees the TV lights illuminating Lovell's clammy skin. Beads of sweat bubble up on his forehead, damp and scaly like a fish.

After hours of searching the entire coastline and surrounds, it's clear that the child drowning was the least likely scenario. Experts had studied the tides, the coastguard divers hadn't found a trace, most of the beaches and coves in the island had been examined multiple times. There had been no further sightings either. In fact, it seems as if Alannah Fitzpatrick had simply vanished without anybody seeing a thing.

Then there was the blood.

A worryingly large crimson stain was discovered on the sand by the small cove close to the tyre tracks. Forensics spent hours photographing and videotaping the scene, taking moulds and removing samples of the blood for documentation and storage. If there was enough, the genetic markers in it would be tested for toxins and other drugs. The DNA would also be compared to traces found on the child's toothbrush, obtained using the Consent To Search forms the Fitzpatricks had signed. But the grains containing the blood would have to be sent off to a lab in St Petersburg, further complicating matters.

Today is all about the appeal for information – the need to rule things in or out. The general line in the media was that the little girl may have tragically drowned or wandered off as her mother was distracted in a bar. That's how it would stay for now. The isolation of the cove meant the details of the blood was under wraps from the media until the investigators knew more.

The initial sympathy and heartbreak for the Fitzpatrick family was also beginning to give way to something else. Blame, in the face of a tragedy involving a child, sells newspapers and encourages clicks. But there is nothing new in tearing down the idealisation of motherhood. Falling angels land with a bigger splash. Not for the first time since the child disappeared, Rolle felt sickened by the sensationalism of such a terribly sad situation. Especially so early in the investigation.

Of course, there's been an undercurrent of speculation about the possibility Alannah has been abducted. Today's news conference is the first opportunity for journalists to probe that further. As Rolle sees it, the investigation now centres around a few things. The first is the sighting of a person walking away with a child, which had been verified by the CCTV footage from the beach club at the Coral Beach Hotel.

The second is the tyre tracks in the small cove behind the rocks – an area hidden from the main beach. Rolle, slumped in his plastic chair at the back of the room, knows that whoever drove over the sand that day must have also had to bounce through undergrowth and steep pebbles to get to that point. There was no road that led to that area, barely a dirt track. That implies someone local may have been there or seen something suspicious. Someone who knew their way around well. Pete Waters from Forensic Evidence in Miami-Dade County is the best in the business when it comes to this type of pattern evidence. He'd already received the castings from those examining the tyre tracks. But they all know that trying to read scribbles from the sand on a windy day is like trying to figure out the meaning from the creases on someone's palm.

Then there's the mother's story. Is it reliable? Her timeline sound? He'd looked her up. Googled Mirren Fitzpatrick + doctor + Ireland. There were articles about her ground-breaking work in paediatric oncology, a photo of her accepting an award in Poland, an obituary of one of her parents, little else. He had a few calls in with colleagues that knew her. Important to get the full story. The father, Nick Fitzpatrick, had been at the pool at the time of Alannah's disappearance. He had a media company in Ireland. Mainly editing advertisements and short corporate videos. Neither had any convictions, but the department had only scratched the surface when it came to what they could uncover about the couple's lives. The problem is that it takes time.

Rolle picks at a hangnail on his thumb as he thinks about some of the other strings he needs to pull on. There was nothing unusual spotted in any more of the surveillance footage in the hotel's private walkway to the beach or leaving the hotel. It was the camera positioned in a more elevated spot that caught the hazy image of what the team agreed was a woman and a child walking down the beach in the direction of the cove. Rolle knew the distance was unhelpful to identify either one of them, but they were hoping that today's press conference might give them some new answers.

He thinks then of the witnesses, effectively everyone else who was there on the day. They'd try to obtain footage taken from their phones at the beach around the time Alannah disappeared – something Lovell Logan and his not-so-merry men had so far failed to do sufficiently.

Rolle looks around the room, packed with journalists and photographers. Most are looking at their phones. He wishes someone would open a window. After Logan's formal appeal for information, there is a gaggle of questions, many directed at Mirren, whose eyes never leave the ground. Logan steps in to take some of them, Candy shakes her head dismissing others. He wonders absently why she appointed herself as the family liaison, PR manager and emergency coordinator. She seems to be enjoying it all far too much for his liking.

Right now, Mirren looks nothing like her professional profile picture that had been lifted by the media and splashed across front pages. Wearing a cream T-shirt and knee-length red skirt, there's no glossy bob or carefully applied make-up, just a broken version, with legs that don't stop jittering the whole way through the press conference. Lovell Logan continues to give curt one-word answers, making it clear that once they get additional information, they'll be in a position to reveal more. Then he motions to Nick to read out the statement the family has prepared.

Silence descends.

It feels increasingly suffocating just by the sheer volume of people crammed inside the room, waiting. The father takes a deep breath to steady himself, and in the staccato voice of a man trying to control his emotions, he asks the watching world to please help them to find Alannah. His strangled words are truly pitiful, and Rolle, in danger of being moved, clamps his teeth together tightly. It wouldn't do to start getting teary-eyed over a kid he never met. But it's hard not to feel the devastation of a father begging for someone, anyone, to help him find his precious eight-year-old daughter. Rolle tries to block out thoughts of all the other desperate parents, and how their stories had played out. This is all a little too close to the bone for him, after what happened in Miami.

'I can't bear to think of Alannah somewhere out there without us,' Nick finishes, finally looking up at the reporters. The cameras click once more – a little less irreverently this time, Rolle thinks. Then there is a moment, a beat, where he thinks Mirren might possibly speak too; that she might reiterate what her husband just said, add her voice to the appeal. But she doesn't and it's a noticeable gap. The reporters also seem disappointed not to hear from the gently swaying mother – those blue eyes remain completely unreadable. Nick reaches over to take her hand and she stiffens a fraction. It mightn't be obvious to anyone else in the room. Most are busy tapping into smartphones about a potential abduction on paradise island, but Rolle notices instantly, and his internal alarm sounds again. Mirren says something quickly under her breath and Nick's head shoots up fast. He recoils as if he's been hit.

Something's off.

It might have nothing to do with the investigation, but Rolle knows he'll have to find out. He'll have to lift this rock and examine everything dirty that crawls beneath. Although he'd tried to steer clear of Lovell Logan, many of the potential witnesses had already slipped through their fingers. There's one more thing worth exploring though. What the media also hasn't been told about, not yet, is the existence of a hotel employee statement about two men hanging around the beach around the time Alannah disappeared. The witness identified two of them as former staff at the Coral Beach Hotel, said they were acting suspiciously.

It's potentially, in Rolle's experience, the turning point of the investigation. They'd since found out that one of them had been sacked just a few weeks before. He was identified as a man called Kata Charles. Known to police.

Rolle had called him in for an interview, and he'd agreed to come down to the station at Calloway the next day. It signified another knot in the complicated strings of this case. But Rolle was determined to untangle every single one. Each moment that passes is a moment Alannah is likely in danger if she's still alive. He thinks of the sticky, almost-black stain on the sand and exhales heavily.

As the reporters file out of the room, Rolle overhears their reaction, the commentary on the lack of tears from the mother, her coldness. *The kid was adopted*, someone beside him whispers.

Weird the way she didn't cry? Something going on there, another offers.

How quickly the tables turn, he thinks. What grotesque arrogance it is to presume there is a right way to grieve for a missing child. The line in the sand between sympathy and suspicion is easily redrawn based on collective assumptions like these. Fractions of reactions scrutinised; the way you sit in a chair, a tilt of your head. That's the fickle nature of humans, Rolle's father used to say. 'We judge so quickly we get blinded by the probablys, the should bes, the how could theys. Never judge too quickly, son. You never know what's really going on, not unless you dig down deep.'

–

Back at the station, Antonio Rolle fires off a quick text to Alice.

> Home late again. Sorry Ally. Promise I'll make it up to you x

Even as he types it, he knows that nothing can make up for what he'd brought upon them back in Miami. But he can't think about that now. In fact, he'd been pushing the thoughts of it away for weeks, ignoring Alice's sad eyes, changing the subject whenever she brought it up. He reruns the footage of the press conference over and over, replaying the moment when Nick jumps back as if burnt. Slowing the tape down, he tries to make out exactly what it was Mirren had said in that moment. It isn't easy deciphering the pixels and lip movements, but with a little help from Jeremy, the station's tech whiz, they finally figure it out just before midnight.

Sitting back in his chair, Rolle swears loudly – the small, huge sentence echoing in his ears.

Mirren's mouth moves in slow motion on the screen in front of him. Five tiny words that add a whole new dimension to the case.

'This is all your fault,' Mirren spits viciously at her husband and turns her attention back to the scruffy patch of blanket in her lap, looping it slowly around her fingers like a noose, pulling it tight.

7

Mirren

The Past

Growing up, my father told me stories about the Tuatha de Danann, *otherworldly islands off the coast of Ireland that could only be found beyond the ninth wave. It was greater than any other wave that came before it, the legend goes, and passing through it was the only way to get to the fog-shrouded land. The sacred sea voyage to get a glimpse of the gods that lived there was known as the Imramma. I loved the idea of that — of running away, of someone trying to make a sacred journey just to reach me. These were the bedtime stories from fishermen like my father. Stories passed down from one generation to another — of fairy forts, lost islands, and brave mermaids. Everything was endlessly possible. Life was big and bold and there for the taking. That frightened and excited me but remained just out of reach from our bleak cottage on that isolated peninsula.*

It was my father who named me after the ocean — his love and his livelihood. On our rare fishing trips, I'd drop my hand over the side of the boat and watch it get swallowed up, the pink of my flesh creating a white trail that followed us wherever we went, ripples across the trapped sky. This was the land of shimmering bogs and earthy-brown scree. Of loose-stoned walls and sheep dotted like low-slung clouds, far in the distance. A life in the wild, but never carefree. The moment I stepped through the front door of my family home; the knot of anxiety pulled tight. The light would fade. After Father died, I spent my life searching for that ninth wave — the one that would lift me up and drag me away from the lone grey shore and heavy hateful horizon. Most of all though, I needed to escape my mother and her brandy-limp body hanging half off the couch each day. My father had spent his life floating far away from me on the ocean, my

43

mother down the neck of a bottle. Somewhere on the horizon, he checked lobster pots while she swigged the dregs. Slowly our childhood was whittled down. Until it was as empty and broken as the upturned boat on our beach. Damaged beyond repair.

The magical otherworld I eventually embarked upon was no fairy tale. It was a tiny flat in Dublin at the age of eighteen, and a job sweeping hair. Sitting on the damp steps behind the salon during my cigarette breaks, I'd squint through the smoke clouds and wonder what I was doing. I'd always been smart, but my mother had raised me in the salt-wounds of her own sadness. 'Worthless,' she'd called me. 'Mirren O'Brien, you'll never be anything.' That's before I shed my name, before marrying Nick Fitzpatrick helped me replace that part of me too. A child believes everything their mother says and her words were my reflection. My gospel. Even though religion for us back then remained tightly coiled around the twin shame of superstition and sacrifice. But more than displeasing God or my bloodshot mother, what I wanted was someday to command real respect. I wasn't sure if that part was more for her or for me. But it was something I was prepared to do.

Whatever that might eventually cost me.

8

Rolle

February on the island is always a mixed bag when it comes to the weather: chilly in the mornings and evenings, with warmth in the middle where it feels as if the sun could last forever. At six o'clock in the evening of the second day since the girl vanished, Alice heads out. Antonio closes the door on her with a gentle wave. A Pilates class, most likely. But he realises too late that he forgot to ask. She deserves to have a nice time, he thinks. She'd been lonely the past few months here, unable to settle in, angry at him for having to leave her life in Miami behind. He heard her crying at night recently and wondered if it was something to do with her age. Or maybe the missing girl had affected her too. He's never been able to understand women – even though his dark lashes had been making their heads turn since he was a teenager.

Rolle spends an hour in the garage he'd converted to a makeshift gym, abusing the punching bag by kicking the hanging dull mass until it swayed in defeat. By seven ten, he's eaten all the leftover roast chicken and too much garlic bread. But his evening's plan of mindlessly watching sport to decompress is marred by intrusive thoughts of the missing girl and her mother with those strange sad eyes. So much so, in fact, that he eases his exhausted legs off the sofa and throws on a sweater.

He crunches the car out of the drive of their rented house and takes the L-45 southwards towards the Coral Beach resort, but not as far. Ten minutes later, Rolle turns off the road and follows a bumpy path that snakes up into the hills and dips down, eastwards. This wasn't on any GPS, nor would it appear on most maps, but Rolle remembers it from the few pointless trips he made here before to warn blank-faced barely-men over hotel break-ins. It's also home to Glades Whitaker, according to the police report. It was her daughter, Mariah, who went out with a friend the previous Halloween night and never returned home.

Ivory Bay is less of a neighbourhood and more like a dirt road littered with once-shiny trailers on overgrown lots. He checks the file balanced on his lap with the light from his phone and turns into number 33. The headlights crudely illuminate the untidy patch of world that Glades calls home. This was the part of the island that the postcards don't show – the poverty-stricken stretches of communities dotted off the main road. Rolle knows places like this. There were plenty back where he came from. Areas of degeneration, where energy seemed sapped by a reliance on government aid, running drugs into mainland Florida… or worse. Opportunities are thin on the ground down these parts, schools as neglected as some of the abandoned burnt-out buildings that stand nearby. Escapism here is smoked deeply or shot into once-youthful veins.

A mongrel runs hungrily to greet him as he steps out of the Audi. A bike lies discarded against the wooden steps, covered in rust and mildew. Rolle raps lightly on the door, mindful of the lateness of his call and the fact that his colleagues hadn't done much in the way of following up on the case. The door opens and a small child stands barefoot in a *Dora the Explorer* nightdress. She's only about six or seven.

'Is your mommy home?'

Footsteps come quickly towards the door and a woman appears frowning.

'Everything okay?' she demands nervously, her hand across the doorway, pushing the child behind her. She looks over Rolle's shoulder towards the car. 'What's going on?'

Glades Whitaker is in her mid-forties and white, like most who live out that way. He guesses her BMI is probably higher than it should be too. Her hair is a garish blonde streaked with grey and she's wearing a faded bathrobe. The cord pulls around her middle like string around ham.

'I'm Detective Antonio Rolle. I wanted to talk to you about Mariah. About her disappearance.'

He holds one hand up in surrender – mindful too of his lack of uniform. With the other he shows her his badge.

'Don't know you,' she decides after a moment, squinting at his face suspiciously. The outdoor light flickers distractingly across the porch, casting shadows against the gleam of damp wood.

'I'd like to talk to you about something and it won't take long.'

He holds up the police file.

'Did you find my child?' Glades asks slowly, with the resignation that comes from too many disappointments in life.

'I'm sorry, we have not. But I did want to follow up on a few things. I've been looking at the case again in greater detail.' Glades stands back and allows him to pass into the tiny cabin. The child sits on a patterned sofa staring at the wide-screen TV. It takes up the entire wall on one side. A cigarette burns a long grey snake into the ashtray on a table next to the kitchenette. 'Coffee?' she asks reaching for the smoke, tipping its ashy length towards the ashtray and missing by a considerable distance. Ash scatters like snowflakes floating gently downwards.

'Tea please, if you have it.'

As she stands, her back to him, waiting for the kettle to boil, Rolle takes in his surroundings. The room is small and a misshapen cardboard box is piled high with toys in one corner.

The noise from the kettle fills the silence.

After placing the watery tea in front of Rolle, Glades sits down opposite him.

'So…' She raises an eyebrow.

'I was looking through Mariah's missing person file,' Rolle explains. 'And I wanted to go over a few things about that night, if you don't mind.' He lifts the mug to his lips, hesitates and blows across the scalding liquid.

'October 31st, Halloween night.' Glades' voice cracks. She raises a hand to her mouth to stop the tumble of emotions Rolle knows he must be triggering.

'She was going to her friend Tiffany's house across the beach over there, right?' Rolle gestures to the cove about a kilometre east – a popular spot for local teens to congregate.

Glades nods.

He'd gone over the report again and again, trying to find similarities between this case and the Fitzpatrick girl. *Mickey Mouse Clubhouse* blares on the TV.

'Never saw her again.' Glades pulls hard on the cigarette, now down to its stump. 'Nobody gave a shit then, and nobody since. Why are you here today, Detective?'

'There's another missing child.'

'Sure, we've all seen it on the news. Irish girl. Just a kid, like Mariah.'

'I'm trying to see if there is anything to connect the two cases. I'm looking to see if there's anything that can help bring them both home.'

Glades emits a hollow laugh. It startles him. Then she slams her empty cup down so hard that the child glances nervously over.

'So, my kid vanishes, and I get kicked out of the station when I go begging for help. They telling me that she's gone and run off herself. And here's a rich kid done same, and they get choppers. Fuck me, choppers.'

Glades wipes her brow on the back of her sleeve. Rolle waits. Silence hangs heavily and instinctively he doesn't want to break it. He notices photographs on the wall instead. Illuminated by the white light from the television, he can see a younger Glades pushing a smiling child in a pram. Another photo, next to it, is of her with a baby and a small girl sitting at a picnic table. There's also a lone framed picture of a blonde girl with a gap between her teeth wearing a flouncy white dress that billows out behind her – probably a Communion. She looks so proud of herself. Rolle feels extremely tired suddenly – tired of seeing beautiful things destroyed, tired of fighting for the innocent and failing. He remembers the satisfying smack of knuckle on bone from that night back in Miami. It feels like a lifetime ago since he made his stand in the name of a vulnerable child. And that hadn't worked out too well. Maybe here in Kite, he could actually do something to help.

Glades uses the large sleeve of her dressing gown to dab at her eyes, taking care not to mess up her already smudged eyeliner. The delicate tapping motion is a stark contrast to the slam of emotions he figures he's just dropped on her.

'I'm sorry Ms Whitaker. I don't know what to say except that we are doing everything we can.' He corrects himself. '*I'm* doing everything I can.'

But he understands this woman's bitterness. Just another demonstration of the second-class status she has to endure her whole life, he imagines. Even worse, Rolle realises, is that it automatically applied to her daughter – tarnished at birth. Her loss seemed inconsequential to everyone expect her mother and sister, and yet Alannah's loss was seen as so vital to many. Both are little girls with hopes and dreams and pretty pigtails and gap-toothed smiles. But he knows that he'd played a part in that grotesque filtration system. Along the way, he's also categorised certain people into who matters and who doesn't. He remembers his father's voice quoting the lottery of birth when he was a boy. 'Antonio,' he'd say in his heavily accented staccato, as he brought him along in his van to help with his furniture removals work. 'When you enter the world, you pick one ticket from a book of billions. That ticket will decide everything about you – your gender, your race, your nationality, whether you are rich or poor, or sick, or American or Greek, whatever. You're going to get one chance to pick and it's the most important thing that's ever going to happen to you in your life.'

'Would you give yours back?' Pops would ask, his eyebrows raised, creating jagged criss-crosses in his forehead as he waited for the answer. 'No, sir,' Antonio would reply dutifully, more interested in his upcoming karate tournament than having a deep philosophical debate with his old man. But these days he's not so sure he'd give the same answer. He'd probably take the gamble. Antonio Rolle is tired of the life he's been given, the path he's taken. He knows Alice can sense it too.

'Ms Whitaker, someone noticed a speedboat on the day Alannah disappeared. There were tyre tracks found on the beach nearby too. Does that ring any bells for you about the day Mariah went missing?'

'I told them a million times that guy Red up at Milton Point was sniffing around girls here. Him and his brother.'

Rolle glances up quickly. This is the first he's heard of somebody called Red in connection with this case. Not that there's much in the way of information about this missing kid at all.

'Nobody even went to talk to him,' Glades continues.

Rolle jots down some notes in the small notebook he keeps in his pocket. He'll have to liaise with Lovell on this one.

'I heard they'd been moving girls too,' she says more quietly now – as if she doesn't quite want to believe it herself. 'Over to the mainland.'

Rolle's pen hesitates in the air a moment.

'Do you know where Red lives, Glades? Do you think he might have taken Mariah?'

'He lives on his boat – moves around a lot. When he's here he stays in a house up by the lighthouse. I went there, to Milton Point, searching for Mariah, but that goddamn junkie ran me off. The brother seems a bit less crazy. They're over and back to Miami with drugs, and… whatever.'

Glades narrows her eyes and leans forward.

'I told the cops all this before and nothing was done. Why you back here now acting like you give one shit about me or Mariah?' Glades starts coughing, a deep smokers cough, that racks her body, and she sits down heavily.

'I'm sorry. I really am. I'm going to do my best to find your daughter.'

But she is lost to her grief. The memory split open by him, like a head against a rock. He returns the notebook to his pocket and retrieves a card with his contact details that he sets down on the sticky table.

He stands to leave, quickly rinsing his teacup in the sink nearby. Before he departs, he puts a hand on her shoulder, promising he'll be in touch soon. Rolle's not even sure he believes it himself. But someone needs to start caring.

He eases his bulky frame past the smiling photos, seeing up close that they're stuck to the wall with scraggy bits of tape. A pitiful shrine, he thinks sadly, and stops to stick back one of the crumpled corners that has come loose.

Pulling the door behind him, he steps back out into the chilly February night.

9

Mirren

The shower taps crank on with a low metallic squeal followed by the sound of water flowing heavily into the ceramic bath. Réa's been in the hotel bathroom for over an hour. Nick and I sit in silence, watching the news, avoiding eye contact. Perversely it makes me happy to know Alannah's clean wherever she is. I gave her a bath the night before she disappeared. 'Make me like a princess, Mummy.' She'd smiled in the bathroom mirror, as I dunked her head back to scrape the suds away. I can still feel my fingers in her damp hair, pressing down slightly a little deeper to rinse it clear. The image of my hands submerging her body are so real to me, I shudder. Closing my eyes, I can almost feel the fragility of her narrow shoulders, her pink skin, the wet slick of her cheek as the water washes over her submerged face.

Stop, Mirren.

Throwing out dirty bath water after dark was something my mother, Nora, refused to do. Nobody in rural Ireland did, for fear of being cursed. It's silly, of course, but we lived beneath the chokehold of superstition. I think of my mother's words to me when I first told her about Alannah. It was she who first referred to her as the changeling. 'She's fairy-struck,' my mother insisted. 'Poor craythur.' She believed that raising someone else's child invited trouble – an omen of sorts. I thought since she'd been given up herself as a child, she might be a little more sensitive to our situation. But compassion wasn't something my mother ever understood or showed.

When I was seven, she sought out her own biological mother. But her rejection, for a second time, was what ultimately pulled Nora O'Brien down the bottom of a brandy bottle.

I force myself to stay in the moment.

The blood they found means nothing, I console myself. We'd given permission for some of Alannah's belongings to be examined and her dental records to be sent over from Ireland. But Nick is dealing with those things now.

Last night I had a dream about Alannah. I watched her roam the beach alone, silvery in the moonlight like a creature from another world. I followed her onto the sand, but then it was the strand by Ballyconnelly, where I grew up. I reached out and felt only the raspy grain of her clothes. She slipped away from me. I got a glimpse of her face as she turned. My daughter looked at me mournfully, accusingly. And it was my mother's face.

The whoosh of alcohol brings a welcome dizziness as I pull myself out of the chair. I put my hand on the wall to steady myself. The taps in the bathroom screech to a stop. Nick walks out to the balcony and slides the doors closed.

'*Don't you think it's a bit odd how the mother is so unemotional?*' someone on the TV studio panel says to the person next to them. '*A strange reaction for a woman who's just lost her child. It just seems "off"*'.' What does a good mother look like anyway, if a bad one looks like me? But their shift to judgement is predictable. It's almost preferable to the growing mountain of soft cuddly toys and cheap plastic roses overflowing on the pavement outside the hotel. Well-wishers, touched by our story, add their relics – ink splashes on cards, sad-looking balloons. As Nick and I crouched to read the messages of support earlier today, I thought of nothing but the cameras trained onto my face. They flashed intrusively, trying to capture our most anguished angles. It seems like no matter what I did or didn't do, my performance would never be hysterical enough. My clothes wouldn't be homely enough, my reactions not sufficiently broken, or tear-stained. I dabbed at my dry eyes with a tissue as I examined the curved ink of kind words on cards and wondered which was worse; that I wasn't crying or that I was pretending to?

I called my big sister the night Alannah vanished. 'She's gone, Tara,' I sobbed down the phone, my head pressed to the wall. It was four a.m. in Dublin. 'I need you.'

'I'm coming,' she replied immediately. My sister, the *banshee* destroyer. I pictured the two of us as children, huddled together under the covers. Nobody in the world knows what went on in that cottage. That binds us.

We've organised posters to hand out to locals too. Disturbingly, they remind me of the missing cat leaflets we once stuck to trees for Alannah's lost kitten. Nick and Candy chose the image for the pages to hand out across the island. It's of Alannah in the garden of our house in Galway. She's sitting on the swing we put in for Réa, squinting into the camera as the sun shines on obliviously in the background. Her hair is loose and her freckles pinch against the crinkle of her nose. She's smiling her perfect Alannah smile.

I glance over at Nick, sitting on the sun lounger on our balcony, texting, his fingers moving across the screen swiftly. He stops as I walk over and lays his phone down on the small bistro table that overlooks the pool. Remains of my room service dinner sit on the table beside him – the sauces congealed like smears of dried blood. Maybe he didn't really mean what he said by the pool that day. I reach for my cross-body bag and linger by the glass doors. I take a breath and slide them open a fraction.

'Off out for a drink?' he says, with such uncharacteristic venom that I almost fall over.

He holds my horrified gaze for a moment, then drops his eyes back to his screen as if he'd said nothing at all.

The sea whispers her hypnotic secrets down below. Réa clicks open the bathroom latch.

This is the moment when I understand that I'm so much more alone in all of this than I could have imagined. How can I forgive him for what he's done to our family? It was never supposed to be this way. I pull the heavy door behind me, remembering that the tiny kitten was never found at all.

10

Mirren

The Past

I spent my early twenties unclogging sinks *at a dingy Dublin salon until Dr Emma Lacey walked into my life. Neither of us knew it then, but she would be the reason I'd become a doctor. Her caramel-coloured fringe balanced on her eyelashes as I blow-dried the ends sharp, just the way she liked it. 'My favourite hairdresser.' She'd smile at me, while I collected her casual compliments like a starved puppy does scraps. Dr Emma Lacey was intimidating without being cruel. Or so I thought. Years later, I'd feel the full force of her frightening wrath.*

When I overheard, one day in the salon, that she needed a childminder, I volunteered immediately. I met the children one Saturday at a local park with Emma, and a few weeks later, I pulled up at a four-storey townhouse to move in. Three little faces peeked out the front door. An autumn wreath hung prettily from its brass knocker. Dr Lacey was a cardiac consultant; her husband Jack wrote books. 'The scary kind' she announced proudly, as she opened the door to a room lined with bookcases, every shelf filled. Their home was a study in cosy opulence. Heavy curtains guarded arched windows and toffee-coloured flagstones gave the expensive kitchen a more lived-in feel. Sometimes, as I scraped the multicoloured playdough off the kitchen table, Emma would talk to me about her life as a doctor.

'Isn't it hard to see all that pain and misery?' I asked her once.

'No, Mirren.' She'd smiled. 'It's wonderful. You get to fix broken things. And yes, it's sometimes grim, but there is nothing more rewarding.' I studied her earnest face as she spoke. 'To be responsible for the life or death of somebody – to help ease suffering – there's nothing more powerful in the entire world.'

At night, lying in my bedroom in the converted attic with windows facing the sky, I'd look at the stars and realise that knot, the one I'd had as long as I could remember, was finally loosening. I knew then it was time to become the person I wanted to be. I'd noticed, in this area of South Dublin, that carrying yourself with a certain air proved increasingly useful. So, I let my Galwegian lilt flatten, and decked myself in an armour of mascara, careful blow-dries and the well-fitting dresses that I saw Emma and her friends admire on each other. I curated myself – a reinvention of the neglected child raised in the waves. All the while, I ignored my mother's pitiful letters. I'd severed the bonds of my ugly childhood, I belonged here now. I knew too, that whatever strange chemistry that had begun between Jack Lacey and I, needed to be suppressed. As the months passed, I felt Jack's eyes on my back more often, as I stretched to put the clean cups from the dishwasher away.

'Listen to this Mirren...' he'd say in his smooth English accent, and read me a few lines of whatever novel he was engrossed in. When his touch on my shoulder began to fizz, I knew there'd be trouble. He was married, nearly twice my age and Emma Lacey had become a role model of sorts to me.

Despite the new life I'd forged, I couldn't deny the tug-tag feeling of the tides of my life. Súitú was what my father called that sucking-out sound of the shoreline at night – the waves that drag the pebbles from the shore and then roll them back in. Living this life, I was one creature pretending to be another.

Then came the evening that changed everything.

'Help me celebrate the arrival of my new book cover?' Jack suggested, wiggling a bottle of wine from the doorway of his office. Emma was working a late shift at the hospital; the children were already asleep.

It wasn't unusual for me and Jack to sit in the large study with the oak panels and roaring fire, talking about books. Sometimes Emma would bring in her tea and sit there too, chatting easily about weekend plans. She was grateful I minded their children so well. She told me so – and that she considered me a friend.

It also wasn't strange to look at the three proofs that lay across his desk under the soft lampy glow. Jack poured a generous glug of red wine into two glasses and handed me one. I tucked my legs underneath me, feeling safe, feeling heard. It was then I knew I wanted this to be the blueprint for my life – not the rotten scaffolding that had come before.

'Which would you choose?' He gestured at the choice of ominous graphics, smoothing his hand slowly over each one.

'None.' I grimaced. 'Sorry.' Glancing up at me, he held his heart, mocking that my words had pierced it.

'So, Miss O'Brien,' he teased, the alcohol making him lighter than his usual gruff self. 'Are you the creative sort?' Sitting behind his untidy desk, he stretched his legs out in front of him and cradled his glass in both hands.

I rubbed the rim of my own glass which balanced precariously on my knee.

'Not at all. I have other plans. I want to be a doctor.'

He raised the glass to his mouth. As I watched the ruby liquid touch his lips, I reminded myself of the ring that circled his finger protectively – the glinting gold of commitment and Emma's trusting face. My declaration surprised even me. But suddenly it was clear; I wanted exactly what Emma had.

'Tell me more,' he smiled, 'about growing up in Galway.'

He'd turned his body towards me, his gaze direct.

That fizz again.

But I'd been caught off guard by his question – unbalanced. How to explain my upbringing in a way that kept me as safe as I felt within those four walls? I could tell him about the view from my childhood window – a sliver of silvery sky, slits of grey from the horizon. Or about the tumbling navy of the ocean, or the shouts from downstairs. I could tell him how we used to draw orange pictures of flames and tuck them inside the hearth to imagine its crayon warmth. Or of my father working weeks at a time out on the boats. I could tell him of my mother's mean, unsteady eyes watching me from her sprawl on the couch, rejection breeding rejection. I'd kept all my memories carefully zipped closed, and his kind words had split them open. Maybe it was the drink, or the gentle glow of the room, or the way Jack sat forward as tears sprang to my eyes, but for the first time, I didn't feel like this burden was mine alone. For a few moments, golden with the glow of the fire and the empathy in the air, I felt my armour weaken. I felt something else too – something forbidden. The rush was tremendous, the dizziness of needing to be as close to Jack as possible. I untucked my legs and walked towards him slowly, trying not think. My hair, much longer then, hung down my back, loose from its usual neat ponytail. Those intelligent eyes were clouded with something I'd never seen before, an intensity I'd created. The spit and crackle from the fire was the only sound as I leaned my face close to his, my cheeks still damp with tears. There was a moment of complete stillness. Of stomach-flipping tension. Of the realisation we were on the edge of a precipice. Then his hands were in my hair, tugging softly as I climbed onto him. Our mouths reached for each other with all the pent-up heat that had been floating between us. His fingers stroked my nipples through my T-shirt, and I trembled with something that felt entirely unstoppable. Leaning back from him, his mouth moved along the length of my exposed neck, his breath hot against damp skin.

'Oh Jesus, Mirren,' he whispered as he stood up, my legs still wrapped around him, lifting me onto the desk in front of him.

'Mirren,' he said again, more urgently this time. And his voice on my name, the rawness of his want, made me pull him towards me, as we clawed at each other's clothes. I welcomed the weight of him, his skin slick against mine as we moved and touched, mouths open, bodies pushing closer and deeper. Nothing in that moment mattered except this glorious stretch and fold. I muffled my moans against his sweat-soaked neck. I remember the stillness afterwards – the salty-skin taste and rough hair of his chest on my cheek.

–

But the man who was to become Réa's dad was a married man. Torn between his admirable loyalty to his wife, and his boyish lust for me, he experienced his own súitú – a push-pull of confusing emotions. From then on, we snatched frantic moments in dark corners, up against walls and in locked offices. But he wasn't mine to hold. Loneliness and desire were Jack's driving forces, which even as a young girl I should have understood. My guilt was quickly replaced with something else. When I missed two periods and my breasts ached, I knew. Even then, I thought that maybe having his baby growing inside me would change things – that I'd be good enough for a life like this. But I saw the boyish fear in his eyes. It reminded me of a fish caught on one of my father's bloody hooks. I wanted to belong, but he offered me cash instead, asking me to leave and to never tell Emma.

'It's better this way,' he told me, as we clung to each other one last time – the lonely and the lost. The Christmas wreath shook as I pulled the front door *behind me. I'd already decided that I'd do what Emma Lacey did — I'd fix the broken things.*

-

I moved to a small apartment in the city and used Jack's cash to begin the first tentative steps towards my medical training. I'd earn the respect I craved, no matter what stood in my way. In late summer, I brought my little Réa star into the world. For the first time in my life, I had something that couldn't be taken from me; Réa was mine alone. And to her, I would always be perfect. The real love affair began. I knew then that I'd do anything to protect her, anything I had to.

I never did see Jack again. I ignored his calls, frightened perhaps he'd try to take what was mine — never knowing that just a few years later he'd be dead. Or that Emma Lacey would blame me.

11

Rolle

Rolle takes the stone steps into Calloway Police Precinct two at a time. Nearby, the early morning bin trucks rattle. The building is just one of many rows of old working-class façades in Calloway – the larger of the two towns on the island. New-build, short-let apartments have sprung up nearby with cheap open-plan kitchens and narrow balconies overlooking the park that marks out its depressing centre. Rolle takes it as a sign that Calloway is on the up. He imagines the small grocery stores giving way to trendy vegan cafes. It's progress of sorts, he supposes – might even create jobs. But honestly, he doesn't give a crap either way. He won't be here that long. The psychologist he was corresponding with was wary about his suggestion of moving back to Miami. His wife was less subtle. 'We're never going back. How can we?' Alice would cry, distraught at the way they'd been forced to leave. He'd failed her too. But he'd clamped his teeth together to try to stop himself saying something he shouldn't. Trying, like the psyche said, to control his temper, to breathe through it. Besides, adding a crumbling marriage to the mix would only worsen his insomnia. The metallic-sweet taste of blood came if he bit down too hard. The taste of when he'd cut his finger as a boy with his father's knife, and later when he attended crime scenes. That same putrid taste on his lips.

The main door to the station is already unlocked. Somebody has tried to make the reception a little festive – tiny paper hearts hang in untidy loops across yellowing walls, reminding Rolle that Valentine's weekend loomed. A lone *Be-My-Valentine* balloon floats sadly by the inner door. He pushes it aggressively out of his path, sliding his key card over the sensor for the officers' entrance. Lovell Logan is already sitting at his desk in the open-plan space, head bowed, reading on his mobile phone. A cup of something steaming sits beside him on his desk. He sits up quickly, as if he's been caught doing something he shouldn't.

'You're in early,' Rolle greets as he slides into his own untidy space.

'No rest for the wicked.' Logan smiles, picking up his drink. He watches Rolle over the rim of it.

'All okay?' Rolle eventually asks.

'It's nothing.'

'Looks like something,' Rolle snaps back, knowing his irritation is more about the lack of progress on the missing Fitzpatrick kid than Lovell's smarmy face.

How the hell is he supposed to get on with anything if people keep thinking he's some kind of mind reader? He has enough of that with Alice. He thinks about Valentine's Day again and the knot of dread tightens.

'You happen to see the papers this morning?' Lovell takes another swig from the take-away cup.

'Why would I give a shit about the tabloids?' Rolle opens his own laptop, feeling the first pang of caffeine withdrawal, questioning why he chose to quit coffee this week of all weeks. But he'd had to do something drastic to claw back his sleep. 'It's turning into a circus. I knew it would.' He taps his password into the keyboard aggressively and glances up.

'Yeah, but how much of a shit do you give about the tabloids if it involves you?' Logan asks, raising an eyebrow.

'Spit it out.' Rolle isn't in the mood for games this morning. He'd spent the night thinking about that poor kid out there alone somewhere. He'd taken to sleeping in the basement of their rental. The official reason was because he didn't want his ongoing sleep issues to disturb Alice. But they both knew it was some kind of strange drift neither could articulate.

'Cat's out of the bag is all I'm saying,' Logan says conspiratorially. 'They're talking about the big shot detective from Miami. Antonio Rolle – the hero who took down that dirty perv Sal Reid.'

'I don't give a damn about any of that.' Rolle tries to keep his voice steady, but he can already feel his heart rate shooting up.

A moment later, he walks over to Logan's desk, deliberately casual. 'Show me then.'

Logan holds his phone up to Rolle. The screen shows a picture of Mirren looking away from the camera, a half-smile on her face, caught in a moment of madness and mania. If you took 300 photos a minute of anyone you could capture any expression you wanted, he thinks, frustrated. He pulls the phone off Logan and scrolls quickly down.

'Can't see a damn thing.'

He throws the phone back at Lovell.

'Bring it up on the computer.'

They read the article together on the screen in front of them. There are a few vague suggestions that Alannah's parents are to blame for leaving the child unsupervised. Then, there's a photo of Rolle in his Miami Police Department uniform. It's at least ten years old – his hair is much shorter. No jowls. Under the picture is a small grey box dedicated exclusively to him and his involvement in the case.

> Detective Antonio Rolle from the Miami Special Crime Unit is supporting recently appointed Lieutenant Lovell Logan and his team in the search for Irish eight-year-old, Alannah Fitzpatrick. Detective Rolle is the former US agent responsible for the arrest and detention of Sal Reid in one of the biggest child sex abuse cases in the state. It saw 14 men arrested on 828 charges two years ago in what Rolle described as 'an abhorrent systemic sexual abuse' of children. There were 25 child victims in Miami, one in Tampa and six in St Petersburg who were subjected to the filming and sharing of abuse videos to a closed online community. It was alleged that Sal Reid was the leader of the networking ring that facilitated the abuse and filming of minors for international distribution.

Rolle tastes iron in his mouth again and pushes the memory of Sal Reid's bashed and bloodied face out of his mind. I'm no hero, Rolle reflects. Not like they think. He continues scrolling to compose himself, though he's read enough. That they were linking his history to this story was typical of the media. Let them say whatever they want, he thinks; he's more frustrated about how they're portraying the Fitzpatricks, twisting their grief like a knife.

'Total nonsense,' he says, turning towards the coffee machine. He searches for the decaf button, knowing too that Logan is probably the type to resent any coverage that doesn't involve him in the case. His fragile ego can't handle it.

'That Sal Reid thing must be coming up soon, buddy.'

Rolle's hand twitches with annoyance. He's not in the mood to discuss any of what happened, what led him here or the impending court case – certainly not with this moron. He shakes his head dismissively and shoves the mug roughly under the machine.

'This place always such a ghost town in the middle of the biggest investigation the island ever had?' he asks instead. Beside the coffee machine, a crumpled printout is stuck to the wall. A motivational quote of sorts. 'Get off your ass and go knock on doors,' is printed on it, in big bold letters.

'Most of the guys were up all night trawling surveillance footage,' Logan replies dryly. 'You know, like you suggested?'

So, the lines are beginning to get drawn in the sand. Good, Rolle thinks, sliding behind his desk again. Fire in the belly always helps. Passive aggression, not so much.

'And I'm sure they've found plenty,' Rolle shoots back. Despite being a foot taller than his superior, he knows he has to go easy on Lovell Logan. That daddy's boy has too many connections. Besides, Antonio Rolle could do without another black mark next to his name. Nobody wants to see this thing blow up in their faces. The politics of it alone are complicated. There are increasingly loud noises coming from the top about Kite Island and its reputation internationally. A swift resolution is expected, but Rolle also can't stand over shoddy policework. 'George fucked it, Logan,' he says suddenly, unable to press that pause button his therapist keeps reminding him about. 'I knew he would. Half of the witnesses on the beach left without us checking their cells.'

Logan goes to say something, but Rolle talks over him.

'Now we've to rely on appeals, as well as a few greasy notes from George, most of which are pretty illegible, if I'm honest. Can he at least write up the witnesses' reports? He can spell, can't he?'

Logan holds up his hand.

'Are you finished?' He looks at Rolle coldly. 'Actually Antonio, this morning I'm speaking to some of the guests at the hotel about the parents' movements on the day before the child went missing. Did you know Nick Fitzpatrick has just filed for bankruptcy? We've done some digging and we've requested the Fitzpatricks grant access to their bank account records.'

Rolle looks up, surprised.

'There's more to that story than we've been told.' Logan snaps his laptop closed and pushes it deep into the sports bag he carries as a briefcase. 'I'm headed there now.'

'What about the blood on the beach?' Rolle asks. 'Petersburg lab shouldn't take this long to come back.'

'When we know, we know.' Logan taps his fingers on the desk impatiently.

'One of the former hotel chefs is coming in for interview at ten, the one seen hanging around Wilkes Beach when Alannah Fitzpatrick went missing,' Rolle continues.

Now it's Logan's turn to look surprised. They weren't his direct orders, true. But Rolle always follows his nose. Disgruntled employees hanging around the place they'd been booted out of, stank to him.

'I want you to do some more digging on the mother too,' Logan says curtly as he zips the bag closed in one deft stroke. 'Check out her work, her patients, the birth parents, the marriage, insurance claims, the usual.'

Rolle takes a slug from the putrid liquid in his cup. He thinks about the complicated levels of bureaucracy that are likely involved in contacting the adoption authorities in another jurisdiction. He'll start by emailing the Irish Gardaí.

'Will do.' Rolle keeps his eyes on his laptop. 'I'm going to get someone to talk to that other witness, the girl who got a look at the speedboat.'

Logan nods briefly but makes a face as if to say it's a waste of time. He starts walking towards the door and holds it open for two arriving officers, who smile an effusive thanks to their superior.

'One other thing worth following up.' Rolle follows him to the door. 'Remember that missing local girl, from last year, Mariah Whitaker? The kid?'

Logan clicks his tongue a few times as he contemplates. After a moment, he slowly nods.

'Yes, that shithole Ivory Bay, wasn't it? Whore's kid?'

Rolle's entire body tenses but he lets the ignorance slide. He'll have to pick his battles with this asshole.

'She says some guy called Red was hanging around there before she disappeared. Possible gang involvement. How come we never picked him up?'

Logan shrugs as he straightens his tie – a grey one today. 'Didn't we?' Either way, he doesn't look like he's lost too much sleep over the case.

'Know him?'

Lovell hesitates.

'Know *of* him,' he admits. 'But I'd be surprised if there was a connection. Small time gangbanger I believe.' He turns to leave. 'One missing kid at a time, eh, Tony?'

Rolle's hand twitches again.

'Oh, and don't forget to book somewhere nice for Alice.' He gestures at the tacky Valentine's decorations. 'Is she settling in any better?'

Slightly thrown by the question, Rolle chooses the easy lie.

'Yeah, yeah… all good.'

'There's a new Mexican place on Delray. Huge waiting list, but I'll get a table for the two of you.'

Rolle smiles through gritted teeth. There's little point in arguing with that smug face. The audacity of Logan not to realise how bad it would look for the investigating officer to be dining out socially while the Fitzpatrick girl is lost out in the Keys somewhere.

No way. He'll book somewhere quiet himself. If at all.

'And we'll get Jess and Alice together one of these days. She'll show her the ropes,' Logan calls over his shoulder. Antonio can't imagine anything worse than spending time with Logan outside of work, even if it meant Alice finally found a friend. The glass door slides shut. And as he watches Lovell's back jog down the steps, Antonio Rolle is overcome with a pang for his former team in Miami. His partners and friends. He realises too, for the first time, the magnitude what he and Alice had to leave behind. The devastating consequences fifty short violent seconds had made on both their lives.

12

Mirren

The Past

I think back to a time before everything got so complicated with Nick – around the time we first decided to try for a baby. It was a few years before Alannah's arrival and Nick had convinced me to take the weekend off work, usually a no-no for junior doctors. We left Réa with my sister and flew to Naples in Italy where we took a boat to an island called Ischia. I got sunburnt on the first day and wore my hair loose. We turned off our phones and spent mornings with our hands wrapped around frothy cappuccinos by the boat-dotted harbour. Hot afternoons were spent in bed, our skin deliciously cool between the fresh sheets. In the evening, I painted on my reddest lipstick and Nick held my hand as we strolled the narrow, cobbled streets. I knew he was my second chance at happiness.

One evening, we found ourselves sitting in a courtyard restaurant surrounded by irregularly twisted olive trees. A pianist leaned on chords that tangled deep in my heart. The waiter waved his hands expansively at our 'bello gioia', our beautiful joy and brought us pizzas in the shape of hearts. The air was garlicky sweet, and the cicadas hummed somewhere above when Nick stretched back on his chair and told me he never thought he could fall in love with anyone until he met me. For a man of limited emotional expressions, that statement was so unexpected, so sincere. I squeezed his hand across the table, overcome. Because he knew me for who I was back then. I'd let him be the only one.

'No really, Mirren – you don't even know what it is that you have. It's an enchantment. I feel like you've bewitched me.' He laughed at his own words, but deep down I understood what he meant. Jack had whispered similar when our bodies were wrapped together. Wildling, he'd call me, teasing me about the current that ran deep inside me – a turbulence not many can see. It took me years to allow Nick a glimpse of who I was. A classic defence mechanism, my old therapist described, when I told him about feeling unlovable. Worthless was my mother's name for me. So, I'd smoothed my riptide with serenity, expensive-looking shoes and a title. To let someone see your true self means added suffering when they eventually abandon you. Except for Nick.

Or so I thought.

A month after our Italian holiday, we made the decision to start IVF. That April I had my first miscarriage – a sad red tear in my underwear at work announced the end of that fledgling life. I finished my shift and cried all the way home. The glow of the streetlamps reflected off my tears as I strode sadly towards the gates of our lopsided cottage.

Then, the careful joy of another blue line, a month later. That faint mark on the white plastic stick was worth a million bruised stomachs, a thousand hormone storms, and a hundred arguments about ovulation windows. We bought a small white cradle and set it up in the room beside Réa's. We painted the walls duck yellow and hung a cloud mobile over the crib. It marked the beginning of our family together – Nick and me. Because although Nick loved her dearly, Réa was mine and I couldn't share her. Nor could I pretend that she belonged to him either, despite the strangers who smiled at us in the park presuming she was ours both. The little baby tucked up tight in my tummy was going to be our first shared thing. During that time, Nick's tenderness with me was when I loved him best. He'd make sure I was eating right, serving me up healthy meals he'd googled after my long day working at the hospital.

'Red cabbage!' he'd yell randomly from the kitchen. 'Spinach and avocado!' Then he'd smile as he laid my dinner before me with a comedic bow. We were his precious things, he told us often. But even he couldn't keep us safe. 'You must take it easy, Mirren,' he'd chide, as we lay on the couch in the evenings, pinching each toe gently as he spoke. Turns out we needed a lot more than steamed vegetables.

Instinctively I knew that the baby had died one morning in my seventh month of pregnancy. It was just a few weeks after our big scan – the one when they check the size of that tiny heart, the brain, the lungs. She had been perfect. That *day she had been perfect. We squinted at the small monitor, trying to decipher the black and white squirms on the screen as the midwife slid the scope up and over the mound of my belly, taking measurements.*

The morning it happened, I lay in bed, fighting the tiredness, psyching myself up for the day ahead. And it dawned on me that I hadn't felt her kick – our baby Alannah, as we'd decided to name her. I was aware of a low, burrowing pain – more uncomfortable than painful. I placed my hand over the warmth of that bump and waited, my heart beating wildly, counting frantically in my head. Then I was heaving ragged sobs and calling for Nick who was up already making coffee. Within an hour, the first blood came. I felt the wetness trickle into my underwear as I sat in the passenger seat of the car, tears running down my face. Then, only silence, punctuated with the cruel beeps of a steel-grey machine at the hospital. A horrible substitute for the gallop of feathery heartbeats we'd grown accustomed to. We listened carefully to that billowy nothingness as the midwife pressed deep into my most private crevices. Her sad headshake was a punishment nobody deserves. This was love crushed, like the mangled cloud mobile I later tipped into the kitchen bin. I dared to try to replace my lost baby Alannah with someone else's child and this is what happens; I lost the babies in my belly, so I lost my adopted daughter on the beach.

The audacity of thinking I could fix broken things when I was so terribly broken myself.

13

Rolle

Ugly, white lighting runs the length of the corridor. Rolle walks into the interview room behind former Coral Beach Hotel sous chef, Kata Charles, and gestures for him to take a seat.

'Thanks for coming in,' Rolle speaks respectfully. He doubts boys like this get much of it – respect that is. Part of the problem, he thinks. They go about demanding it yet have never been taught what it really means. Through martial arts, he'd learnt its importance – the bowing, that mutual dignity, win or lose.

'I'm Antonio Rolle. I'm a detective here at Calloway. I just want to go through a few things with you if you don't mind.'

Kata Charles clearly hits the gym, observes Rolle. Not too much though – things are in proportion. Brown eyes, a little over thirty, baggy jeans and a T-shirt, close-shaved hair, gold chain to match a couple of his teeth.

He nods stiffly at Antonio Rolle.

'Need anything – water, coffee?'

The sous chef shakes his head.

'We're working on the investigation into that missing kid.' Rolle bowls straight. He rolls his sleeves up over the curves of his own tan muscles. Hopefully Kata would also realise that the introduction is intended as a warning – code for I'm not here for any bullshit, buddy. Fight fire with fire, his dad would say. Kata shifts in his seat slightly, rearranges his legs under the table.

'Got nothing to do with me.' Kata leans forward, his hands flat on the table in front of them.

'You got a cell phone, Mr Charles?'

Kata looks up.

'Can we see the photos or videos you might have taken on the beach that day? Or messages? You were there that day, weren't you?' Kata nods slowly, as if trying to figure something out. It's likely he had another cell, thinks Rolle. Easily led, yes, but these guys are never dumb. 'I'll get one of the officers to take a look when you leave,' Rolle says, looking down at his iPad. 'And I see you are no stranger to the system?'

'I've been inside, yeah. Long time ago.'

'That was last year, Kata. Can I call you Kata?'

'I guess.'

'Do you know what it means?'

Kata looks at him. He barely moves.

'What what means?'

'Kata's a Japanese word. The name for karate exercises.' Rolle had spent enough years working on his kata. He welcomed the repetition of the movements, the whoosh of air as he bent and stretched, finessing, concentrating on every fraction of movement.

'Ma told me it meant pure,' Kata says quietly. 'Part Hungarian.' He shrugs by way of explanation.

He almost feels sorry for this kid who he knows from his criminal record was sent into the foster system aged just eight.

'Kata, where'd you go on Monday evening after the beach?' Rolle looks down at the iPad deliberately, as if he knows a great deal more than he does.

'We stayed around with my brother and a couple others.'

'Where's that?'

'Just round.'

'You used to work at the Coral Beach Hotel, right?'

'Yeah, a while back,' Kata answers, looking directly at the detective now.

'And you were fired?' Rolle asks politely, meeting his gaze.

'Boss was an asshole.' He shrugs.

You and me both, thinks Rolle. He scrolls confidently through Kata's digital details.

'Which friends did you say you were there with?'

Rolle is scanning the document but absorbing all of Kata's uneasiness. He looks like a man who had something to lose.

'My brother, my girlfriend.'

'Names please.'

Kata stalls and stammers as he tries to work out if he should share such information.

'Names please.' Rolle's tone is sharp.

'Lottie, my girl and, eh… Red.'

Rolle looks up suddenly from the screen. His heartbeat quickens.

'Red is your brother?'

'Half-brother, but we didn't see nothing. What's this got to do with the girl anyway?'

'Wilkes Beach is where the child vanished.' Rolle emphasises the word child. Not girl. No minimising. He feels a buzz of electricity too – a current that ripples through him. He loves it when a hunch pays off.

'We were just chilling. Not illegal, is it?'

Beads of sweat now dot Kata's forehead. There's a simplicity to the boy, but he's definitely hiding something. Would he be stupid enough to slip up, wonders Rolle. Or was he just caught in the crossfire of this situation – an unintended sidebar?

'What kind of work you do now?'

Rolle has seen people like Kata all his life. Young men who fell into gangs to find a community, a common sense of purpose, a misguided cult that happened to shower you with cash and power. He knows the pattern: men like him struggled to fit it, to keep jobs, they fall into flogging illegal fakes, sunglasses, handbags… then drugs, trafficking, prostitution, petty theft. Where there were tourists, especially rich tourists, there would always be those looking to scoop up some of the scraps. The plankton they shed was tempting, Rolle knows.

It makes him sad for the boy he imagines Kata had once been, but Rolle has no sympathy when the line is crossed, no mercy. Not in life, and not on the karate mat. He takes a slug of his third decaf of the day.

His head throbs. Nothing but sweet, sweet caffeine is going to get rid of this killer headache.

'I'm looking for work,' Kata explains, but he can see Rolle clocking his designer trainers.

'Not doing too badly.' Rolle raises an eyebrow, gesturing at the pristine kicks.

Kata doesn't answer.

'And your brother Red. What was he doing Monday night?'

Kata hesitates again. For the first time since they sat in the small interview room, he looks away.

'No idea. Ask him yourself.'

Rolle notices the change in Kata's demeanour. He seems uncomfortable, torn in some way. Rolle glances down and scribbles something on the lined pad balancing on his lap.

He thinks suddenly of the CCTV. The woman walking along with a child. Towards the rocks.

'Was Lottie with you the whole time?'

Kata doesn't look up.

'Yeah,' he says to the floor. But the spark is gone. The interview will fade to black now. Rolle knows the beat of them, and that he wouldn't be getting much more. No harm trying.

'Does your brother live with you up at Milton Point?'

'Lives on his boat mainly.'

'What's his full name?'

'Red Roccio.'

'Did you know the girl Mariah Whitaker, who went missing a few months ago from near there?'

'Don't know the names of every kid that hangs around up there, do I?'

He'll get nowhere else today. But there's one thing Detective Rolle needs before he leaves the room.

'I'll need to interview Lottie too, of course,' he continues, thinking of the shadowy figure on the beach that day with the child. 'Okay, Kata, I've two last questions for you and then we're done for now.'

Usually, Kata would be put under surveillance for the next few days to see his movements, verify his answers and speak to his former boss at the hotel again. But that requires manpower, something they don't have much of around here – especially when there are search parties to coordinate, fields and forests to be raked through. Rolle has a feeling he'll be spending a lot more time in his car. They have to find the brother too. But otherwise, they couldn't hold him for much longer.

'What car does your brother drive?'

Rolle leans forward to study Kata Charles' eyes. His Good-Boy-Now act is solid, but the eyes usually give it away. He's so close now he can smell his warm breath – grassy and stale.

'I think it's eh, one of those… like a Ford,' he finally answers, uncertainly. 'Used to be a labourer so…' Kata trails off, sounding unsure if he was saying something he shouldn't. Rolle knows that giving cops information, any type of information, would probably have been a big no-no Kata's whole life. No way he's going to start elaborating now. But Rolle has heard enough. Behind those dark pools of eyes, he's also seen something. And he doesn't like it. Bowing in karate had a double benefit – as well as respect, it was the way to look into your opponent's eyes – to really see who they were and what they stood for. Skittish or impulsive, stubborn or petty, he could see it right there in their eyes in those final moments before a battle commenced. Reading people had won Rolle a lot more matches than muscle speed and brute force. Although he had plenty of that too.

'Where is he? Where's Red?' Rolle demands, glaring at the man, an equally dangerous glint in his own eyes now.

14

Red Roccio ends the call. He sits for a moment staring out through the water-speckled windshield of the speedboat. Then he turns the key and the engine roars angrily to life. A decision has been made. He rubs his lips with his fingers, distracted. Swirling tattoos snake up one arm. Mythical creatures with thrashing serpent tails. On the other is a fake Rolex Daytona. It hasn't worked in a year, but he knows it looks good. The sun is beating down – February weather is always unpredictable: too warm in the sun, too chilly in the shadows. Red eases the boat out of the small jetty at Milton Point, making sure the blue tarpaulin covering the back of it is secure. The disappearance of the kid was hitting too many headlines for his client's liking. It was bringing too much heat. Maybe they should have thought of that before they did what they did. Red glances behind him a few times as he speeds up and cuts through the waves. The boat bounces, its belly slapping the water as he heads north up the coast. Out of habit, his hand gropes the underside of the driver's seat, making sure the Glock semi-automatic pistol is still there. He touches the loaded hunk of it, cool and smooth under his fingers. He told Kata the plan was to lie low for a day or two, until the coastguard stopped circling the island. Then they'd make their move. Red pushes down harder on the throttle, speeding now, exhilarated by the thoughts of what lay ahead.

15

Mirren

Lunchtime in Calloway is humid and hurried. Bodies press together as they scuttle towards the market stalls and cafes of the small port town. Somewhere nearby, a speedboat propeller cuts into the day. An exhausted-looking mother pushing a pram walks past, asking her trailing toddler to please move faster.

My fingers curl around the white sheaves of paper I've clutched to my chest.

To my left, a woman lingers for a moment by the pharmacy. She looks vaguely familiar, but the moment passes and when I turn, she's gone. Candy dropped us here at Calloway, beside the cafes, to hand out missing person leaflets. 'Back shortly to help,' she'd called from the window of the hotel-branded Jeep, her ruby nails blurring as she waved. I pictured her glancing back at us in her rear-view mirror as she drove off, eyes alternating between us and the road ahead – our little search party growing smaller until we disappeared completely. I look at the cafe in front of me and will myself to go in.

–

The mornings are the worst – the torment descending the minute I wake, like flies to a corpse. Réa wouldn't get out of bed again today. She's in a worse state than I am, lashing out in grief and shock. I picture her eyes, empty and sad. They remind me of my own, when I was admitted to the treatment centre a few years back. I'd stare at my reflection in my cubicle at The Residence realising I could never undo the things that had led me there. I knew I was being punished for my actions when Nick refused to bring the girls to visit. Then three weeks in, they arrived. Alannah jumped on my lap, smothering me with kisses I knew I didn't deserve. Réa hung back, eyes down, shoulders hunched. She refused to hold my hand. Nick's expression was sour, and I immediately felt that familiar pang of guilt. There's a selfishness to seeking help that others don't understand. How could I give them everything they needed when I'd nothing left for myself? That's the true burden of motherhood, having to abandon yourself constantly. 'Exposing your dark side shouldn't frighten you,' one of the therapists said, her words sticking with me long after I left The Residence. 'But hiding it might.' Still now, if I look in a mirror, those same eyes stare back accusingly. Bad mother, they say. Bad daughter. Bad wife. But I wasn't brave enough to acknowledge my feelings towards Alannah back then. It was my mother's death that brought it all to the surface. The realisation of the competing frequencies in my love for my daughters. The slamming reality that I turned to alcohol to numb.

–

A sudden sound startles me – unnatural, like a bird hitting a window. But there's not time to dwell on anything but pushing open the glass door into the cafe in front of me. I've a job to do. The air changes – the whoosh of new perspective quivers, and then I'm inside. The warmth of the vodka blunts the sharpness of the moment. Smells of cinnamon and grilled cheese waft towards me. Locals look over at me and then quickly away, but not without pity. I imagine what they see; a small woman hidden behind a curtain of unwashed black hair, a puffy face, a suitcase-crumpled jumpsuit. Huge dark sunglasses place an additional layer between me and the rest of the world. The attention Alannah's disappearance has brought to the doorstep of locals is unwelcome, but it has been the islander search parties that have been the most sympathetic to us. The kindness of strangers has always appealed to me. I figure people can't judge you if they don't know you. But I'm not sure that applies to this situation – to people like me. Because I'm starting to feel them measuring the authenticity of my grief. I bend forward and hand one of the leaflets showing my daughter's face into the outstretched hands of the teenager on the till. She makes a fuss, promising me she'll put it in full view. 'You'll find her,' she calls after me dramatically, as I trudge out the door, smells of brioche and toast turning my stomach.

One foot, the other foot.

If I concentrate on placing my left flip-flop in front of my right flip-flop and repeat, time will pass, the inky nothingness will give way to the moment I have my arms around Alannah again. I picture her swinging from my limbs with the casual confidence of a child who trusts she'll never fall. Or that I'll never drop her. I think of those freckles across her forehead, the chipped tooth she cracked during gym class. I can almost smell her soapy softness.

I did my best to love past that early unease. But she was both trigger and target for my resentment. I admit that I felt at times over the years that I was capable of hurting her. That frightened me – the rough throw onto the bed, the twinge of fleeting satisfaction when I registered fear on her face. Then, being instantly flattened with the shame of it all. I'd watch her sleep at night, her stillness mesmerising, dazzling in her innocence, and I'd hate myself. I'd hate myself so much.

Guilt and grief competed to pull me under. Was that intensity a product of our tenuous bond or because I was floored with the exhaustion of motherhood? The thing is, I don't remember being that way with Réa.

A bead of sweat trickles down my forehead and I smear it back into my skin with my thumb. I try to count the days Alannah is gone and fail. Three, maybe four days? Thoughts of the conversation Detective Rolle had with us claw at my mind as I walk along the street holding the leaflets. Another little girl lost alongside Alannah gives me no comfort – the thought of twin ghosts roaming the shores of Kite Island unbearable. But the suggestion that Alannah has been deliberately taken from us has opened new possibilities. I shudder, incapable of letting my mind go to that disgusting place. But alive… that's a spark worth kicking down doors for. Or knocking on them as I am here in this dive of a town on the other side of the world.

Detective Rolle also mentioned a man's name, Kata. 'Small-time thug,' he told us. 'He's been picked up for drugs and robbery before. He and his brother were at the beach that day. Rough guys pretending to be tough guys.' The detective had tried to sound gentle, but I could hear the worry in his voice. 'But it now looks like they skipped town. We're going to search Kata's house up at Milton Point, and then try to rule out some other people who were on the beach that day.' Rolle glanced sideways at me when he said that, not mentioning that golden sand stained with somebody's blood.

'I'll keep you updated. I know how hard this is, Mirren.'

I try to imagine this shadowy figure, Kata or whoever. But I can't see beyond my own grief. The coastguard divers had found nothing. Blurry images of two figures from the CCTV walking down the beach haunt every waking hour. Rolle asked us to look at the jumpy sequence the day before. Two people, one taller than the other, walk past the screen in black and white. The taller person makes unmistakably female movements as she moves. Her head is lowered towards the smaller figure, as if they are talking. I've watched the eight-second sequence over and over trying to see if it might be Alannah. She is skipping slightly, trying to keep up.

Where are you going, 'Lana?

I wrestle with the fact I'm in the bar at that very moment, drunk on despair and Corona Lites. 'It's her,' I told Detective Rolle when we were in the small room behind the reception of the hotel watching the footage. Nick agreed, but Réa was adamant that it wasn't her sister. 'Why would Alannah ever go off with someone?' she'd pointed out angrily. 'She's not a complete idiot.'

Maybe Réa is right. Hadn't we warned Alannah about things like this?

My phone beeps. It's clogged with hundreds of anything-we-can-do-to-help texts and emails asking for my digital signature to release files on our entire lives. They even want to speak to Alannah's birth parents. But it's Tara sending a picture of nearly all her leaflets gone. I thrust another missing poster into pitying hands and walk to the next doorway. My big sister stepped off the boat this morning, her bloodshot eyes brimming with tears, her bulky frame holding me tight, chiding me for not eating enough. I haven't seen her since Mother's funeral. Has it really only been a few weeks?

'We'll find her, Mirren,' she'd promised, as she held me tight, reminding me of those tangy nights wrapped up together in our child-hood bed.

Suddenly I'm disorientated – the lack of sleep and constant panic drilling holes in my brain. Nick was right to warn me that my mother's death could trigger something big. Since her funeral, I'd medicated with alcohol. An act of solidarity, perhaps. Because like her, drunk-Mirren is blind to consequences. She doesn't see what came before or what comes after. She doesn't care.

The next shopfront is shabby and discoloured with paint that curls away as if trying to escape its neglect. Across the road, photographers follow, clicking, clicking. I catch sight of my wretched face in the glass. The woman in the reflection distorts against the door pattern. Multiple faces, each layered against the next, give me the look of a rippled creature, inhuman. I shake off the grotesque creature looking back at me and push the door open. With each flat page containing my daughter's face that I give to strangers, part of me is erased. Like a chisel against the hardwood my father repaired the boats with, smoothing and reshaping, turning one thing into another. I wonder what happens when there are no more places to search.

Then, just as I step into the shop, somebody grabs me roughly from behind. My sunglasses fall to the ground.

'Mirren.'

Nick, at forty-seven, has grown greyer with each year, but remains a tower of a man – imposing, the moment you lay eyes on him. He has that familiar rugged face; a face you think you know before you even know him. People always remember Nick. He speaks my name so softly, so deeply in his throat, that the sound seems to come from somewhere else. It comes from a time when we weren't angry with each other about everything. We stand there a moment, facing each other on the street with the camera crews flitting around us. I try to see the old Nick, my Nick, in his narrowing eyes and fail. There is no gentleness in those eyes that bore into me. They are hardened like stone, flinty rough. I crouch to pick up my sunglasses, keen to use anything to shield myself from the commotion that follows me everywhere I go.

Grabbing my arm, he steers me away from the photographers. We walk without speaking, towards a pretty cafe with a seating area, cordoned off in a small blue courtyard, away from the prying eyes of the media.

'You are eating something. And then we are talking,' he commands.

As my husband browses the sticky laminate menu, I admire the edge of his jaw, the crease of faded laughter lines fanning out from his eyes. Tears roll down my face, salty streams stinging my skin as I try to dab them away. I've lost him too; I know I have. A startled waitress comes to take our order and Nick hands me a neatly folded tissue. 'Two cappuccinos – not too hot – and two chicken Tropicana wraps, only one with red onion,' he says curtly and turns to look at me.

'Would you like to see the Valentine's menu?' the waitress asks hesitantly. Nick swats her away and I continue to stare at the ground.

After the second miscarriage I was grief-stricken. I pushed Nick away, mainly to see if he'd come back – that thing we do. Réa was the one who soothed my soul and her little-girl innocence was all I could bear to be around. She was happy to have me all to herself. Like before. But I was too consumed with guilt to notice the deterioration of my marriage. Nick took responsibility for mending the fragile fragments of our relationship. He was the one who gently suggested adopting – a new way to reach our goal, a less damaging one perhaps. But none of us realised that the steps we took back then set in motion a chain of events that brought us to this miserable moment. We reclaimed our happiness for a time in between – our love was too strong not to. But my mother's death was the exact second I should have steered our ship a new way. Instead, I allowed it to drag me back to a place that I never wanted to return.

The waitress brings the coffees and sets them down quickly. Then Nick begins speaking. I watch his lips move but can't focus on the words he's saying.

'Mirren, are you even listening to me?' Nick taps his fingers in frustration on the polka-dot tablecloth. Immense sadness dampens the hot flames of my anger from the previous day. I'm too exhausted to think of anything at all, so I force my eyes to rest on my husband's and I try to answer him without keeling over. The smell of reheated food makes me even more nauseous and my head throbs.

'Tell me what happened. From the moment you left me by the pool.' His face is as serious as I've ever seen it.

'What are you asking, Nick?' My voice breaks as I try to make sense of it all. Everything feels very far away suddenly. I grip the table, but his face is scaring me.

'Mirren, you were hammered drunk. You left Alannah to have a fucking drink, or ten. You are still drinking.' Nick practically spits the words. He takes a slug of milky coffee as if to wash away the cruelty in his voice. My nails dig onto the cheap plastic table – I look at the veiny roads of blue and purple that track my hands. A red half-moon gash interrupts their network on the back of one wrist. I wonder how it got there; the injury looks fresh.

A few of the other customers glance over, embarrassed by Nick's agitated tone.

'Are you going to say anything? For fuck's sake, Mirren, Alannah is gone.' He drops his head into his hands, completely overcome. His shoulders shake as he tries to steady his emotions.

'She's gone,' he whispers.

'You swore you were still sober.' His voice is muffled now, far away. He stays like that for a minute – but eventually raises his eyes to look at me.

'It's just like before,' Nick says. I bite my lip, feeling like the lobster in the tank.

I push my chair out suddenly, scraping the legs along the wooden decking. I'm breathless with anger and indignation and something else too – something I can't understand. How dare he suggest this is all my fault. How dare he, after everything he'd said to me the other day. He'd started all of this. He'd sickened me with his words. He wasn't the one being dragged through the media mud.

'You're so arrogant,' I shout, frightened by the power in my voice. I swat hair away from my face with trembling hands and think of the *tápholl* from my childhood beach – the unsteady water where the currents meet and changes direction. The oily bubbles that are left behind. I open my mouth and look at Nick and his unforgiving face.

'You left me with no choice,' I shout. 'Can't you see?' My tears are falling so fast, they miss my cheeks completely and plop miserably onto the table before us.

'Be quiet,' he says, his voice low with warning. But I can't stop myself. I can't stop now.

'This is on you,' I say, pointing close to his face. Then too many people are staring. Everything is spinning. I'm exhausted and over-whelmed.

'Be quiet, Mirren,' Nick growls, even angrier this time. 'I need to talk to you about something. About something that might come out.' I open my mouth to speak again, but Nick suddenly moves towards me at lightning speed. I try to step back but the startling burst of camera clicks disorientates. I start to fall, too dizzy from all of it to stop myself. The last thing I'm aware of is Nick pushing the photographer away roughly. Protecting me, of course.

But he doesn't get to me in time.

Then I'm falling, falling onto the courtyard floor, sinking down into the ridges of the hard boards underneath, and out through to the other side.

16

Rolle

Rolle hates the smell of hospitals. It reminds him of his childhood visits to his mother as she lay pale and gaunt against oversized hospital pillows. That was in Miami General Hospital over a period of a year, as Magda Rolle battled the cancer that would eventually separate her from her husband and small son forever. That mother-shaped hole in his life remained wide open, even to this day.

The pungent smell of disinfectant catches the back of his throat as he walks down the corridor in St Anne's ward searching for the nurses' station. He tries to identify the emotion, like his wife Alice taught him, and realises it reminds him of the helplessness he'd felt as a child. His wife wasn't a bad shrink, all the same, especially considering she was a history teacher.

He got the call just after lunchtime to say that Dr Mirren Fitzpatrick had been brought by ambulance to the local hospital, a blocky pale building squatting half an hour from town. It's a miserable place, one he usually avoids at all costs. The officer who rang hadn't said why Mirren collapsed, but he presumes that grief and worry have taken their toll. He isn't surprised. She'd looked fragile and broken from the get-go.

Tormented.

At the nurses' station he introduces himself and is directed to one of the dingy wards just off the corridor on his right.

'She's exhausted and half-starved,' the pretty young nurse answers when he inquires if she is able for visitors. 'Been drinking too,' she says, dropping her voice and moving very close to him. Antonio Rolle tends to have that effect on women. Not something he'd have noticed unless

Alice had pointed it out, teasing him, years back. Irrelevant really – he'd always been a one-woman kind of guy. He nods, trying not to act surprised at the information about Mirren's drinking. But finding respite from a bottle was something he'd been familiar with after the Sal Reid debacle. He listens to the nurse note the treatment Mirren has received so far, then strides into the ward where he immediately spots Mirren in the bed closest to the window. Her eyes are closed, her face turned towards the early evening light which tries in vain to flit through the cracks of the blackout blind.

'Dr Fitzpatrick,' he calls quietly.

There are three other people in the ward, all with their privacy curtains pulled closed. Mirren looks at him blankly for a moment and then, as she registers his face, gestures for him to pull the curtains around her own bed. She sits up with effort and slowly adjusts the snake of transparent tubing coming from the back of her left hand. She looks drained and fragile, her dark hair is pulled back from her face into an untidy plait, and he notices a large purple gash on one side of her forehead – presumably the result of a pretty nasty landing.

'How are you?' he asks gently, pulling the plastic visitor's chair a little closer to her bed.

She opens her mouth to speak, trying to compose herself but her face crumples in deep pain, and she puts her hands up over her eyes to hide the gulf of her misery. Her shoulders shake as she cries. She looks so fragile – the alpha male in him feels useless.

'I can't… I just can't think.' She grabs a tissue from the almost empty box on the locker.

'Everything is destroyed. I don't know what to do.'

A pile of crumpled tissues sits next to the box, like a collection of sad snowballs. The nurse warned him that they had given her calming medication – he can see it now in her eyes which are a brilliant drug-filled blue. As they talk, she remains slightly off beat, her words thick and her movements slow – like a movie with misplaced tracking.

'Where's Nick?' he asks when she seems calmer. He's never met anyone which such delicate features; she's petite, almost childlike herself. Her face is smooth despite her age, and her accent is melodic, even in its misery.

'Do you have children, Detective?' she suddenly asks, looking at him with those indecipherable eyes.

'I don't. Alice… well, we couldn't,' he replies. Antonio Rolle had long made peace with their family situation. He'd committed himself instead to trying to protect other people's children – especially from predators like Sal Reid. But he wasn't sure Alice had fully come to terms with it. Not that he was about to spill his guts to Mirren. He thinks of his wife's sad eyes and shakes his head slightly.

'It's a love like no other,' the mother continues, dabbing at her eyes. 'That's what everyone says anyway.'

She squints at him, her head lolling slightly.

'But do you know what Alannah used to say?'

He shakes his head again.

'That there are four types of love. Mummy, she'd say to me… there's peaceful love. That's blue.' Mirren is smiling now, distant, remembering her daughter's words. 'Peaceful love is when you don't have to do anything but be loved. Then red love is true love. That's two.' Rolle's phone vibrates in his pocket, and he slides it out quickly. A message from Logan.

'Go on,' he says to Mirren, so she doesn't think him rude. Her eyes are far away, unfocused.

'Green is never-ending love and yellow is happy love – a kind of laughiness, Alannah would say.'

'So, like a rainbow,' he suggests, distracted, as he clicks into his message inbox as discreetly as possible.

'Yes, Detective. Exactly like a rainbow. She'd always text me love heart emojis, a row of four different colours. I'd know it was her.' Mirren is smiling but her eyes are closing.

A long pause. Then her eyes snap back open.

'There is a spectrum of love that can only be applied to children. It's not black and white like romantic love. Do you understand that, Nick?'

She looks directly at him.

'Detective Rolle,' he corrects her.

She ignores him and keeps talking, faster now.

'Mothers will do anything for their children. I see it all the time where I work. They'd kill for their child. They come to me, and they trust me to save them but sometimes their little bodies just aren't compatible with this world. Sometimes all the medicine in the world can't save them. Sometimes dying is better than the pain they experience every single day.'

She sits up. His finger hovers over the link Logan just sent to him. He notices Mirren's hands are shaking and wonders if there is more history behind the drinking than he thought. Or maybe grief is making her seem so fragmented. He nods agreeably and finally clicks into the link that Logan has messaged him. It brings him to the photos of Mirren crumpled on the floor of a cafe; her body crowded by strangers. The indignity of devastation. Above the image – a strap across the screen in red shouts Breaking News...

Rolle's heart sinks when he reads Lovell's next message.

We just got a witness who says the mother and husband were fighting by the pool the day the kid went missing. That she assaulted him.

Typing again.

Update on her condition pls.

This case isn't black or white either, it seems, thinks Rolle. This was starting to get a lot more complicated. But Mirren had said something else important. Damn, what was it?

'Mirren,' he says more sharply than intended. 'I need to speak to you about Nick for a moment – did you have an argument?'

She falls quiet for a few moments. Then, softly, 'Yes.' Clearly fatigued now, Mirren lies back against the pillow. 'At the cafe.'

'No,' he continues. 'At the hotel. Someone says that you and Nick had an argument by the pool of the Coral Beach Hotel. Just before Alannah went missing. That you were both shouting.'

There's a long pause, Mirren's eyes are closed, and Rolle thinks for a moment that she might have fallen asleep.

'Nick is leaving me,' she says finally, breathing out deeply.

He looks at her, some strands have escaped from her plait, her eyes are unnaturally bright.

'He told me that day, I made him tell me. I guessed and I confronted him. He said I pushed him away.'

Mirren's head doesn't move, but even with her eyes shut tears stream down her face and onto rivulets below her throat. Rolle watches them seep down along the length of her neck.

'So, I pushed them all away.'

She looks at him for a reaction, but Rolle has nothing to give.

He's at a loss. Should he tell her that her picture is all over the internet? He scans the main news sites quickly on his phone. It makes a horribly clickable story and an uncomfortable undercurrent to the tale of a family already in turmoil. This doesn't look good. Not at all. This plays right into the image they wanted to portray – the unhinged parent. Grief or madness, who gets to say? Rolle also knows the tabloids will now only dig deeper. They won't just find all the skeletons, they'll do their damnedest to position them strategically first. Now it's only a matter of time before this argument by the pool is exposed.

'Mirren, I need to know everything about that day, or I can't help you.' His voice is stern. 'Do you understand that any distraction whatsoever means the focus on finding Alannah is compromised?'

The woman in front of him seems like a fighter, despite her current demeanour. He has to help get her shit together or the media will rip her asunder.

'Mirren, is that why you went to the bar? To get drunk?'

'I haven't taken a drink in almost eight years. I started drinking again a few weeks ago, when my mother died.'

Slurring from the medication, she raises her arm heavily into the air and mock clinks her invisible glass. 'Cheers.'

Something's bothering Rolle, though. Something Mirren had said earlier. He tries to think, but Mirren keeps talking.

'Said he was going to tell me when we got home. He thought we'd have one last happy memory as a family. Blamed me, the bastard.'

There's fury in her eyes – and sadness, real sadness.

'And then Alannah…' she trails off, looking off towards the window again. 'And then here we are.'

Rolle massages his eyelids, both palms to his face, buying time, as he considers what to say next. He'd kill for a flat white right about now. He feels desperately sorry for Mirren Fitzpatrick, but what she's saying raises questions that he knows, from experience, will be problematic.

His priority is finding Red Roccio and his brother, to try to link them to this conclusively. But that isn't proving straightforward either. The last address Red had given to his parole officer didn't exist. The one before that was some halfway house in Miami. Of course, nobody had checked he was going to be where he said he would. Under-resourced, both financially and morally. He sighs, wondering how anything ever gets solved here on Kite. Fucking backwater.

They'll have to cast the net further. They need to refocus this circus, away from the tempting Dynasty-esque storyline the media was about to capitalise on. But the threat of marital separation, loud arguments, a catatonic mother staring blankly into the distance; none of this is good. They have another thirty or so CCTV tapes to trawl through from businesses around Calloway and at the main port, but right now Alannah's a ghost. It's as if she's simply vanished.

His phone vibrates again in his hand, and he sighs. *What now?* Two new emails sit at the top of his inbox, envelopes closed, waiting for him. Alice was right – they definitely needed a holiday. A cruise might even be nice.

The first is from the Irish Gardaí noting the Fitzpatricks had been in touch with the Department of Foreign Affairs. Rolle scans it quickly. They recommend he contact the Adoption Authority of Ireland to get background on Alannah's biological parents, but they note in the final paragraph that Nick Fitzpatrick had been in trouble with the country's tax authorities as recently as three months ago.

Financial problems always interest Rolle.

The second email is from Dr Eddison Sterling at the Clearways lab in St Petersburg. He clicks in, realising he's praying as he does. Scanning the report, his heart sinks. According to DNA, the blood found on the beach by the cove has a 98.4 per cent chance of belonging to young Alannah Fitzpatrick. Dr Eddison would like to set up a call with him to discuss the findings. At his convenience, of course.

Rolle sighs heavily. They were increasingly looking at the likelihood of a murder investigation – a whole different ball game. He glances at Mirren, feeling desperately sorry for the situation she's found herself in.

He can't tell her any of this now, not with those dark circles under her eyes. God, he hates feeling so helpless. But there's only so much he can do to protect her.

Rolle stands up to leave but stops suddenly. Something floats right at the edge of his thoughts, something important. He's motionless for a beat, as he grasps at it, tugging it gently back into his consciousness.

Then it clicks – the thing he couldn't quite put his finger on. He spins around and locks eyes with Mirren.

A pause.

'You said Alannah would text you,' he states abruptly.

Mirren nods, more alert suddenly, a strange look on her face.

'Yes, we got it for her, so she'd be safe.' She shrugs at the obvious irony of it.

But she looks frightened suddenly, caught out. No sign of the earlier confusion. Her face is flushed.

'Mirren, you never told me she had her own phone,' Rolle says sharply.

She pushes back a few strands of hair that have escaped from her face, her eyes considerably more focused now.

Rolle takes a step towards her and rubs his hand over his jaw.

'Where is it, Mirren? Where is Alannah's phone?'

17

Mirren

When I open my eyes, I see Réa. She's perched on the side of my bed, pencil in hand, sketching. From here, I'd like to draw her myself – her sharp profile, the angular nose, those high cheekbones that I know off by heart. Her hair is pulled into an untidy bun, tendrils curling, creating a halo of black fuzz at the nape of her neck. My beautiful, silent daughter. She's always been slender but now, at sixteen, she's grown into that skinny frame. Her limbs are long and graceful – even her fingers are elegant as they flit and skit over the page, the nib smoothing some parts and shading others. She's wearing the dress we bought in Zara for the holidays, the black one with the long sleeves. We both know it's to hide the path of faint scars that ladder untidily up her arms, but it's never been acknowledged – no time ever feels right to expose that particular wound.

She looks up, slightly startled as I stir. Every movement is painful. I touch my heavy head lightly with my fingers and wince.

'Mum,' she whispers. 'Are you okay?'

The paper falls from her lap as she jumps up. Woosh, one direction, woosh, the other. Then her drawing skims the floor, landing close to the bottom of the privacy curtain.

I smile at Réa and attempt a weak thumbs-up.

'I'm sorry,' I whisper back, my voice thick and slow. I clear my throat and she hands me a glass of water that she's refilled from a jug by my bedside table.

'Sorry Roo,' I manage, a little louder. 'I'm all over the place. I don't know what's going on.'

She nods and holds my hand. We both watch her thumb tracing mine.

Out of nowhere I picture a tiny, curved scar, white against freckled arms. A fingernail stamp that lingered after a burst of frustration. I shake my head and focus on Réa – the daughter I can see.

'Any news?'

She shakes her head.

I've often wondered if Réa's silence in life is because of the silence she was born into. We never talked about her dad – not until much later. Even then, she didn't say much. I know she went to Jack's grave. She had all the books he ever wrote – searching for something to cling onto – some hidden sign or clue planted among the print about who she had come from. He'd not had the same opportunity to find any breadcrumbs from her life. I stole that from both of them. Only now, on reflection, I realise my pride was their loss. Maybe that's why Réa and I had forged this most special of bonds. Because we'd both suffered the loss of those we'd never met. We were infatuated with the ghosts of relationships that might have been.

The nurse interrupts us. Falsely bright, she fusses over my drip and hands me a small paper cup with two painkillers.

She greets Réa warmly. 'Your older daughter?' she asks kindly, and I appreciate her candour. Too many people tiptoe around tragedy.

The nurse breezes out, promising to organise my release as quickly as possible, and leaves Réa's fallen page on the seat of the chair. I lie back on my pillow and exhale deeply. Réa looks at me nervously.

'Mum, there's a picture online…' she starts, but then stops, as if considering something.

I look over at her, but she glances away.

'Please, just get better so we can go home.' For a moment I think she means Ireland, but the thought of leaving this place without Alannah is unthinkable right now.

Réa falls silent again. The quietness I brought into our lives was borne out of necessity. Evenings were spent focusing on my textbooks, my eyes raw from concentrating on diagrams of bile ducts and artery networks. Réa had been such a good baby. I'd feed her, swaddle her tightly and she'd sleep until morning. When she was older, she'd spend hours colouring or playing with dolls. It was like she knew that I needed that silence. For both of us.

And perhaps our perfectly fine but relatively joyless lives would have continued had we not met Nick. My gut twists when I think of him. It always has. He brought out a vulnerability that helped me love myself – like his love was a reflection. Maybe that was the problem – I'd absorbed all of his love and then used it up on Réa.

'How's Nick?' I turn to Réa, who shrugs.

'You both need to get your shit together,' she says, anger unfurling. I recognise the beginning of one of her outbursts. They've been less frequent in recent months, but we're all teetering on the edge with Alannah missing.

'You're making all this so much harder for me.' Her breathing quickens, and I watch as her foot jigs beneath the visitor's chair. This was how her panic attacks sometimes started.

'Breathe,' I coach her. 'It's going to be okay, Roo. Breathe.'

How could I tell her that he was planning on walking out on us? Especially as it had taken so long for her to let him in.

The problem with a relationship as tightly coiled as Réa's and mine, is that there isn't much room left for anyone else. Introducing Nick to my child wasn't straightforward. Réa found it hard to accept that loving someone else wouldn't dilute my feelings for her. And she made it known. She'd never had to share me before. Back then, I'd wonder how much of my own life imprint was stamped on her. For she was the seed of a twice-rotted apple.

I notice the drawing on the chair. It's the beginnings of a set of eyes, the curve of a face. In just a few lines of grey squiggles, Réa has captured perfectly the girlish crinkle of her sister. It's mesmerisingly accurate. She watches my reaction and then quickly folds it into her bag. I feel the tug of her yearn for approval – the need for validation that began as soon as she realised that there was someone else who needed my love. How could I ever show her how pure my love for her was? She was my

Imramma – she lifted me up and over the ninth wave and transported me to another world. But what I said to Réa, it never seemed to be enough. She'd never know that my love for her was part of the reason I felt so guilty about Alannah.

'It's breathtaking,' I tell her, and she squirms contently under my words. Suddenly I think I might choke on all these feelings. They bubble to the surface, a surge of regrets, of what-ifs, a wave of emotion that engulfs. I reach for Réa's hand to steady myself, but she's already turned to pull on her cardigan, she doesn't see.

'I'm going for coffee, want one?' She refills my glass again and steps closer to me. I shake my head, biting back tears. I haven't told her I've been drinking again; I couldn't bear to disappoint her. She lays a warm hand on my head, touches the wound gently and bends to kiss my cheek. I put my hand over hers, keep it there for a second, pressing her warmth against mine. I feel the gentle crush of her fragile bones against my skin, the surge and thrum of a pulse that was once mine.

Mine.

'I love you, Roo.'

'I love you, Mum.'

When she leaves, I reach for my silver phone charger on the other side of the locker. The painkillers are kicking in. I hover over Nick's last message, the one he sent hours ago. But I'm too tired to think of the appropriate response to the news that it was our daughter's blood that spilled on the beach that day. There's no emoji for numbness or shame or grief. Everything is surreal – I can barely remember even being in that scruffy beach bar anyway.

Instead, I text Alannah. I told Detective Rolle earlier that I didn't even think to tell him about her phone. In all the commotion, I hadn't registered the fact that the phone companies might be able to locate it. He'd hurried off after I explained this to him.

I'm sorry, I text Alannah now. Then, four different coloured hearts. Our rainbow love. I press send. I'm about to place the phone down when two blue ticks appear.

The air is pulled from my lungs.

'She's seeing it,' I cry out to the empty room, the phone shaking in my hands.

I check again. Did I get it right? My vision blurs as I try to steady my breathing and look again.

Unmistakable. Her profile says she's online. Right now.

'Oh my God, she's there.'

'Alannah.' I fumble to press the call button, but the online status disappears. I try calling over and over, but there's no answer.

There's nobody there at all.

18

Rolle

The waves lick at the bright sand rhythmically, staining it dark. The voice-over explains that it is six days since Alannah Fitzpatrick vanished from This Very Spot. The camera zooms in on a couple walking hand in hand – Nick and Mirren, their twin shadows long against the light. They've been told to look sad and longingly out to sea by the producer. The crew works on cut-aways and close ups of their faces. Millions have tuned in to watch the Fitzpatricks' heartbreaking story. But also, to watch them interact.

Rolle watches the interview at home with Alice. He was against this idea. A recreation of the day the child went missing can't harm, Candy had suggested, enthusiastically. The hotel liaison had organised a child actor, extras and even an interview with the couple, a bid to take the heat off Nick and Mirren's demeanour and back onto finding Alannah.

Mirren was horrified when the idea was first floated – mainly by the idea of a child playing at being Alannah. Then, by the idea of a one-to-one interview on the biggest US cable news show, *24-Hours*. But Nick quickly agreed. He understood that reports of their display of violence that day by the pool could jeopardise the search for Alannah. Plus, the photo of Mirren's collapse needed managing. The couple had to appear solid, drama-free and entirely focused on appealing for information. The search continues either way, Rolle had explained, when Nick pressed him on the blood findings. How could he tell them anything less? Hope was all they had left. He wouldn't bring up Nick's finances. Not yet. Not until he gets the full picture.

Mirren, after being released from hospital with medication, remains understandably jumpy. Nick, aware of the fragility of his wife's state of mind, seems happy to steer the logistics. Réa sits quietly during every interaction, her aunt Tara clutching her hand tightly. Candy's idea to take control of the media might just work, Rolle hopes.

'They want to hear from you. You need to be accessible. Then they'll leave you alone.' Candy had shrugged, as if it was the most obvious thing in the world. Her contact in *24-Hours* jumped at the chance to organise a sit-down interview with the Fitzpatricks who hadn't done any interviews since their youngest daughter's disappearance. It was to be with ice-queen Sarina Bindra – a no-nonsense journalist known for her powerful human interest stories. But Rolle wasn't so sure truth was the motivation here. This was entertainment masquerading as concern. Heartbreak porn. Social media was now awash with drastic home detectives spinning conspiracy theories. *She's clearly hidden the child to keep the husband around*, wrote someone on one of the hundreds of forums about the missing girl. *She was smirking at the press conference. That mother is a nut job*, wrote another. There were thousands of similar posts strewn nastily across the internet. Others claimed both parents had killed Alannah and had disposed of her body somewhere on the island.

Did the police even search the hotel properly?

Can you believe she left her kid alone and went to a bar? Doesn't deserve to have kids at all.

Lock her up and throw away the key. Her kids should be taken off her.

It was frightening how some of the public had turned on Mirren, just because she wasn't weeping prostrate before them. Or perhaps it was just that the trolls were the ones shouting the loudest.

The cafe photo had depicted Dr Mirren Fitzpatrick as troubled and unfit – character traits a mother cannot be. But being a bad mother isn't a crime. Of course, there were other theories hashed out in whispered conversations. Concern and gossip, the most dangerous two-headed beast. It was pointed out that a few of the hotel staff had questionable pasts, others suggested a trafficking ring involving the US and Mexico. That thread interested Rolle the most, but until they found Red and

Lottie, it was difficult to know where the next stepping stone lay. He'd made some calls to former colleagues in Miami. It would be interesting to see if anything came back considering the rumours that Kata and Red were regulars in and out of there. But the most worrying part for Rolle is the fact that Red Roccio had been convicted of a violent sexual assault on an eighteen-year-old university student, five years ago. He'd been indicted on further false imprisonment charges and had been released the year before. Rolle's alarm bells are clanging, and he doesn't intend to let this strand go without yanking it hard first.

While a missing kid and a rap for violence doesn't necessarily tally, in Rolle's experience there usually wasn't smoke without fire.

More importantly, the brothers seem to travel with a woman. Rolle thinks of the grainy CCTV images again. Another concern of Rolle's is his boss. Lovell Logan seemed to prefer wading through some of the tips that had come in off the back of the press conference earlier in the week. The obvious route, Rolle thinks. He knows Logan's feeling pressure from the top. And although Rolle isn't sure what would come out of this sit-down interview, he tries to swallow the knot in his stomach. The news on the blood wasn't good. Not at all.

He'd spent an hour on the phone to Pete Waters in Forensic Evidence. Presumably, if the tyre tracks on the sand in the cove were made by the perpetrator, figuring out which type of tyre was the objective. Maybe they could match it to Red's Ford. The problem with pattern evidence like tracks, and Rolle had seen this before with footprints on gravel outside a nightclub shooting in Daytona, was that they were notoriously difficult to identify. Not only that, but they are difficult to create castings from, especially on sand, difficult to interpret and even more difficult to match to a potential suspect.

Pete explained that to be able to declare a match that would hold up in court, it would have to contain more than just general characteristics created by the manufacturer. Besides, he said, there were millions of Goodyear and Michelin tyres. Not even anomalies in the grooves, like nail marks, wear, uneven fitting were as helpful as one might think. On hard ground perhaps, but certainly not on soft sand.

It was frustrating. That was the problem with TV shows like *CSI* – they created false expectations people had for investigators. No computer existed where you entered the results, sat back and waited for a name to pop up. Ultimately, getting an exact match would rest in the eye of the beholder, and they both knew that no judge in Florida, or anywhere else for that matter, would ever go for that.

After the mournful montage on the beach, a live interview back at the hotel with Nick and Mirren follows. Alice, sitting beside him on the couch, sighs and stands up to leave. 'Can't we turn this off?' she says, surprisingly emotional. 'This isn't a spectator sport, you know.' But they both know that everyone will be watching the segment, perversely enthralled by the horror of such a thing as losing your own child. Rolle hears her starting the car and pulling out of the driveway. She's almost never home these days. Maybe he should have mentioned the Valentine's dinner.

On the screen, Dr Mirren and Nick Fitzpatrick sit in matching armchairs in a hotel suite with carefully placed flowers and studio lighting. They look almost technicolour, unreal. The heavy make-up makes Mirren look older than she is, but the bruise on her forehead is just visible under the layers of thick foundation. She is undeniably beautiful, with her black hair blow-dried in that bouncy way women love, and a white shirt tucked elegantly into jeans. Nick wears a pale blue shirt, his silvery hair brushed back, exposing a slight receding hairline, his face gaunt despite the stage lights. The camera tracks a wide shot, showing Bindra sitting opposite the couple, notes balancing on her lap. The angle changes and it's a close-up of her carefully managed face.

'There has been criticism of you, Dr Fitzpatrick, because you were in a bar at the time Alannah went missing.' Bindra smiles compassionately, her brow furrowing in trained sympathy.

It's an awkward moment, but also excellent television. Especially because of Sarina Bindra's reputation as the ultimate smiling knife. The camera pans the couple's faces slowly. It rests on Mirren's. The question everyone is asking hangs in the air.

Mirren's hands are folded in her lap. Eyes down.

'What do you say to people who blame you for your daughter's disappearance?'

The tension is unbearable.

Jesus, go easy on her, whispers Rolle, noticing that Nick has also turned to look at Mirren, the camera flicks to his face to monitor every tiny reaction. The live production team have obviously been briefed that this is a contentious issue. Climatic, he guesses you'd call it. But the problem is that this isn't a movie, or a TV show conjured up for entertainment. This is a real-life tragedy. A little girl is out there missing somewhere. The vulgarity of it sickens Rolle. He turns to say as much to Alice, but remembers she isn't there. He thinks of Alannah's missing phone. Dead now, just like most of the leads.

'She usually just left it in the room,' Mirren had explained wide-eyed in the hospital when he asked about the phone. 'I didn't even think to look for it. I don't know what I thought.' The last time it had been switched on was later that day. Mirren had called him, jubilant. 'Proof she's alive,' she'd cried. To him, it was proof that somebody had the kid's phone. It was proof something sinister was going on. The last geolocation for the phone was within a 10-mile radius of the Coral Beach Hotel. In other words, it hadn't gone far. Yet.

Mirren considers Sarina Bindra's question. Rolle prays the strength of her character will finally emerge, so that the public can see what he sees – a mother's devastation, a family's obliteration. Conspiracy theories fucked him off – all that waste of time judging and second guessing. And for what?

'I was just yards from my daughter when she went missing.' Mirren finally speaks. Her voice is firm and clear – the first time Rolle has seen this confidence. Her timing is spot on. 'It could happen to anyone. It could happen to you.' Mirren looks directly into the camera. 'My eyes were only off her for a few moments. Right now, the media is painting me and my family in a concerning light and it is nothing but a distraction.'

For the first time, Rolle can picture her on a ward, or reassuring the family of one of her patients. Cool and collected. No sign of the desperate, ethereal creature he'd spoken to in the hospital. In fact, it doesn't seem like the same person at all.

'Our daughter is lost, and we need help finding her. Not questions about our sex life.' On a screen in the background, an image of Alannah appears. She's wearing a pink and white outfit, smiling. She's looking just beyond the camera and squints into the sun. The montage shifts to a picture of younger Alannah and Réa dressed up at Halloween, two cute witches – one tall, one small, holding up bags of sweets proudly to show the camera. Another slide, this time of Mirren with her daughters. She looks younger, her hair longer. Alannah, about five in the picture, is draped around her neck, their cheeks pressed tightly together. Réa, a mini version of Mirren, stands behind, her hands on her mother's shoulders. She has the beginnings of a self-conscious teenage pout but she's holding bunny ears behind her sister. The last picture on the loop is Alannah's Communion picture. She is surrounded by buttermilk-coloured taffeta. The background is muted grey, obviously a studio portrait. She looks bewildered, as if the flash just went off and a beat later, she realised what had happened, that she was supposed to smile.

It's cute, really cute. And totally heartbreaking.

At the centre of all of this is her, thinks Rolle. Some seemed to have forgotten that. He feels that lump in his throat again and looks away quickly before it turns into something unmanageable. It didn't bear thinking about such innocence shattered. Overwhelmed, Rolle turns the volume up to drown the images in his head of a different time, a different tragedy.

It's also impossible to erase the pictures he spent the morning examining – the other missing child. Mariah's case file was pathetic-ally thin. Coverage was even thinner, except for the lone report on a mother's quest for justice one of the smaller papers had run a few months back. Online, he'd found a picture of Glades photographed outside Calloway police station, a framed picture of Mariah in her hands. The article alluded to the two-tiered justice system and the questionable police investigation into Mariah's disappearance. *How this mother earns a living shouldn't have anything to do with the search for her child*, the headline reads.

Nothing came of it. A sex-worker who waitressed part-time at Marla's Pancake House and her fatherless kid were no match for a renowned oncologist from Ireland and her doll-like daughter. Glades was also right about another thing: according to the police report, nobody ever investigated Kata and his brother. The only people interviewed were Glades herself, Mariah's best friend Tiffany, who'd been with her on the beach the Halloween night she'd vanished, and a teacher at Ivory Bay Middle School. No follow-ups, no arrests, no other statements. There was a paragraph in the file on Glades causing a scene at the police desk when she'd come in demanding answers last December. They'd considered filing harassment charges but never followed up on that either. Rolle felt sick to his stomach. People like the Whitakers had little on their side. Mariah was just twelve years old for goodness' sake.

Rolle had gone over Mariah's file carefully. She was a smart kid, the teacher had said. She loved cheerleading and helping teach the younger kids the more complicated flips. She wanted to be a baker.

Not just some kid, but a person with dreams, a future pastry chef. Rolle would now need to go back to speak to Tiffany. To try and fill in some more of the blanks from Halloween night.

On the TV, Mirren continues to answer Bindra's questions. And like Candy had coached her, she keeps steering the conversation back to the same vital appeal.

'Today my husband and I want to ask you, each of you, to please think of anything that might help to bring Alannah back to us.' Her sincerity is mesmerising. She glances back at the images of Alannah behind her and hesitates. She inhales deeply and turns to the camera once more.

'Have you seen her? Were you near here that Monday? Did you see anything that might help us? Anything at all.'

The camera switches to Bindra again. She glances down at her notes, perhaps giving Mirren a moment to compose herself. More likely to build suspense, Rolle thinks cynically. Poor Glades Whitaker didn't have a chance.

'Dr Fitzpatrick, what can you tell us about the argument you had with your husband shortly before Alannah disappeared? There are reports that you struck him in an altercation by the hotel's swimming pool.'

Rolle notices Nick shifts in his seat slightly. He's not said much throughout the interview. His silence is curious. Why is Mirren the only one having to fight against this judgement? Where's his contribution in all of this? Then Rolle catches himself, annoyed – now he's doing what everyone else has been doing. Judging for how something seems.

Bindra speaks again.

'We heard a witness say that you were both extremely angry that day, the day Alannah went missing.'

Rolle sits back on the couch, anxiously. Please Mirren, please remain calm… sane, he pleads.

'As I've already said, Sarina, our private life isn't of concern,' Mirren states simply. She knows she's on show, she's switched it on.

Then, Mirren turns to Nick and reaches for his hand. He smiles back at her, and they both look at Bindra.

'All we want to do is find Alannah. Anything else is simply a distraction. Please help us find our daughter. We miss her so terribly.'

Her voice cracks and she looks down at her hands. Sad but demure. The image people want. The image that they expect.

Sarina Bindra smiles her thanks and the lights in the makeshift studio fade. The image of Alannah disappears. The well-known news sting plays, and they cut to the ads.

19

Mirren

I excuse myself from the hotel room to throw up. The hot lights, fake smiles and smell of make-up have turned my stomach. When there's nothing left to heave, I flush the toilet and sit on its lid. I've never felt so exposed in my entire life. I focus on the imperfections in the white tile grout and practise tapping my pressure points, the way they taught us at The Residence. Using pressure as a way of balancing my body's energy system was an ancient Chinese method at odds with everything I'd learnt at medical school, but it was the only thing that had helped release negative emotions in ways I couldn't fully understand. I notice as I press down that the injury on my hand has started to heal. After what seems like ten minutes, but could be an hour, I slip past the TV crew members who are busy dismantling lights. We've been filming in a junior suite on one of the top floors of the hotel. Sarina, on her phone in the corner, is no doubt lining up the next heartbreaking tragedy for the network. I realise I've just been consumed by the general public. It feels draining.

I creep down the hotel corridor, to a door leading onto the roof garden. People come here for the views, but ten years ago we'd been too wrapped up in our own wedding reception to notice them at all. I imagine the ghosts of Nick and I, gliding up the flower-strewn steps, frothy champagne in our hands, jaws sore from smiling.

The evening is soft and warm. Oaky BBQ smells fill the air. I'm alone on the open-air terrace, which should normally be packed with well-heeled guests enjoying icy sundowners. But this area hasn't reopened since Alannah went missing – to keep the ever-present media at bay, I imagine. Grateful to have the place to myself, I finally cry. Stumbling around the corner of the landscaped garden, I collapse into the first rattan chair I see, my body shuddering with sobs. It feels cathartic. I curl my legs beneath me and lean my head against the cushion. It smells faintly of sun cream and old sweat.

Holding Nick's hand like that was a cruel punishment – pretending we were good when we weren't. But I know that sometimes playing a role is the best way to get what you need. And I need to find Alannah. I tried to look sad enough for the public to lay off me, disgusted that I felt compelled to act. Once again, my true self isn't good enough, so I had to pretend to be someone else.

The door to the terrace clicks softly open and I stiffen. Somebody's there. I really can't face Nick at this moment. I'm exhausted after our display of happy families.

'Hello?' I call out, frustrated. I can't even get a moment to myself.

I wait a beat for someone to appear, every muscle in my body tense.

The day Nick and I got married on this terrace, the look in his eyes told me he loved me as much as I wanted to love him. That person now seems to be as lost to me as Alannah.

The irony is that this trip was supposed to bring us closer.

I sigh and clamber out of the sunchair, rearranging my shirt which has untucked from my jeans.

'Is somebody there?' I call out again sharply, an undercurrent of fear beginning to curl around me as I glance towards the corner that conceals the door. I inch closer to see who might be there, trying to contain the prickles of panic that have started to bubble up.

'Hello?'

'Mer.'

I exhale. It's just Tara.

My sister gathers me into a huge embrace. 'You did amazing.' She breathes into my neck. I tighten my hold. She smells like the wrinkly damp of almost dried clothes. She turned fifty last year, but she's always had an old soul – reserved too, only speaks when necessary. Her presence draws me back to my other childhood smells.

That's why Tara's embrace here, on the top of the building over-looking the sea, is bittersweet. Her presence is another push-pull of tide that I've felt throughout my life. She is a relic of my long-locked youth. But she is here now, and she means well. She hands me a tissue and I blow my nose.

Réa stands quietly behind her.

'Réa.'

I open my arms and reach for her, but she steps quickly back, shaking her head, paler than usual. She says something so quietly that I have to move towards her to hear. I want to pull her close to me – she looks sad and lost with her arms wrapped protectively around herself.

'Is it true?' she says, her entire body trembling. We are standing on the same spot Nick and I cut our cake.

'I'll be back at the room,' Tara mouths silently and disappears out the door of the roof garden, pulling it closed behind her. As it swings shut, the reflection of the sea mirrors dizzily in its glass. And then, there is just me and Réa.

Above us, the sky is mostly clear, except for white flashes of birdwing and wisps of aeroplane contrails. No rainbows today. A storm ahead somebody said earlier. Before all the rest of everything, it was just Réa and me. But she looks at me now with sparks in those eyes and I recognise the look of betrayal.

'Come here, girl,' I whisper.

Réa stands a few metres in front of me, hugging her slender frame miserably. In her pink jumper and denim shorts, she reminds me of the ice-cream photo of Alannah in our garden. She looks half-little, half-big. She is beautiful. I remember the way she'd insist on telling her little sister her bedtime story every night. One night I overheard her telling Alannah the story of the changeling, interrupting subtly when Alannah's fascination turned to horror. To distract Alannah's tears, I told them the fairy tale of Oscar Wilde's *The Nightingale and the Rose*, about a student who cries because his garden does not have a red rose to give to a girl he loves. The little nightingale understands the strength of his emotions. Thinking about the mystery and power of love, she flies off to solve his problem. The learning is that sometimes a heart breaks, not only because of happiness, but also because of grief. Because of the love you wanted so badly to feel.

'They said you were drunk,' Réa says to me, slightly less hysterically now. I get a glimpse of the fine lines that criss-cross up one arm – an indecipherable language neither of us truly understand. Pain, just below the surface, healed and reopened. I start to cry again, blinking back mascara tears which I tap at uselessly with the crumpled tissue. It falls apart in my hands. It seems even Réa couldn't escape the shadows that have followed me all my life.

'It's all over the internet, Mum,' she says, shaking her head in disbelief. She rubs one hand up and down one of her arms.

It's excruciating how much pain she seems to exude – this sixteen-year-old trapped in the shadow of her missing sister. All I feel is shame that I couldn't protect her from this one thing.

'I'm sorry, Réa. I was angry.'

I reach for her again, but she pushes me roughly away.

'You promised me. You swore. You said that day that you swore on all the stars in the sky that it would never happen again. I thought they were just headlines. I didn't believe it was true.'

'Réa, hang on—' I start, but she shouts over me.

'Are you drinking now?' She looks me in the eye.

Silence.

'Are you?'

I can't meet her eyes.

'Oh Jesus Christ, Mum.' Réa turns in circles now, her hands over her head, as if she is protecting herself from bullets raining down.

'I'm getting trolled about you online. I'm afraid to pick up my phone. You and Dad are arguing all the time. I can't deal with any of this. Why did we even come here?'

She's shouting, her chin pushed up, defiant. She's backed me into a corner. I feel a surge of something dark emerge and escape my lips. The words are out of my mouth before I realise what I'm saying.

'He's not your dad.'

The instant I say it, I regret it. She knows of course, but we've never really gone there. That's the moment I feel Réa's heart break. I see love injured right in front of my eyes – pink and jagged like the scar across my belly. But I can't stop myself.

'Where were you that day?' I demand, hating myself. 'I told *you* to watch her.'

Réa's face crumples in front of me.

Another familiarity, just like every time my own mother promised things would be different. This is the cycle of hope and despair that I never wanted for my own child. The ugliness of it passes. But Réa turns around and walks quickly out the door away from me. I don't have the energy to go after her. Ours is a complicated entanglement. Maybe we are too alike. I know she needs to go somewhere alone – to feel her feelings in whatever way she chooses to release her pain.

I look over at the endlessly mocking sea. An image darkens my mind again; Alannah's face trapped underwater looking up at me, her clean blonde hair fanning out, blurred fear in her eyes. Her arms are flailing, clawing. I gasp in shock and search the horizon frantically to rid myself of such a desperate vision.

Please God. *Not that.*

Suddenly I don't want to be alone. I think about following Réa down into the dark corridors of the hotel, but for what? She's right. I've betrayed her too. Instead, I step closer to the edge of the roof, a thick sheet of waist-high glass is all that separates me from nothingness. All around, beautifully planted gardens overlook similarly stunning vistas. Other humans sun themselves on balconies, eating lunch, hanging wet towels, strolling on phones. I crave their mundane lives.

I suddenly hate it here. This rotten place that has swallowed up a small child. Nothing is as it seems. Reeling still from the devastating vision of Alannah, I reach into my pocket, pull out a slim silver-foil packet and swallow another of the tablets the nurse gave me at the hospital. I have to swallow a few times to get it down. I think of the minibar. Of sweet oblivion. Dread rolls into the monstrous creature that Judy the therapist had warned me lurks within: guilt, shame and fear. A terrifying beast I've been battling for far too long.

My mother is dead. Nick is leaving me. Réa hates me. Alannah is gone. I had a slip, at the worst possible moment. My family is disappearing while I watch on helplessly. To love is to grieve – the nightingale from the story had that part right.

The sea below looks soft, inviting. I inch my torso over the glass edge. I can see the tops of the news satellite vans, the scraggy crowns of mismatching palms. In the February twilight, the water mirrors the still expanse of the sky. I imagine floating down, into the huge nothing. I imagine not feeling the pain of the decisions I've made in my life… the sins.

Then behind me, footsteps. I close my eyes and pray it is Réa, or Nick. They'll scoop me up and press me to them. But the steps are too heavy, and there are too many of them. Spinning slowly around, Lovell Logan, the lieutenant overseeing the search for Alannah, stands before me. Two deputies trail behind. All have frighteningly serious faces. Candy is there too, of course, hovering nearby, dying to catch a scrap of exactly what's going on. She hangs back by the door as Logan walks towards me. Her face colours as I meet her eyes.

'Help me,' I want to scream at her.

'Did you find those brothers?' I immediately demand. There's an unmistakable shift in the air. Something is different. The senior detective strides closer to me, past the potted frangipanis dotting the perimeter of the roof garden. He ignores my question.

I hear his loud American drawl, but it takes a moment to register exactly what he's saying. I try to absorb his words, noticing his tie is the same shade of blue as the sea, and that he missed a spot above his lip when he shaved this morning.

He repeats himself, more urgently this time.

Then his words finally hit, with a slamming intensity. A surge of bile floods my mouth.

I bow my head.

Jesus Christ.

'Dr Fitzpatrick,' he says, and I raise my eyes slowly to meet him.

This is it, I think, my heart pounding. The moment I knew was coming.

'We've received some concerning information. I need you to come with me to the station.'

At that moment, there is nothing left to say.

In one hour's time, I will see Alannah's face.

20

Rolle

Milton's Point stretches out from Kite towards Cuba like a beck-oning finger. It's a tacky seaside town on the tip of the peninsula, now catering to a live-and-let-live breed. It's popular for kitschy daytrips, home to families escaping the Miami rat race and ageing hippies. It's the end of the line – both figuratively and literally. Next stop Havana.

Rolle drives past the bucket-and-spade town out towards the quieter, more run-down patches of scrubby beach, towards the address Kata Charles had given him for Red. He's in a marked car. Donut patrol, as the guys call it, tends to command a little more respect around here. The sea is deathly still, reflecting the grey swirl of sky as Rolle drives along the single lane road, cursing his GPS. Not far from the lighthouse, Tiffany had also said, close to a long wooden jetty, she'd described, when he visited her earlier in Ivory Bay.

The girl had cried as she talked about her best friend Mariah Whitaker, the local girl who'd been missing since Halloween night. The party that night was on the beach next to their home, just fifteen minutes' drive from Milton Point.

'Everyone was in masks – frightening masks, with animals, monsters. We sat around the bonfire drinking,' she'd told Rolle, glancing at her father standing protectively by the door of their trailer. 'Drinking beer,' she continued.

'The music was loud. Mariah was beside me.' Tiffany's eyes brimmed with tears. 'We knew one of the guys from around, Kata, that he was in some kind of gang. His girlfriend used to babysit us.' Tiffany scratched at the chipped enamel on her nail beds. She had pink dye running through the tips of her hair, which hung limply down her back.

'Would you like a glass of water?' Rolle had asked gently, knowing how awful this must be for the child. He looked up at Tiffany's father. 'Would you mind? And could I trouble you for a mug of tea?' The father slouched off into the kitchen reluctantly. Tiffany looked up and Rolle smiled at her. Time wasn't on his side and speaking to twelve-year-olds about their nocturnal activities wasn't exactly straightforward.

'Tiffany,' he spoke more urgently now. 'I cannot find Mariah unless you are honest with me. There's something you're not telling me.' He said this matter-of-factly. The illusion of knowing more than you do.

A quick glance into the kitchen. The man was thumbing his phone, leaning against the counter as the kettle sheeshed.

'They gave us something else.' Tiffany looked frightened. Her voice barely audible. 'Like pills or something. Then the masks seemed to come to life. They were like phantoms, and the flames...' she trailed off, her voice trembling. 'They were dancing around the fire, with sparks everywhere, the faces of horrible creatures. It felt like everything was spinning...'

'Who gave them to you?'

'The other guy with Kata. The man with the tattoos. I think he was called Red?' Rolle could see the memory of the night reflecting on the girl's face, her eyes were distant as she darted her tongue over her cracked lips.

He scribbled down all she was saying, loath to interrupt her recollections.

'Then we were in a truck somewhere.'

'Like a pick-up?' Rolle asked, thinking of the Ford Kata had mentioned.

Tiffany nodded. 'My head was banging against the window. They said we were going on a boat. They were arguing. They still had the masks on, they looked so scary. Then, I threw up.'

He noticed she was trembling. The sound of hot liquid pouring into a cup came from the kitchen.

'What then, Tiffany?' Rolle urged.

'Because I was sick they kicked me out of the car in the middle of nowhere. Everything was dark. I couldn't walk, the world was moving too fast. I think I fell asleep somewhere and when I woke it was almost morning.'

Tears spilt down her cheeks. Rolle heard the triple-clink of a spoon against ceramic in the next room.

There was nothing in Mariah's file about any of this. Rolle guessed Tiffany had never breathed a word of it to anyone until now.

The gentle thunk of a fridge door closing.

'When I got home, she wasn't there. Mariah was gone.'

Rolle leaned back to signal the hard part was over. He wanted to pat her on the hand but it didn't seem quite right.

'Thank you, Tiffany. That's been so helpful.'

'Will you find her, Detective?'

Her small expectant face was a punch to the stomach. Too hopeful. Too trusting.

'I'll do my best.' He frowned, uncomfortable still with making promises he wasn't sure he could keep. Her father walked in with the tea on a flowery tray, a mini-Mars bar next to it, a napkin folded into a triangle. The effort was touching, and Rolle was grateful for the much-needed sugar rush. They shot the breeze for a bit, Tiffany silent beside them. Then, as he got up to leave to head up towards Milton Point, Tiffany began to say something but stopped.

'What is it, Tiffany?'

'It's probably nothing,' she said shyly, shaking her head slightly, leaning against the doorway. Her powder pink hair made her look even younger than she was.

'Nothing is nothing,' Rolle said patiently, stepping forward to emphasise his point. 'Anything you remember is helpful to us.'

'The guy Kata was with, he kept saying something about rain. That he was bringing us somewhere where it was always rainy.'

Fresh eyes on a case were always important. But when it was almost five months after Mariah disappeared and no actual policing had been done, it was hard for Rolle to get a grip on the case and see how exactly it related to Alannah. What was indisputable, was that one case had never been taken seriously, and the other had become an international obsession. No wonder Glades was horrified by the coverage of Alannah's vanishing, the days-long search parties, the frenzy across the island, prime-time TV interviews. It wasn't just income divide that fostered bitterness, a culture of dependence on the state, the same state that was failing the underprivileged was disorientating; the confusing act of both loving and hating the hand that feeds you.

Needing and rejecting.

Rolle remembered his father's voice quoting Thomas Jefferson when he went on one of his rants. '*No one is born either with a saddle on his back or with boots and spurs to ride his fellow man.*' In other words, no one's birthright should trump another. Yet that was the way of this world. He wondered why he had never noticed it as much before.

–

The sea to his left mesmerises as Rolle follows the red GPS line on his phone. A woman's robotic voice tells him to stay straight for 4.8 km. Fewer cars pass him as the lighthouse in the distance grows ever closer. Suddenly, Alice's name cuts through the tangle of map lines on his screen. He swipes and her voice fills his car.

She must be out for a run, she sounds breathless. Then he remembers the dinner.

'Ally, I've booked us dinner,' he says triumphantly. 'For Valentine's.'

But she's not running, she's sobbing.

'I want to go home.' His wife cries. 'Tony. I just can't do this anymore. Tony, I can't… please. It's all too much…'

He's never heard her like this before – so completely devastated. It's a shock. Alice had always been so accepting, so steady, despite everything.

'I can't pretend to be okay anymore. Tony, I'm not okay. I'm not okay. I need your help.' Her voice shakes with increasing hysteria. His heart sinks. But there is too much to say. So, as usual, he says nothing at all. There are no cars at all on the road. He's completely alone for miles in every direction on the narrow coast road.

'Alice, honey, can we please talk about this later?'

He hears how hollow that sounds, but breaking down the past year into one emotional phone call while he hunts a missing kid isn't right either. He's horribly aware of how much she needs him and how little he can give her right now.

The speakerphone fills the car with her ragged breathing. He imagines her shaking her head in frustration, but when she finally speaks there is no anger – just a sad desperation to her voice that he's never heard before.

'It's always later with you,' she whispers, and he doesn't think he's ever felt worse.

'Later, it could be too late, Antonio. I need you to help me right now.'

She sounds hoarse, as if she's been shouting.

'Please, Alice… you know I can't,' he says, trying to think of something else to say, something that will make her feel better. But she's gone, and the lighthouse looms.

21

Mirren

Laura Bennet had no idea that the shaky thirty-second video she took on her phone that day on Wilkes Beach would have a million views within an hour of posting it. When it reached two million, her friends convinced her she should contact the information line for the Alannah Fitzpatrick appeal. It was that decision, and her bouncy montage that brought me here to this dirty waiting room at the station at Calloway.

But I don't know that. Not yet.

Uneasy, I pace up and down, convinced the pale walls are closing in on me. Lovell, that asshole, framed this as an informal chat, as if I have a choice in all of this. That didn't stop them marching me down the polished steps of the hotel an hour ago and into the car in front of the media like some kind of criminal. As the camera lights flashed, the media scrum jostled to get a comment. This is Lovell Logan's glory parade, I realised, a little too late. He marched beside me, hand on my back, helping me into the waiting car. He held his hand up importantly, blocking the reporters, aware this was going to be the top story at all the major news channels. I understood then, as they sat me into the car, that every case needs a focus and this time I'm it.

This isn't about finding Alannah at all. It's about allocating blame.

Where's Nick? I thought wildly as I shielded my face from the blazing glare of cameras. Some were being pushed so close to the car windows that they clashed against the glass.

'Is this really necessary?' I called, but my voice was too quiet against the cacophony of chaos. I felt the medication ooze out into my bloodstream, a gloopy release, stripping the chill from the moment. Even so, my frontal lobe was screaming that this was bad, this was really bad. I asked to speak to Detective Antonio Rolle, but the officers who craned their necks from the front seat assured me they just had a few questions. Nothing to worry about. I heard someone talk about mobile phone networks and my ears pricked immediately. Why weren't they out hunting those brothers that Detective Rolle had told us about?

They put me into the first car – an unmarked BMW – while Logan followed behind in the police SUV. When I asked the officers about Nick, they looked at each other quickly, as if they knew something I didn't. It was dark by then – an inky void where the sun had once been.

I peer out of the glass door of the room, into the hallway of the police station. Despite my studio make-up, my reflection looks ghostly, my features overly distended, the yellow glow of the overhead office lighting stretching my face into something I don't recognise. I need a drink, I decide, to blur all of this.

They've given me a synthetic-flavoured coffee in a thin paper cup. I pace up and down, matching time to my throbbing headache. If they need to speak to me this urgently, they must have found something significant. But surely, they would have called Nick too? We should be here together.

I smooth my hair back, forcing myself to breathe deeply and to stay calm. I want to know and yet I don't want to know. Could they have found Alannah?

That's when I see the shape of Lovell Logan simultaneously knocking and opening the door. He looks at me coolly, rearranging his face into his version of a smile. His eyes remain hard. He suggests I sit down.

'Did you find her?' I ask, my voice high-pitched with fear.

Lovell shakes his head, grim-faced.

Across the table, he hands me something – a phone, and there's a video playing.

He raises his eyebrows as I grasp it, confused. For a split second I think it's Alannah's phone, and gasp. 'How did you…' I trail off as Lovell shakes his head slightly.

'Watch this, please,' he commands.

I hesitate a moment and then look down.

It's footage of a beach and a group of girls. The sound is off, but it's obvious they are giggling. It's like an advertisement for a sun holiday. The girls are posing for the camera, and just as I'm about to throw the phone back at him, it starts to dawn on me that I'm looking at that day on the beach.

I swallow. Close my eyes for a moment. Suddenly I'm back there. The stinging sun, the whoosh of the waves. The girls are struggling to hold onto a yellow umbrella that's been stabbed into the sand. It fights them, the breeze tugging it sideways. The view is unsteady. I'm disorientated watching it.

I remember the wind that day – sudden and strong.

'Keep watching,' Lovell instructs. He's watching my face, but I'm standing back on that beach.

The umbrella obscures most of the background, but whoever is filming moves slightly and I see someone walking along the sand behind it.

It's Alannah.

I see my child.

I cry out. My hand shoots up to my mouth and then stretches towards her. I'm watching her walk past me. Before the moment I know her blood spills.

My other hand shakes as I try to keep the phone steady. My daughter is so animated. She's talking, her hands moving as she chats to the person walking alongside her. She doesn't look frightened, I realise, and relief floods me.

I see her moving and laughing, heartbreakingly within reach. She's only on the screen for seconds. Then the camera angle shifts again, moving erratically, as the girls scramble to rescue their flying clothes.

Suddenly, I see clearly the person walking alongside Alannah.

I freeze.

The footage stops abruptly, cut off. The screen goes blank. I'm back in the room with Lovell. Suffocating.

I imagine what happened next: the giggling girls continue to chase after errant towels, flip-flopping over the sand as the breeze captures their belongings. I picture Alannah, continuing to walk towards the direction of the cove, skipping happily as she slips her hands into the woman's. I can almost feel her hand in mine; slim and warm, our fingers interlocking, the zigzag of flesh. Our palms pressed together. I close my eyes to enjoy the feeling for a moment. It's the most peaceful I've felt in days. She's with me for those few seconds.

Go back, I whisper. Just in my head.

When Logan speaks, that peace shatters. There's a strange tone to his voice.

'Dr Fitzpatrick?'

I look up at him. The meds tickle deep. Everything seems slower, heavier suddenly, as if I'm underwater.

How can I try to explain what I am seeing when nothing makes sense at all?

Logan's jaw is clenched.

'Mirren, can you identify the people you see in this footage?'

Something in his voice chills me.

'Is that Alannah?'

I sit back into the chair and nod weakly. My head feels heavier now. I think of Nick and how I'd lie my head on his shoulder and he'd stroke the top of my head, like I was a child.

There are others in the room now, the two officers who were in the car with me.

Someone is filming me. Have they been there all along? The confusion panics me. I try to stand but my legs refuse to cooperate.

'Can you identify the woman walking beside Alannah?'

My mind whirs. I try to remember that day. Screaming at Nick by the pool.

'I won't let you leave us,' I'd screamed. But the man I loved stared back at me with a strange new expression.

'You can't stop me.'

That's when I'd hit him.

Then I remember crying in the little beach bar, drinking. Drinking some more. Everything was crooked. The awful image of Alannah's face struggling to breathe from underneath the water laps at the edges of my mind.

'I love my daughter,' I suddenly cry.

But it comes out as a wail, a banshee wail. I need them all to know that I love my children – in my own way. Maybe not a rainbow love, but I was trying. I had been really trying.

'Dr Fitzpatrick,' somebody repeats, more firmly this time. I turn my head wildly from side to side, trying to understand where the voice is coming from.

'Can you please identify the other person in the footage – the woman?'

And I close my eyes. I feel the shallow water lapping around the half-tides of my mind.

'It's me,' I whisper, choking on my grief.

My voice is small. Everyone in the room is looking at me, judgement in their eyes, and now something else too.

'That's me with Alannah.' I let the phone fall onto my lap. Exhausted. Defeated.

The problem is – we've skipped a step.

22

Rolle

Rolle pulls up outside the run-down bungalow by the lighthouse – Red's place, as the light trickles into evening. There's not much out here – an old jetty, a few burnt-out cars, misshapen outhouses dotted in the distance. Unholstered, Rolle tucks his weapon into the waistband of his pants. The whoosh of sea against rock whispers behind him as he steps over the mounds of stringy grass. It was wilder than most spots on Kite, but Rolle had always favoured the less-loved places. His sharp rap cause birds to lift in frightened flight. The house is unlocked. The mustiness is pungent as he flips the light switches inside the door uselessly.

'Police.' His voice reverberates throughout the empty house.

A creak behind him suddenly startles. Rolle spins around and something sticky brushes against his face. He claws at it frantically, momentarily blinded, but it clings. He manages to fling the twisted thing to the ground, his hands on his gun in a split second. Breath steady, mind sharp. Antonio Rolle – always ready for a fight.

Then he lets himself laugh. He'll tell Alice about this later, to lighten the mood. The big bad detective scared of a fly. Well, a fly catcher. The sticky paper lies mangled on the floor, covered with the twisted bodies of trapped bluebottles. Rolle rubs his face in disgust. The relief dampens the adrenaline rush, but it's clear as he surveys the house, that whoever was here had packed up and moved on. But it's what he finds in the outdoor bin that really chills: thick masking tape bindings, layers of them, as if something was wrapped or unwrapped in a hurry. He finds the remains of a fire too, a dark ashy blemish on the grass. They'll have to get forensics but it's already nearly dark and the weather's picking up again. He spots a battered outhouse at the end of the property. His impatience trumps fear. Nudging the door open with his gun, he examines the splintered wood around the top hinge. Recent damage. He knows a thing or two about how wood could tell a story after years helping his father with furniture removals. Inside the small work shed there are tools scattered on shelves, rusted paint pots and a makeshift table fashioned from an overturned crate. At the back of it, a freezer chest. He turns on his torch and, setting his gun on the shelf next to him, tries to pull it open. It's stuck fast. Using every fibre of his strength, Rolle grits his teeth and yanks the lid. With a stiff squelch, the freezer lid releases, and he uses his torch to light up its dark corners. He covers his mouth with his elbow, tries to breath into his sleeve as he goes. It stinks, but there's nothing but a few thawed-out sodden pizzas.

His phone vibrates in his pocket. It's not-so-curious George.

'What's up?' He leaves the shed and walks the perimeter of the broken fence, examining the ground as he goes. It's starting to rain, and he needs to wrap things up and call Alice back to see if she's calmed down.

'You told me to talk to the prosecutor in Hatton County about Red Roccio.'

'And?'

'He was charged with indecent assault and sexual assault after the girl was attacked in her dorm. First year psychology student. She was sleeping off a concussion and he accessed the room.'

'She was unconscious?' Jesus fucking Christ. What's wrong with people?

'Girl woke up to the assault and managed to escape when a friend heard her screaming. Similar charges were brought by another girl, up in Tampa, but there was a lack of evidence. It was dropped.'

'Thanks, George,' Rolle says, as something catches his eye in the grass.

'One more thing, Detective Rolle,' George is saying. 'I spoke to the witness that saw the boat that day. He says it was white with a red stripe.'

Rolle tries to sound patient. Maybe it wasn't George's fault he was so completely clueless. 'We had that already, George.'

He hears the pages of a notebook flipping in the background. The shiny thing Rolle had seen was the gold label from a crumpled beer can. He kicks it in frustration.

'Eh, he says there was writing on the side of it. Like a… like a name.'

Rolle stops walking and glances out towards the distant horizon. He'd always loved the moment day turned into night. Soon the long beam from the lighthouse would start to skim the inky water, cast far out to sea, always close but never illuminating the ground on which he stood.

'Spit it out, George. What did it say?'

'Said he thinks the name on the boat was…' More sounds of flipping pages.

'Something like *Rainy Day*, or *The Rain Day*.' George stammers. Rolle closes his eyes briefly. This might just be the alignment he needs to inch things forward. The name of the boat. And what Tiffany had said about the brothers bringing the girls to where it was always rainy. The connection he needs between the two cases. This might be it.

Then his phone sounds again. It's Candy from the hotel with one heart-stoppingly ominous question: '*Did you hear the news about Mirren Fitzpatrick?*'

Rolle is almost back at Calloway police station by the time the last raspy light bleeds from the day.

23

Not much scared Kata – the result of fending for himself ever since he watched his mother overdose on the kitchen floor when he was just eight. But the thing that petrified him most, was the billowy shadows of the crocs he'd come across more frequently since he'd started this Kite to Miami run.

There was something about the power of them, their knobbly impenetrability, their hunting instinct, it made his stomach lurch. This is what he is thinking about as he and Lottie approach the boatyard repair, 50 km north of Miami for the drop-off. There are no shops or restaurants, just a few warehouses and the odd shipyard. This far north, the postcard Miami beaches have thinned out. Up here, the sea crashes aggressively against ugly rock, blighted by orange-red algae – a stinking mess that leaves people sick with gastro. Kata keeps his mouth closed as he swims, guiding *Rainy Day* in towards the mooring. Bioaccumulation, they called it on the radio. The dangerous bits become more concentrated in the bodies of the top-of-the-food-chain animals because they eat the big fish, who've already eaten the medium fish, who've eaten the small fish. Kata already knows that he's the tiny marine critter barely visible in this entire process – an invisible but necessary link in the chain that's led him here to the boatyard this evening. Lottie whistles gently to signal the mooring is ahead. She's been here before, but never with cargo this valuable. Together they drag the boat against the rough pockmarked wood. The waves punch in stronger as the wind rises.

'Stay on the boat,' he tells her, concentrating on the knot in the rope but inclining his head towards the tarpaulin.

'What happens now?' she asks, wide-eyed, though they'd been through everything multiple times since they left Kite.

'Don't worry, Lotts. It's a quick in and out. Red's meeting us here. We'll give those guys what they want and then get out. Any problems, head to Osprey, like we planned.'

The rain falls heavily as he picks his way past rows of damaged vessels, towards the huge aluminium-clad building. The workshop, they called it. The boatyard is a sprawling jungle of cranes and overturned boats, that look like beetles upended. Ducking around the end of one of the three rows of jetties, he moves towards the dark building. Once inside, Kata crouches low under one of the small windows that faces out onto the empty car park. Ten minutes later, headlights, like a pair of glowing eyes in the dark, catch his attention a distance away, they sweep through the window as they get closer, casting distorted shadows across every wall. He glances at his watch. Almost midnight, as agreed. Outside an engine dies, a car door slams, then heavy footsteps crunch towards where he lies hidden.

24

Rolle

He's waiting in the bar, 10 p.m. on the button, three hours later than planned. Harris, smaller than Antonio Rolle, is smart in jeans and a pale-yellow shirt. He wears his hair short, a cropped military haircut that makes him look like somebody's uncle. That's new, thinks Rolle as he eventually walks into O'Shea's.

After everything with Mirren and the footage, Rolle needed a drink. He'd taken a taxi directly from Calloway police station to the bar, unable to face Alice and her sad eyes. A delay of the inevitable, he knew. But all he wanted was cold beer, a friendly face and someone to bounce the Fitzpatrick case around with.

Promise we'll talk once I'm done with this case, Ally. Things will be better then.

She hadn't texted back.

The taxi driver flicked on the radio on the way to O'Shea's, talking endlessly about the missing kid and how its mother had been taken in for questioning. 'Storm is on its way too,' the driver clicked his tongue, and the radio anchor switched to reporting another gang hit – rival drug cartels swapping routes from Mexico to some of the Florida Keys' closer islands. Are local police failing because of a lack of resources, the reporter asks, or is there another reason not to go after these networks?

'They're all in it for the cash,' the driver announced, knocking the radio off. 'Cops turning a blind eye to these traffickers – they're all at it.' The wisdom of taxi-drivers, Rolle thought, as he handed over the notes. But the driver wasn't wrong. Nothing as dangerous as a dirty cop.

Like half the world, Rolle's former partner Sam Harris had been following the Fitzpatrick case from Miami. He'd jumped at the chance to meet, picking up on Rolle's enforced isolation, perhaps. He'd be that type.

O'Shea's is a dingy Irish pub nestled down a side-street of Tilbury – a town the opposite side of the island from Calloway. Its ring-stained tables and whiskey mirrors draw crowds of meaty-faced fourth-generation Irish over from Miami.

Bono croons from the speakers.

Rolle breathes in the slightly sweet-sour smell of what islanders call one hundred rabbits – an acrid *poitín* brew named for the numerous behaviours it could trigger after a few glasses. But Rolle isn't here to forget, he's here to remember. In order to move forward with one case, he has to take a step back into another.

The two men embrace theatrically, clapping each other's backs.

'Coffee?' suggests Harris, and they both laugh. It feels good to be back together.

Rolle gestures to the barman and points at Harris's beer.

'How's Matt?' he asks pulling the bar stool closer to the table.

'In love with the quiet life.' Harris takes a generous slug of beer from the bottle and shakes his head slightly. He was a Miami city-slicker himself.

Matt had been the third member of their tiny team at Special Crimes. He'd moved to Albany, New York after the Sal Reid case. It had taken a lot out of all of them. And from them. The barman places the fresh bottle down in front of Rolle and the former partners clink bottles. 'Good to see you, Tony.' Harris grins, slipping right back into their familiar banter. 'You can tell Alice for me that she's a terrible liar. You couldn't have been at work every time I called.'

'Workaholic, that's me,' Rolle smiles, before turning serious. 'I didn't want anything to do with back then. It's a head fuck, you know?'

On good days, Alice described taking down Sal Reid as a victory, but Rolle knew it was only a matter of time before more scumbags popped up to take his place. It was an exhausting, never-ending game of whack-a-mole. And he was the big, dumb mallet. But his main regret was not keeping a lid on his emotions. Because of that, he'd become as monstrous as those he was paid to catch.

'Wanna talk about it?'

'Not really.'

But Harris's presence had brought it all back.

-

Their team had been working on the case for almost two years when the intelligence came in; the ringleader of the child abuse ring they'd been investigating had shown up at one of the addresses on their list.

If they pulled off this operation successfully, it would be a major coup for the department. Every last detail was planned out.

Once darkness fell, the specialist teams pulled up two blocks away. Rolle, operation lead, went over the plan one last time with Matt and Harris. The three of them had formed a unique bond. Cook-outs together, shared family trips. Hell, Rolle was Matt's kid's godfather. The thing is, when it comes to child abuse and people trafficking cases, there is nothing in the world comparable. What you see, what you share, it binds you. After years of watching computer screens filled with harrowing images and swapping details of horrifically graphic crimes with other jurisdictions, Rolle's mind was shredded. He should have seen the signs – the jumpiness, the insomnia, constantly depressed. He told the therapist that he thought PTSD was only for war veterans. That night it accumulated in the perfect bloody storm.

Harris approached the front door of the bungalow silently with three other agents. Rolle and Matt crouched along the side of the dirty stucco walls. Slowly, flat on their bellies, they crept along the grass towards the back of the property. Rolle gave the command to enter.

Then everything moved at once, like a firing gun at the start of a race. Teams ran in, from the front and the back of the bungalow simultaneously. Those inside the house scattered like rats, bodies flailing on the floor as they were restrained one by one. A large bald man curled around the doorway, whipping out a pistol, but Matt, running towards him, got there first. It always amazed Rolle that something so small could have such a large impact. With the twin crack of the blast, the wall sprayed red. The man slid downwards; eyes empty before his head even hit the ground.

Still running, Rolle burst into the next room. An open-plan kitchen-lounge, the TV was on, and two teenage girls on the couch pulled filthy duvets up to their necks in fright. Grease-stained takeaway containers were stacked on the coffee table, along with overflowing ashtrays. The stench of congealed food would cling to Rolle's hair for days. According to Rolle's investigation, about thirty girls had been trafficked in and out of that house in the past five months. Now years of work came down to this one moment – a stark responsibility.

Twisting the handle of another door, he pushed it open wide, bracing himself. It was empty. But inside he made out things that made his stomach lurch. Some of the girls back there were barely adolescents. Rolle barged against the next locked door with his shoulder, the cheap lock gave easily. What he saw in that moment is what had haunted him ever since. The rest of the team crashed into the room behind him. Harris took over immediately, arresting the acne-faced man who they identified as ringleader Sal Reid. Even lying face-down on the grubby carpet with his arms twisted behind his back, Reid smiled lazily at Rolle, as if to say, 'I was done here anyway.'

CPS and an ambulance crew entered the house as Rolle eventually stepped outside to remove his riot gear. Once deeply religious, Rolle knew at that moment that he was done with imagining some kind of goddamn karma chain. What kind of God abandoned children like these anyway? He'd been too late; he couldn't save them all. Matt found him crouching beside the back tyre of the patrol car, his head in his hands, coughing to conceal his emotion.

–

'Why do I get the feeling that this isn't a subject you want to dwell on?' Harris is sitting in front of him at O'Shea's, still probing.

'Cut the psychoanalysis, Harris. It's bull, everything you heard is bull.' Rolle looks out of the window. The frosted glass obscures the view. Neither of them talk for a moment. Then, looking directly at Harris, Rolle begins.

'I'll tell you what really happened that night.'

There's a pause. Harris stays perfectly still.

'When we got him to the station,' Rolle admits to his ex-partner, 'I brought Reid to the room at the back, and I lost it. I beat the shit out of that... that, fucking monster. And you know what? I loved every minute of it. I loved wiping that dirty look off his face. I wanted to kill him.'

Rolle's blood pressure shoots up at the memory of it. Fresh anger grows. How could he ever put this behind him, as Alice had begged. She was right, of course, it had ruined everything.

Harris's expression hasn't changed. But he leans forward and places his hand on Rolle's arm.

'We knew all that, Tony. Did you think we didn't?'

Rolle stares back at him for a moment.

'No, I never told anyone. Turns out the only cell I could have sworn didn't have cameras, mysteriously had cameras. Reid squealed, and I was sent here to Kite. I only came back to testify against that bastard. Apparently decking someone wearing handcuffs is problematic – especially when you happen to have a black belt in karate.'

When his mother died, Rolle's father guided his son away from the impulsive street fights he'd start, and towards mixed martial arts. He said it was for distraction, but they both knew Antonio would end up in jail, or worse, if he'd been left unchecked. His rage was too great to be stopped completely, so his father channelled it instead. He'd spent his adolescence hearing the slap of his opponent's back on the school gym mat. But he'd also taken an oath – like all those who hold a black belt rank – the responsibility to respect the tenets of the art: integrity, perseverance and, most of all, self-control.

'Tony, if it wasn't you, it would have been one of us. We all saw what he was doing to those kids.'

'You don't get it,' Rolle says, quieter now. 'I was made out to be some kind of hero. Especially in the media. But I was just the man who failed to stop him sooner. I lost it with him. I lost my place over there.' Rolle shrugs and drains the last of his beer. 'He got less time because of me. It was part of the plea deal. That fucker sued the department anyway. It's up in court next month.'

'Hang on.' Now Harris was animated. He tapped the table with his index finger sharply to emphasise his words. 'You were out anyway. You'd said it for months. You were done with it all, and I was glad. You'd had years of it, Tony.'

He aligns two beermats side by side, his voice softer now.

'You were a hero to us. You always were. Plus, you got him in the end – a year shaved off fourteen years isn't important.'

Rolle hadn't expected anything less from Harris. That's what he'd always liked about him – 100 per cent sincerity, matter of fact. No drama with Sam Harris. He'd give it to you straight.

'But there are always more of them. And I can't axe-kick every low-life who wants to traffic a kid.'

'We don't have to, Tony. We just have to put them away, one at a time.'

Rolle nods, feeling the warmth of support that he forgot came with a partnership like theirs.

'That's why I'm struggling with the missing kid case here,' he admits. 'I can't see another kid messed up. I just can't, Sam.'

'Heard there were developments.'

That's an understatement.

They order more beers and a plate of a mystery, deep-fried meat they take turns dunking in ketchup, while Rolle fills him in.

Mirren is the woman in the footage from the mobile phone, he tells Sam. She'd admitted as much to Lovell Logan who was standing waiting for Rolle as he arrived back to Calloway station, straight from the lighthouse.

–

'She lied to us, Rolle,' Logan had stated smugly. He may as well have added 'I told you so.'

'But it doesn't mean she had anything to do with Alannah's disappearance,' Rolle insisted, annoyed with Logan for unnecessarily parading Mirren in front of the media over this. 'Since when do we arrest someone for being drunk or having a history, or walking across a beach? By that logic, I'd be down for life. As would you.'

Why was he so quick to want to blame her? *Glory hunter*, Rolle wanted to add.

'Not arrested, no. She was always free to go,' Lovell Logan answered. 'But why lie about it?'

Rolle knew that Logan's eyes were on a different prize. His motivation for wrapping this up was a pat on the head from above. From Daddy, Rolle figured, and to go down in media history as the guy who got the mother who left her kid unsupervised.

In fact, none of this was ever about finding the girl.

Logan wasn't enthusiastic about Rolle's find at Kata's house either. 'We'll wait for forensics,' his boss said. 'See what they say. It doesn't mean much yet, Antonio.'

'We need to find the *Rainy Day*, and those brothers,' Rolle urged. But Lovell Logan was more concerned with the Fitzpatricks right now.

'Nick Fitzpatrick admitted there was an incident between Alannah and Mirren a few years ago. He agreed to speak to us, but I want you to do the interview.'

Nick was in a separate room at the station waiting to be interviewed.

While Logan spoke to Mirren about the footage, Rolle spent two hours hearing from her husband about what happened a few years back. If it was difficult to hear, it was even more difficult to watch Nick break down, explaining how baby Alannah was found dehydrated and hysterical in an empty house while her mother roamed the streets falling-down drunk. There was no doubt Nick loved Mirren, but you could see the pain in his face as he explained the damage she'd caused to their family. 'She's a complicated person,' was how he put it.

But that didn't mean she'd harmed Alannah.

What about the money problems, Rolle had pushed Nick. His financial problems with the Irish Revenue?

But Nick just shrugged. 'It is what it is. Social media gave people the power to make their own videos advertising brands. We didn't adapt in time, is all. I didn't declare the right amount because I didn't have it. And I got caught.'

'And does Mirren know the extent of it?'

Nick had shaken his head slowly.

'She has no idea.'

Rolle wondered suddenly what else Nick was concealing from his wife.

There was no sign of Logan by the time Rolle was finished speaking to him.

One of the other officers was going to drop Mirren back to the hotel, but Nick would spend the night elsewhere. The cracks in their relationship were widening. And it was making Rolle uneasy.

'That Logan's a real asshole,' is Sam Harris's blunt prognosis, as more locals stream into O'Shea's laughing. A band sets up in the corner. The friends have progressed to spirits by now.

'That's why I need to ask you to find this guy Red's contacts over in Miami,' Rolle explains. 'You know the lay of the land over there. This smacks of trafficking… your patch. Heard of him?'

Sam shakes his head. 'I'll ask around. There's been a lot of restructuring since we clamped down on a few of the usual routes. But every time, those bastards find a new way to bring stuff in. It's relentless.'

Sam has the same propensity to get to the bottom of things as Antonio. He knows he'll be back with something.

'His brother Kata is involved with him, and a girlfriend called Lottie. We think they've been bringing drugs and girls into Miami. I need to know for who.'

The band has started soundchecks. Rolle leans forward, tries to speak above the synthesised twangs.

'There's another girl missing too, and I promised her mother I'd find her.'

Sam raises an eyebrow.

'Oh Tony, you are going to get your heart broken,' he says, grim-faced. 'It's the very best thing about you, how much you care, but you have to stop taking everything so goddamn personally.'

Rolle shrugs.

'Saviour complex, I guess you'd call it.' He smiles dryly. But they're both thinking the same thing.

Sam had also lost his mother to cancer. Something they'd bonded over in the early days of investigations when they were paired up. He'd been older than Antonio when it happened, just fifteen at the time. But the mother-shaped hole in their early lives lingered into adulthood.

Sam says something else about Logan, but they were too many whiskey-sodas in by then. Rolle tries to make a point of remembering. He knows it's important.

A while later, a text pings through. It's Logan: *Meet me in the morning 8 a.m. at Marla's. I've something important to discuss with you.*

Rolle only notices then the five missed calls from Alice. It's better to talk face to face, he tells himself, feeling like the coward he knows he is. He turns to the barman and indicates with a flick of his wrist, that they'll have two more Jameson's please. Yes, doubles.

The guitar strums mournfully on.

25

The footsteps crunch across the gravel, as whoever is out there comes closer.

Kata tries to steady his breathing, his hand on his gun. The workshop reeks of petrol fumes. Strange objects cast shadows across the industrial floor: boat parts, hunks of metal, a jagged generator. He's crouched low behind the rusting carcass of a small Gibson trawler.

There's a light tapping on the metallic door he'd locked from the inside.

'Kats?' It's the unmistakable voice of his brother. Kata nudges open the small office door of the boat repair shop. He embraces Red. Fostered separately, they'd grown up with different degrees of love. Money and adrenaline became Red's substitute for family. When they reunited years later, they'd vowed to stick together, but Red's capacity for violence made Kata deeply uncomfortable. There was something broken in his brother's eyes, a glint of something he couldn't place. Now he's standing in front of him, but the only thing he can see in those eyes is fear.

'Kata man, I've fucked up.' The same words Kata has been hearing for years.

Outside, more headlights stream in through the rain-splattered glass. Their contact for the exchange is here. Red's confession would have to wait.

An extremely tall man steps out of the car. He has a thatch of straight blond hair and surprisingly full lips. The brothers stand unsmiling. 'All okay?' the tall man asks, holding out a pack of cigarettes. Kata waves it away impatiently – keen to get the package unloaded as quickly as possible. He and Lottie planned to abandon *Rainy Day* once the cargo was exchanged, and they'd all leave in Red's car. But Red is looking at him, shaking his head. There's something very wrong.

A tiny spark in the parked car, catches Kata's eye – almost imperceptible. Is there someone else there too? But the boatyard parking lot is too dark to make anything out.

'Let's go,' the tall man commands.

The clink–clink of boat masts grows louder as the three of them walk towards the boat. Red hisses something at him, and Kata glances over uneasily. The rain gets heavier as they navigate the west pier.

'Piece?' he's mouthing. Kata nods, feeling its bulky weight in his belt. Making their way towards Lottie, Kata hears the unmistakable sound of a car door closing, far back in the distance. He and Red fall back a little and let the tall man continue a few steps ahead.

'I got some info,' Red explains quickly. 'It's really fucking big.' The whites of his eyes flash in the dark and Kata knows something's definitely off.

Fucking Red. He should have known that trouble is never far behind. At the turn for their mooring, Kata makes the decision. He realises this is likely a set-up, feels foolish. What did he expect getting dragged into something this huge?

He whispers back to his brother. 'There's someone behind us. We'll take them at the other side.'

They've one minute until they are at *Rainy Day* to exchange the package.

'Hang on, wrong way,' Kata calls loudly, holding up his torch and changing direction abruptly. His other hand creeps around to his back, his fingers find the gun. He hopes Lottie can hear him, can keep quiet.

'Sorry, it's like a maze in here,' he laughs, every muscle in his body tense. He wipes the rain from his face with the back of his sleeve.

They walk a different route – towards the east pier, the one leading out to sea. It's much windier here. Broken boats pull violently against their moorings, swaying and creaking as the waves try to tumble them over. Out of the corner of his eye, Kata spots another person, a shadowy figure creeping low around from the opposite port wall. The driving rain gives an ethereal effect. The tall man stops, he's behind them now.

'Got that cash?' Kata asks breathlessly, his fingers slipping as he unlatches the safety on his gun. No answer. Kata whips around to face him, gun in hand. But the tip of the man's gun barrel is just inches from Red's head. At least Lottie and the *Rainy Day* are safe on the other side of the port, he thinks. But Kata couldn't see them even if he looked; the air is thick with fog – blanketing the collection of masts in its wispy shroud. Kata takes a lungful of breath, forces his brain to engage. Red is moving his mouth, saying something, urgently about the police. But there's no time for that now.

'Shoot him!' his big brother commands. The shadowy figure is almost upon them.

One final desperate decision is made.

Kata screams Lottie's name in warning as he swings his gun upwards and shoots towards the tall man, who squeezes his own trigger at the same time. There's a double explosion. One shot each. Red's hit first. His body teeters backward over the edge and into the water below. Kata's shot catches the tall man in the stomach. He twists as he falls awkwardly to the ground but manages to fire at Kata as he lands. Kata feels a searing sting in his left hip. He drops heavily to his knees. His head hits the wet dirt first, his face just inches from the watery drop below. The shadowy figure finally reaches them.

Squirming on the ground, the tall man holds one bloodied hand up towards the shadowed person desperately – grasping uselessly, as his lungs fill with blood. A close-range pop and the pleading stops. The shadow man uses his foot to roll the tall man's body closer to the sea wall. Then, one push and a sickening splash. From his position on the ground, Kata sees the body being swallowed up by the inky black water. He holds his breath, desperately praying Lottie would have the sense to get out of there fast.

Then the shadow man stands over him. His voice suddenly familiar. Their contact for all the deliveries into Miami to date.

'Fucking scumbag.'

Kata's last thought is for the crocs, as the man with the voice he'd only ever spoken to on the phone, pitches him heavily into the depths. Then Lovell Logan straightens up and adjusts his glasses.

Logan watches the commotion he's created below. The blood attracts the smaller fish first. Their frenzy will bring the bigger predators – the sharks and eventually the crocs. He walks slowly back down the pier towards the empty car park. He doesn't notice a trembling Lottie crouching low in the small white-and-red boat, her hand clamped over her mouth to prevent the scream lodged in her throat. The rain has eased a little, but the fog lingers. Lovell Logan sits for a moment in the car, staring straight ahead. He texts Rolle:

Meet me in the morning 8 a.m. at Marla's. I've something important to discuss with you.

It's time to wrap up this shitshow once and for all. His eyes dart quickly back to the boats. Logan puts his left hand on the door handle but seems to reconsider a moment. Then he starts the engine and repositions the car, so its headlights are illuminating the entire west pier of the boatyard.

He loosens his tie, gun in hand, and steps back out of the car.

26

Mirren

The Past

I think of Nick's face, always so serious now, and remember a different one; a concerned face when he found me crying on the steps of the house a few weeks after Alannah had come to us. I struggled so much in those early days, trying to cope with the demands of a small baby and a jealous eight-year-old while still grieving my loss. Alannah cried and cried. I took it personally, of course. She's rejecting me. I looked down at her blank face. My changeling. Who are you? Whose are you? I announced to Nick one evening that I was cutting my maternity leave short – I want to return to work to the place where I can make things better, I said above the sound of the baby screaming. He shushed me, made me sit on the couch while he fed her and put her to bed. His gentleness a stark contrast to the rough handling I sometimes couldn't help. 'Don't worry, it will get easier.' He smiled and pulled my legs towards him, rubbing my feet, the way he knew I loved.

But it didn't get any easier.

Each day, I'd drag myself out of day-crumpled sheets and pretend to play with the baby, just before Nick came home from work. The truth is that Réa was the one spending the most time with Alannah. Maybe, I'd think sometimes, it was a ploy to keep me apart from the new baby. If she was with Alannah, it meant I wasn't.

Escapism in those days came in a twist cap and a high alcohol content. I began to consider the convenience of pouring vodka into a soft-drink bottle to bring to the park earlier and earlier. What difference would it make if I had a few at four p.m. in the park, or at five p.m. at home? How much less respectable is it to drink vodka from the bottle rather than pour over ice? Is the lemon justification perhaps? It struck me that the mummy jokes about wine-o-clock and birthday cards about drowning in gin were more like one giant primal scream. But the hot trickle of irresponsibility did make the day more bearable. I fooled myself into believing I was a better mother if I'd taken the edge off a little. I imagined it made me less abrasive. But then I'd see those red grab marks on Alannah's small arms and legs and realise my failings. I wasn't handling things well at all. Some days, I'd visualise dropping her on her head. I'd jump in fright at the horror of my own thoughts, afraid I'd do it simply because I'd thought it.

Then, one day in the playground after school, I thought I saw Emma Lacey. As far as I knew she'd left the Dublin hospital where she practised and transferred to a private clinic in the Midlands. But, convinced it was her, I jumped in fright when I saw the woman watching me from a distance. I grabbed Réa and stumbled home leaning hard on the handle of the pram. The grey sea churned beside us as we strode towards our sunken house, my feet heavier with each step.

Nick had no idea how bad things were getting. He had no idea I'd spend hours looking at Alannah's little face, blaming her for replacing the baby I should have had – the baby that my body rejected. Later, in writing therapy, when I admitted these awful truths on paper, the psychologist nodded gently after reading them, absolving me from being the ogre I was sure I'd become. But I couldn't say them out loud. Not until the week before we left for Kite Island. Not until after my mother died.

The therapist explained the term Maternal Bonding Disorder, sometimes known as Anybody's Child Syndrome. She explained that although rare, it was common among those who had miscarried multiple times.

'You've blamed yourself for too long,' the psychologist explained gently, setting the box of tissues down in front of me. 'But having someone else to blame now, in this case Alannah, means you have transferred that rejection.'

It made sense that my rejection of Alannah was anger at myself for losing my babies. But understanding that wasn't the same as living it. Back then I felt safe in that room at The Residence where I tried to come to terms with those intrusive thoughts. I never told anyone, but in the deepest dark of night during my time at the treatment centre, I questioned if it was those losses that made me the way I was. Or did these problems come from the tumultuous tide within me – the one that had been there for as long as I remember, waiting to be unveiled?

The incident that landed me in The Residence started like most days; Alannah was howling and clinging to me, her face damp with sweat and snot. Nick took Réa to school and went to work as usual, while I collapsed back onto the sheets. But she wouldn't settle. I tried the cot. I tried rocking her, singing to her, nothing was working. My head ached, fuzzy with the lack of sleep and dread that I wasn't doing anything right. As someone who was well-respected and good at my job, I wasn't used to failing. Feeling useless triggered something. This, I only learnt later – some would say too late – that I was taking my past out on my child.

'You felt helpless,' one of my psychologists explained. 'As you did, so many times as a child.'

Helpless and hopeless.

I don't remember much of that day but there are moments that stand out, as crisp and as colourful as if I was watching myself in a movie.

I remember the scrunch of her face. The balling of her tiny fists. The determination with which she was screaming. I thought a bath might help. I sluiced the water around her body uselessly.

She was so small and yet the noise was so great. I just needed to dull the pain of all the jumbled-up thoughts. I had to dim the lights on the intensity of the day. I gripped her too tightly, watched the shock in her face as the water washed over her. It was only for a second, before I pulled her out. Only a tiny second. Then, shaking, I wrapped her in a towel and placed her on the bed, afraid to touch her at all. Horrified, I walked downstairs, opened a bottle of something – I can't even remember what – and poured glass after glass, sloshing the liquid across the kitchen table in my haste to numb every last feeling.

I thought of my mother and poured some more. My last clear thought was that she'd been right after all.

Then there was only silence.

What followed next was relayed back to me later. I turned up at Réa's primary school. 'You drove there,' they told me, 'smashed out of your mind, and tried to take her out of school.' It's all a complete blank – even now. They said I tried to drag her out of the classroom. The teacher later told Nick that I was cursing and shouting that she was my daughter and I'd remove her if I wanted to remove her. In my version, Réa is oblivious to this – all she sees is her *loving mother needing to be with her and not the demented drunk grabbing her arm and pulling her away from her friends. I know that's not what happened. I could see it in her eyes for years afterwards. The school called the police, and I refused to give them anyone else's number for hours. When they finally contacted Nick, he asked about the baby. The police admitted they had no idea what he was talking about. He got home just minutes after the police had broken down the front door, driving the fifty-minute journey in just thirty.*

They'd found Alannah lying in our double bed, six hours after I'd walked out on her – starving and inconsolable. Everyone said it was a miracle she hadn't rolled off the bed or choked or any of the numerous things that could have happened. I never mentioned to anyone what happened in the moments before I placed her on the bed, but I noticed I'd placed pillows around her. To keep her safe. That wasn't the first fracture in our bond, but the damage I caused to my life in the space of those hours was hard to fathom.

In rehab, I begged to see Alannah and Réa, my totally opposite-in-every-way daughters. Those weeks were some of the emptiest of my life. All shakes and nightmares. I spent hours thinking about my girls, about their beautiful faces. As the guilt eroded. Hating myself was part of the problem, the therapist said kindly, leaning forward during our sessions to pat my knee. I learnt that hating and hiding, and then being swallowed up by the guilt, was the vicious circle that made me drink. When Nick eventually brought Réa to visit me, we sat in the rose garden behind the converted castle watching the birds fighting over birdseed someone had left out.

I reached for her hand, but she shifted her little body away from me. Her face struggling with something I couldn't place.

Of course, at almost nine years old, she couldn't possibly understand what I was going through, but I had guidance on what to say, which involved letting her know that none of this was her fault. It was like speaking to myself as a child – a strange irony that wasn't lost on me. 'I promise, on all the stars in the world, you will never have to worry about Mummy like that again,' I reassured her, tears streaming down my face.

I needed her to look up to me, like she always had, to show me that I was everything to her. She had always seen the best of me. Without that reflection, I knew I'd be adrift.

But her eyes remained on the birds, spitefully squabbling now, trying to grab the seeds while chasing the others away.

A long time after I returned home, sombre and sober, Réa eventually accepted my promise to her. She slowly lost that worried expression anytime she was alone with me. She placed me back on the pedestal, gave me back my light.

I never touched alcohol since that day, not until my mother's funeral.

I tried to remember for all those years in between that it wasn't Alannah's fault that I felt entitled to a different child. In fact, it wasn't about her at all. And I had a responsibility to love her with the same ferocity as I loved Réa.

A bright green love. A never-ending love.

27

Mirren

I am now a person of interest in my daughter's disappearance.

After hours in that claustrophobic room, I'm eventually released from Calloway station just before midnight. Not under arrest exactly, but something that means they get to question me again, to examine my life in every tiny detail.

It's almost one a.m. by the time I drag myself into the lobby of the reception. The officers dropped me off at the service entrance, ignoring me as they drove, talking about how the Dolphins were set to top the league. I sat in the back, hunched low, as we navigated past the waiting media scrum. The night manager shakes his head a little too sadly when I ask him if the bar is still serving. 'Room service?' I ask quietly, shame creeping up my scalp. I see what he sees as I ride up to my room in the elevator – the heavy mascara, carefully applied hours ago for the TV interview, smeared beneath my eyes. My crisp white shirt is grubby after an evening sobbing into my hands in a miserable room with men who didn't care. I glare unhappily at my *banshee* face in the mirrored walls of the elevator. Then I'm thinking of my mother and the emptiness of her face – in life and in death.

I slide the key card over the door handle and, once inside, place it gently into the card slot on the wall. Light floods the room and I blink for a moment, still trying to get my bearings. Part of me still expects Alannah to pad sleepily towards me, golden hair mussed, arms outstretched. I kick off my shoes and peep into the adjoining room. Tara is in one of the twin beds. Réa is in the other – Alannah's bed. Mouth open, legs kicked out over the duvet. I envy her oblivion. But it will be short-lived. I think of why I need to speak to her so urgently and consider waking her but decide against it. It's too serious to do when I'm this exhausted.

There is no sign of Nick. The bastard's probably in another hotel, I think, trying to quell the anger that squirms in my stomach like a beastly thing. I swallow it down. I saw him at the station a few hours ago. I looked into his eyes as I walked past and knew he'd told them about what happened all those years ago. One of the junior officers confirmed it later when I pressed him about it. 'They're saying you left your daughter alone when she was a baby,' the uniform finally admitted uncomfortably, his eyes never meeting mine. 'Mr Fitzpatrick said you left her unsupervised and, eh, went drinking.'

I flick open my laptop. The envelope icon screams 1,600 new messages at me. The hospital's assigned many of my patients to Leonard, another doctor on the team, but he needs a steer on some of the sickest patients. I spend half an hour replying and sorting, ignoring all the well-wishing, first lines of every email. Apparently, everyone is there if I need them.

But the distraction is helpful. When my eyes blur from exhaustion and I've finished my drink, I know I need a shower and a long sleep. Letting the hot jets stream over my aching muscles, I rest my head against the marble-effect tiles a moment and then bang my head gently against them. The dull pain feels good, so I do it again, harder this time. I decide I'd like to do this to Nick's head instead. I want to cause him deep hurt, like he's done to me. Perhaps it makes it easier for him to leave me if he believes I'm such a bad person. But honestly, I never thought he would be capable of throwing everything we've been through back in my face. I turn the taps even hotter.

Wrapping a giant cotton towel around my body I wipe a gap in the foggy mirror over the sink to get a glimpse of my face. Without the make-up I look old, I think sadly. Touching the fresh bruises on my forehead I wonder when was that moment when I crossed from being one thing into another? From daughter to mother, from wife to drunk?

That's why I don't think Nick ever forgave me. At family therapy, the extent of my secret drinking was laid bare.

I shake the towel off. My hair hangs like a dark veil around my shoulders. I wonder what comes next. Nick has told them about all I've done – and leaving Alannah alone. That, along with the footage, didn't exactly paint the picture of the perfect mother I'd portrayed in the TV interview. So where do I go from here? I wrap myself in a fluffy white robe I find hanging on the back of the bathroom door and throw myself on the bed to focus on my breathing. It's two a.m. Try to concentrate on what we can control, rather than what we can't, I was told by every therapist. As if life was black and white and we were robots, instead of humans who live in the greyest grey edges every minute of our lives.

With one arm flung across my face, I try to drown out the noise of my thoughts. Focus Mirren. Focus, or you will never see Alannah again. That's all that matters now. So, while the police focus on me, I'll have to focus on her. Because time is running out. I curl myself into the crisp bed sheets, my body still damp from the shower, and give myself permission to finally think about Alannah. I let myself remember her for a moment – to force myself to feel something, to pierce the numbness that I've submerged myself in. Alannah is eight, I say to myself. She has long blonde hair with a natural wave which she definitely doesn't get from me. I only recently told her about Noelle, her birth mother. I told her that she had extra mums to love her. She liked that, smiled her gap-toothed smile and pressed her nose to mine. But you are my real mummy, she said gently and skipped off leaving my heart sore. Her favourite food is pizza, half plain, half pepperoni. She loves baking and hip hop – anything hip hop. She wants to be a waterslide designer when she is bigger. 'You mean an engineer,' Nick said hopefully when we talked about the future, one evening over a fish and chips supper. 'No, I mean a waterslide designer,' she quipped back, making us all laugh. She is definitely a daddy's girl, I'll admit that, bitterly. But I loved her in my own way. She brought out a side to me, a playful side that nobody had before. I'd never hidden in closets with Réa playing hide and seek or played tag when she was little. But I found myself seeing life through Alannah's eyes and it was so simple, so free. I was never given a childhood like that.

I fold my knees into my stomach and tuck my body up tight. The pain of thinking about her is immense. That day at the treatment centre, I vowed to Réa on the stars, but I also made a vow to myself about Alannah; that no matter how confused or flawed I was, that I would try to keep from her how I really felt. I'd push that ugly thing down deep inside me, into my darkest depths. I think I succeeded in doing that, for a while.

I pull off the damp robe and let it plonk softly on the floor beside the bed where it folds in on itself. My phone ran out of battery earlier this evening and I have no urge now to charge it up, no urge for the fight I will have to have with Nick about the new complications he's brought. That wasn't his story to tell.

The TV's digital clock tells me it is 2:30 a.m. I stretch my naked body out across the crisp sheets, more tired now than I've ever been, woozy from drink and enjoying the gentle ache of my muscles as they yawn open. My limbs feel heavy – ready to rest. I place my hand on my stomach for a moment, enjoying its warmth, and practise breathing deeply, trying to keep my mind blank. I hold my breath, enjoy the swell of the air, tight in my chest, the softness of my skin, and after a beat, I exhale slowly. I feel the release, my body loose for the first time in days. Then I let my hand slowly slide downwards closer between my legs – in that gentle curve beneath my stomach.

It's a pleasant heat, comforting. I move my palm from side to side slowly, slowly. After a few minutes, something starts to stir. Exhaling again deeply, I let fingers slip further down and the warmth spreads. It feels forbidden, wrong at this moment and yet, I have an overwhelming need to fly away from myself, just for a bit. My feet squirm as I stroke feathery circles. Turning onto my stomach, I close my eyes and imagine I'm back in our bedroom in our cottage at home. The girls are downstairs watching TV, and Nick and I are having a lazy morning in bed. Arching my body against the cool sheets, I'm surprised how quickly the heat builds. I think of Nick's soapy smell and his strength, and the way the light from our bedroom sometimes makes his silver hair look gold as he lies beside me. My fingers are his fingers, and they move more quickly now, faster, and deeper until I'm on the edge of myself. I muffle throaty moans into the pillow, climbing out of the feeling with short shuddering breaths, savouring the jolts of pleasure, stretching them out. I relish the disorientation, floating for a moment in that perfect twilight between dream and reality. I push my face deeper into the mattress, a huge sob shaking my entire body. Then another and another. My tears flow fast and hot and then I'm crying, like a child cries for its mother. But it's the wrong way around. I stay like this for a long time. Until my body eventually stops shuddering and things feel strangely calm. Then, just before I reach across to switch off the bedside lamp, I feel under the locker for the tiny pouch I've tucked underneath, to retrieve something secret. It glints seductively against the soft lamp light.

Mesmerising.

I turn off the light. Then I wrap my hand around the cool ridge of Alannah's gold heart necklace, feel the sharp piercing edge of it against my palm as I close my fingers around it.

Imprinting.

My head finds the deepest crevice of the still-damp pillow. I hold on tight.

I fall asleep wondering where all the lost things go.

28

Rolle

He stands outside a closed Marla's pancake house at 7:45 a.m.,
watching the Kite birds soar over the churned-up foam of the morning
sea, searching the waves for whatever the storm has dragged up.

There's a reason he doesn't really drink much anymore, Rolle
remembers, and this is it. Seeing his old friend had been cathartic, a
chance to lay to rest some of the ghosts he'd been carrying for the past
year, and to catch up with the news from the rest of the gang. He didn't
realise how homesick he'd been.

'Stay in touch, man.' Harris had clapped Rolle on the back as
they said goodbye. 'Assholes like us need to stick together.' Rolle had
laughed, but Harris was right – there were only a handful of people in
the world that understood just how heavy the burden of responsibility
they'd been tasked with was. Without the anchor of them, Rolle was
adrift.

Alice had been asleep when he finally arrived home from O'Shea's
and peeked in at her. Or pretending to be, at least. He couldn't
remember the last time they'd gone out together – just the two of them.
Or even had a proper chat.

Rolle rubs his temples and tries to focus on anything but the whiskey
he's sure is still sloshing around his insides. Just before eight, the first of
Marla's employees arrive to unlock the door, to mix the pancake batter,
he supposes, feeling nauseous suddenly at the thought of fried milk and
eggs. They smile politely at him, and he scans the road for Logan's car.

7:58 a.m.

There's no sign of the unsettled weather of the last few days. He checks his phone for updates. He's expecting a call from forensics about the house at Milton Point. He'd put a rush on things. But in truth, he wasn't feeling optimistic about finding either of the girls – especially after his conversation with Sam Harris. You don't find a puddle of blood and expect the kid to be alive. Not logically anyway, he'd said. But hope was a powerful thing. Besides, Antonio Rolle's job was to find them either way.

He gulps some of the salty morning air and sets a reminder to buy Alice a Valentine's card.

At 8:20 a.m. Logan pulls up, shades on, and lumps his police SUV up onto the kerb outside the cafe. There's no sign of his usual neat appearance.

His tie is askew, and it looks like he needs a shave. Rolle knows he doesn't look much better either. This case is weighing on them all.

'Rough night?' Rolle asks.

'Could say the same about you,' Logan shoots back, throwing his half-smoked cigarette onto the ground.

Rolle's stomach flips at the smell that assaults him as they walk into the cafe. Logan of course, is practically salivating because of Mirren's revelations about being the woman in the footage. It suits Logan perfectly to wrap up the investigation by blaming the drunk mother rather than have the public think the island is unsafe in some way. Rolle gulps down a glass of warm water, trying not to get annoyed by Lovell's tone. Ignoring the trafficking and corruption side of things was so typical, he thinks. NIMBYs his dad called them – the 'not in my back yards' of the world. Those who preferred to bury their head in the sand rather than admit there was an issue or even confront it.

Their breakfast arrives; greasy pancakes that slide across the plate, as the waitress sets them down in front of the men. Rolle watches Logan mop up some of the slimy smear with a forkful of blueberries. As he chews with his mouth open, he explains to Rolle that he wants to push forward with Mirren Fitzpatrick's second formal questioning.

But there's a snag.

Until a body is found, nothing can really change.

On one thing they both agree and that's the overwhelming pressure to make some kind of move – from the public, the media, the authorities.

The problem is that, fundamentally, Rolle and Logan disagree on which way to go.

'Mirren's obviously not under arrest for forgetting she walked her kid across the beach,' Rolle snaps, trying not to focus on the fatty rivulets of butter oozing off Logan's pancake. 'She was drinking, she told us that,' Rolle says, shrugging.

He takes a sip of peppermint tea. Anything but decaf coffee.

'I've a contact looking into Red and Kata,' he tells Logan. 'I've a few of the team scouring for that speedboat, the *Rainy Day*, too.'

'Sorry, Tony. I need as much background about Mirren Fitzpatrick as possible,' Logan says sharply. 'There is obviously a reason she lied to us about where she was taking the child that day. She was seen in the bar just before the kid disappeared, then next thing she's seen walking her down the beach. Which is it? What happened in those ten minutes?'

Things don't add up – another point they agree on. The timeline has never been exact.

But there was no such scrutiny for the girl from the trailer park, Mariah. Rolle also should have remembered that Glades worked at Marla's part time.

He doesn't blame her for laying her tray on the table halfway through their meal and begging them to do more to find her child. It's no longer the whiskey hangover leaving him nauseous. He pushes his pancakes around the plate, watching them soften under their syrupy weight as she shouts at both him and Logan, hands on hips, her anger giving way to tears of frustration, until someone comes and leads her away, a comforting arm around her shaking shoulders.

Logan's demeanour sickens him too – the blatant disregard as Glades pleaded sorrowfully for answers. His glee over the footage of Mirren and the subsequent interviews with Nick, had blinded him to all else.

Rolle makes a note on his phone to update Glades Whitaker on what Tiffany had told him about going off with the brothers that Halloween night. She needs to know the full story. He glances at the time. Forensics should be back to him by nine a.m.

Later, he thought about the $20 tip he left peeking from under a glass for her.

It felt wrong somehow. Given the circumstances.

29

Mirren

The Past

The first night I came home from The Residence, I slept in Réa's bed. It reminded me of the nights we spent wrapped around one another. Before Nick. Before everything.

'Like old times.' I smiled, willing her pale face to lose its pained pinched look. 'It was easier when it was just us,' she said quietly. I glanced at her face, but she was lost in her thoughts. 'After the babies in your tummy…' she trailed off. 'And then Alannah came… and you were always so cross.' I knew my drinking and treatment had been a huge bump in such a small road for her, but I'd never really thought that she'd associated it with Alannah's arrival. 'I'm so sorry, Réa,' I whispered, as familiar guilt clawed at my insides.

I'd been so wrapped up in how Alannah made me feel, that I'd neglected Réa and her feelings. She'd resented being left alone with Nick for all the time I was getting treatment. It was hard for her to be pulled from our thorny embrace and catapulted into a completely alien life with Nick and then Alannah. I knew she preferred when it was just us two. 'Do you want me to tell you the story of The Nightingale and the Rose?' I whispered, as she wrapped herself around my arm like a vine. 'My favourite,' she sighed happily. 'The little bird wants to help the student woo his one true love.' I began reciting the story that by now, I knew off by heart. But it's my own damaging behaviour I was reflecting on as I spoke.

'To find the red rose she seeks, she spends the night singing with a thorn in her heart.'

I glanced over at Réa who was curled up beside me, her eyes closing. 'The nightingale's music will create the flower and her blood will dye its petals.'

I brushed the dark hair from my daughter's face, still talking softly.

'Losing life's pleasures saddens the little nightingale, but she believes that the sacrifice is worthwhile if it's done out of love.'

How could I ever have put my relationship with Réa in jeopardy? She represents all that is good in me.

'So she sings of love through the night, gradually pressing her chest further onto the thorn, then further still, until it's too late.'

Réa's breath was even, and her arm slackened against mine. She was fast asleep. Somewhere in the house came the sound of Alannah crying. A low mewling that I tried to ignore. I remained wrapped up beside Réa, our heartbeat matching time. Nick will take care of her, I think as I curl around my eldest. Nick loves Alannah *best.*

30

Rolle

Rolle checks his phone immediately after he gets into his car outside Marla's. The white light is harsh on his sleepy eyes, but the headlines jolt him awake. The transcript of Nick's interview from last night has been leaked to the media. And they know about the blood. *Goddamn it.*

This has Lovell Logan stamped all over it. He slams the steering wheel in frustration.

Flicking through the other headlines, his head continues to ache. This is so much worse than he thought. After days of speculation over what exactly happened to Alannah Fitzpatrick, the court of public opinion had settled on her mother being responsible for her daughter's loss. Ostensibly it was because of her 'strange disconnect' during her media appearances, he reads. But also because of the series of bizarre interviews obtained by the police from Nick that pointed to some 'concerning behaviour' in relation to Alannah.

This is exactly what he was afraid would happen. He could almost hear the talking points that would pop up on discussion forums everywhere. She'd left her kid alone before. To drink. In other words, this mother had form.

It will make his next meeting particularly interesting, he thinks wearily, as he weaves through traffic. He sticks on WKCP and pretends to enjoy the melancholic piano swells. 'It's relaxing,' Alice used to laugh as he playfully smacked her hand away from the dials when they used to go on drives together. 'It calms you without you even realising.'

Nick's words are on the front page of every newspaper in the super-market that morning. Rolle lingers in front of them as he drops into SuperMart to buy Alice a card. All that's left on the selling stand is one with a couple in a hot-air balloon shaped like a heart. Corny, not at all Alice's style, but it will have to do. He knows if he doesn't buy it now, he won't get round to it later. He throws some gum onto the conveyer belt alongside it – anything to curb the caffeine cravings.

Vanished Girl's Mother's Secret Mental Health Battle, he reads, sick to his stomach. The picture of Mirren crumpled on the ground under its cruel splash.

Blood on the beach IS little Alannah's, screams another.

He stuffs the minty roll between his teeth and bites down hard, trying to banish the distaste in his mouth. This, on top of the Instagram footage of what seemed to be Mirren walking along the beach beside the Coral Beach Hotel with the child, now offered a plausible explanation to the who-done-it millions were seeking. It wasn't just the media either, amateur sleuths on almost every social media platform had weighed in. Overnight, the mobile phone footage had been slowed down, poured over, analysed. Every post Mirren had ever written online had been picked apart. *Her mother died just a few weeks before*, he'd read on a *Reddit* thread yesterday, after he'd fallen far down the rabbit hole of various online detective-wannabes. *It could have been some kind of sacrifice. Have they even examined the rental car for DNA?*

As he put down his basket at the grocery store conveyer belt, he could hear locals discussing the case.

'*Something went wrong, and she panicked, I guess*,' is one comment that floats over to him. '*Where was she taking her that day?*'

Everyone has an opinion.

This was Logan's masterplan, Rolle realises, as he reads the paper's confirmation that a 'close family member of the child is being questioned, according to senior police sources'. Kite Island was fast becoming the centre of the media universe. Rolle knew that the Irish media had it front and centre too – opinion pieces on leaving children unsupervised, spotlights on the couple's relationship, speculation on

Mirren's access to medication. Even interviews with former house cleaners and a distant cousin that painted Mirren as an aloof academic, cold and unfeeling. One of her former mentors at the hospital where she first worked had described her as unstable. It had also led to a flood of hoax calls to the incident line, off-the-wall sightings and bizarre explanations: Satanism, cults, celebrity involvements. One woman had even called to say that Jesus Christ came to her and told her the child was buried at the back of the church grounds. Every report, no matter how zany, had to be investigated, which took up valuable time and police resources. No stone could be seen to be left unturned for the child with the blonde curls that strangers had fallen in love with. Alannah was easy to fall for, unlike Mariah, whose awkward adolescence and perceived lack of status rendered her almost invisible. To the media at least. Pretty sells, Rolle thinks resentfully.

Back in the car, he tunes the radio to Easy 93 and taps the steering wheel as he drives towards the Emerald Plaza Hotel. He hums along to Phil Collins and tries not to think of the meeting ahead. For a moment he allows himself to feel like his old self – before Alice's eyes were sad all the time, before he had this knot of anxiety living in his stomach. Before Sal Reid. Sunny evenings on the beach, cook-outs with friends, trawling car boot sales at weekends to find clutter for their home that Alice excitedly called treasure.

The radio news beeps to signal the top of the hour news, dragging his mind back to Alannah.

The transcript of Nick's interview is mind-blowing stuff. No wonder it's the top story across most of the stations. Amazing what grief can trudge up – and anger. But some things are sacred among couples. He could never imagine Alice blindsiding him like that. But Rolle knows that Nick's words have been twisted – an undercurrent of implication that simply isn't fair.

He leans on the horn as an electric scooter whizzes carelessly past, making him swerve towards the pedestrian path. This is the worst time of the day to drive on the island. Now that the missing child story is rolling twenty-four-hour coverage, the extra media traffic, satellite vans and rubberneckers on the roads are causing chaos for locals.

Antonio turns off the turnpike and indicates towards Tilbury. Rolling down his window, he gulps some air, ignoring the faintly mildew smell in the wind. The algae blooms are particularly voracious this season, especially after a storm. As he chews his gum, he thinks of his boss, whom he has no intention of informing about this afternoon's meeting. His phone buzzes insistently beside him on the seat. It's probably the update he's expecting. Only two hours later than he'd have preferred. One of the guys at the lab puts him on speaker phone.

Forensics had found old burnt clothes at the lighthouse shack in the remains of the fire. They were trying to establish if they could be children's items perhaps. But it was almost impossible to tell, the team leader explains. The plastic containers, also found inside the house, held drug traces. Not unusual for a gang house, he figures. Testing for blood traces are ongoing, and DNA samples are being cross-checked with Mariah's sister and mother – something Rolle was horrified hadn't been collected earlier in the case.

He thinks about Mirren again as he hangs up. He felt as if they'd made a connection that day at the hospital. Like the media, though, he still couldn't get a complete take on her. She'd presented herself initially as vulnerable, a child-like victim of a devastating loss. But there was an edge to her too. Nick described her as damaged but seemed pained to say it – as if the words were being drawn out of him against his will. Of course, Rolle reminds himself, it is entirely possible to be both damaged and devastated. But did her problems in the past mean she was capable of something as unspeakably sinister as harming her own child, or having something to do with her disappearance?

He doesn't think so. Besides, grief distorts. Rolle has never dismissed his capacity to go with his gut feeling. And in this case, it is yelling at him to do things his way for a bit. But he can't help feeling frustrated for not getting a better handle on this case. He pictures all the children Sal Reid had destroyed – young and frightened. Then, the pictures of Mariah on the walls of her mother's trailer. The toothless smile crumpled carelessly into her thin file at the police station. He had let them down; he couldn't bear to feel that again.

Selfishly, solving this case was also Antonio's ticket out of Kite. Being with his pal Sam Harris had convinced him that it was time for him and Alice to return home to Miami, the sooner the better. Once the impending court case was behind him.

He leaves a voice note on Alice's cell reminding her of their Valentine's date later that night. It's time to make things right.

Easing the Audi carefully around the tip of the coast road, Rolle spots the Emerald Plaza in the distance – the hotel Nick Fitzpatrick had moved to after his police interview. It's a slightly downmarket aparthotel, a ten-minute drive from the Coral Beach Hotel. The beaches aren't as pretty here, but like all the island's resorts, they are quieter now since the child's vanishing. Rolle is meeting both Nick and Mirren there. He'd described it to each of them as the chance to give them an informal update on the investigation.

Nick was initially reluctant, especially when he woke up to the media screaming about their relationship. But Rolle explained that he needed them both there – that this lunch date wasn't negotiable. The optics of having it at the station wouldn't be good. Plus, Logan's intentions over leaking Nick's interview were becoming increasingly concerning. His boss was blocking every connection Rolle tried to make to the trafficking network between Kite and Miami, between Kata and Red. And Rolle was starting to wonder why.

The Emerald Plaza is a bright white building made up of ten floors of curved, green-tinted balconies overlooking the rockiest part of the coast. This is the busier side of the island, with a crowded boardwalk that runs directly outside it, linking the hotel to Calloway, a thirty-minute walk away.

As he drives towards the car park entrance, he sees couples power-walking along the coast, children on bikes, and a few brave souls attempting the outdoor exercise machines that dot the boardwalk.

There's a generic cafe and bakery at the ground level of the Plaza, a small lobby and no-frills swimming pool on the roof. Rolle chose it because he knew the media were mainly staying on the other side of Kite, camped out near the Coral Beach. The cafe, which has private booths, is usually empty too. He doesn't feel like a scrum today.

Rolle parks badly underground and walks heavily up the stairs to the ground floor, removing his chewing gum and carefully folding it into a SuperMart receipt he finds in his pocket. Inside the white-tiled cafe, he glances around briefly before making his way towards the last booth in the row.

It's clean and the décor is kitsch, in a candy-stripped way, he supposes. Ignoring the glass display case filled with elaborate cupcakes, he dips down towards the first bin he sees to deposit his used gum. He's the only person in the place except for the waitress, who also happens to be the daughter of one of Alice's clients. Jagger is the one who keeps him updated about who is coming and going from the cafe. She also showed him *TikTok* and how to access *Reddit* – she's the one who showed him all the online sleuthing – a whole new world to him.

'Ma still away?' he asks, taking the menu from her. She's wearing cut-off denims and her hair is pulled back into a ponytail revealing an earful of piercings. He concentrates on not wincing as he looks at it. Alice looks after a handful of properties on the island, managing their short-term rental when the inhabitants are away. Jagger's mum, Tracey, is among her clients. A way to keep busy, he supposes, during her teaching post secondment.

'Yeah. Mom's thrilled. The guests extended their stay.'

Rolle raises his eyebrows. Alice never said – then again, she hadn't said much to him since her outburst. Still, they have a nice candlelight dinner planned for tonight. He should probably get flowers too, he decides suddenly.

But never roses. 'Too obvious,' Alice once said, and he never forgot. He'd get her pink peonies, their wedding flowers. 'Did you know they are called *sho yu* in Chinese,' she'd read aloud to him from some wedding brochure, as they prepared for their country club ceremony all those years ago. 'It translates as "the most beautiful".' She'd smiled happily, and he'd scooped her to him, kissed her hard on the neck – called her his very own *sho yu*.

Rolle orders an orange juice and a decaf from Jagger and tries to ignore the uncomfortable feeling in the pit of his stomach. He pulls out his laptop and updates his investigative report while he waits. There are still a few documents he's waiting on; including insurance details for the Fitzpatrick family and the Red Roccio case file from the assault charge.

At exactly one p.m., Mirren steps out of Tara's rental car and walks the short distance to the cafe. He can see her from the window. She looks exhausted. She's wearing one of those wrap dresses with pale yellow flowers and a wide-brimmed fedora. She spots Rolle who has strategically positioned himself at the back of the cafe, next to the kitchen. She raises her hand, hesitantly. She still has Alannah's blankie clutched in her hand.

Sliding into the booth opposite him, she places her hat on the seating beside her and smooths the wrinkles from her lap. She seems a lot more put together than she did that first morning on the beach. Rolle studies her face as she sits there in silence, no stomach for small talk most likely, and he doesn't blame her. There are new red marks across her forehead that she's attempted to cover with make-up. Rolle tries to imagine her having something to do with her daughter's disappearance. Sipping the bitter pulp of the juice, he reminds himself that judging anyone simply by appearance is a weak way of getting the measure of a person. He sets down his glass, rubbing the moisture off the side of it with his thumb, and begins to talk.

'Mirren, I know things with Nick are bad. But I need to speak to you both without any drama. Do you understand?'

'I've nothing to say to him,' she whispers back, her eyes filling with tears.

'Plus, I'm not ashamed of my past,' she continues. 'What I can't forgive is him letting it interfere with the search for Alannah,' she says, her chin quivering as she speaks. She takes a menu off Jagger politely but sets it to the side without reading it.

Two minutes pass.

He deliberately doesn't mention the footage of her on the beach that he knows already has 4.5 million views online. Not yet.

Nick walks in, his face entirely passive. Rolle knows he needs to focus all his Mad Dog instincts on this meeting. From the corner of his eye, he senses Mirren breathing out quickly as Nick approaches. She cradles one hand in the other, squeezing her fingers together tightly, as if holding herself together. He can't tell if she is about to cry or attack.

'Detective Rolle,' Nick says curtly, and then, nodding at his wife, 'Mirren.'

Nick is paler than the night before; his eyes are bloodshot, and his hair stands in wild tufts. Folding his large frame slightly, he slides self-consciously into the booth beside Mirren, opposite Rolle. He glances at her again, as if to check how his wife is doing – concerned, perhaps, how she's holding up. Rolle watches him take in the injury to her forehead. Then Nick turns his attention to Rolle to ask him about his leaked interview. Rolle shrugs.

There's no proof it was Logan, besides not much they can do about it now. They've more important things to discuss. He watches the air between the couple ripple with tension. Rolle sure as hell isn't here for a marriage counselling session. God knows he's had enough of those himself. But he needs to know a lot more about all of this before Lovell and his guys take things to a point beyond return.

Rolle wonders, for the hundredth time, if the TV interview had been a mistake. The media got a taste for blood and now were even more frenzied for morsels about the couple and their private lives. The narrative was too tempting to ignore – a rocky marriage, the troubled mother, a stellar career. Mirren's take-down was soap-opera territory. No wonder she looks so shell-shocked as she sits motionless before him, her tiny features sharper and more delicate than he's seen.

'Have you anything more on those brothers?' Nick asks quickly.

Rolle shakes his head and smoothing the table in front of him with both his hands, starts his oratory. He doesn't look up as he speaks. 'Nick and Mirren,' he begins. 'I understand this is hard for you, but there are some serious issues we need to get straight before things derail completely.'

There's no point going into anything about the *Rainy Day* or Tiffany. Not yet. Not until he gets some firmer lines drawn in this ever-shifting sand.

He raises his eyes. 'It's almost a week since Alannah disappeared, and I think we can all agree, the last few days have been...' he searches for the right word, 'distracting.'

A crash from the restaurant kitchen interrupts his sequence of thoughts, and he grimaces, eyes to the ceiling, waiting for the commotion to subside. Mirren beats him to it. When she speaks, it's with the slow deliberation of a drinker trying to seem sober.

'Why would you bring all that up, Nick?' Mirren says too loudly. Was that the trace of a slur? 'Now it's all over the papers – what I went through.' She stares at him, tears in her eyes. 'They are now talking about me instead of Alannah. Do you get that?'

Mirren sits back, shaking her head. Then leans forward suddenly and speaks more quietly.

'Do you really think I'd actually hurt her?'

Rolle puts down his glass, suddenly afraid he's made a huge mistake by hosting this meeting so informally.

He's about to speak, but instinct stops him. Sniff the air, Dog. Wait a beat.

They both wait for Nick to respond.

'No... I don't know.' He looks miserable, defeated. She waits for him to say something more.

'Now it looks as if I neglected her – left her alone to drink back then, and again here in Florida.'

She's peering into his eyes.

When he speaks again, his voice is so low that Rolle has to lean forward slightly to hear him.

'But you did,' he says, holding her gaze.

'Being a shit mother doesn't mean I did anything to harm her,' she cries, flinging her hands up in the air, agitated.

But Nick has a right to know what happened – why she lied about walking with Alannah up the beach towards the rocks.

'Mirren, why were you walking with her? Where did you go? At the pool, you slapped the glass right out of my hand, and then you stormed away. Then Alannah's gone. It's hard to know what to think. It's all just...' He shakes his head again, despair written all over his face.

Mirren glances at her hand, she traces the wound on the back of it.

Nick looks broken in every way, Rolle thinks, watching him running his hands through his hair, over his jaw.

'I just thought...'

'What did you think?' Mirren demands, more forcibly now. She blinks too slowly. Definitely drinking. Rolle sighs.

'Just because I had a drink that day, a slip, you think that I'd hurt Alannah? You're the one who decided to destroy our family. Then you throw me to the wolves?'

'I thought what I was saying was private...' Nick trails off. 'I thought it might help. I didn't think they'd use it against you, Mirren.'

Rolle takes his cue to interrupt.

'Enough,' he commands.

'Mirren, talk to me, please.' Rolle holds her gaze.

'Do you remember walking Alannah that direction after you left the bar? Nick, stay quiet.'

He holds his finger in the air as a warning. Unconsciously, both men shift slightly closer to hear Mirren speak.

Mirren twists her hands together and steeples them over her nose. Under the table her leg jigs violently. Rolle can feel its vibration against the plastic booth. She opens her mouth to talk, but nothing comes out. She buries her face in her hands.

It's hard to watch. Rolle glances over at Nick. His face is the picture of desperation.

'Mirren?' Rolle says her name gently. He knows whatever she has to say will need to be coaxed out. Then, her words tumble out in slow shudders as she pauses between each breath, as if it hurts. It is impossible to decipher what she's saying, and for a moment, Rolle wonders if he should be recording this officially. He swallows nervously, as Nick catches his eye. He realises this is probably a mistake. But it is too late now.

'I couldn't tell you,' she's saying, her eyes closed, and she puts her hands to her face again. 'I couldn't tell anyone. I was trying to protect her.'

Jagger starts walking towards the booth. Rolle frowns at her fiercely and shakes his head.

Suddenly he feels completely out of his depth. Had his instincts been wrong all along?

Mirren picks at the half-healed scar on her hand, ripping it back to its rawest pink as she struggles to speak. Nick turns his body towards her, coiled, ready for whatever was about to come next. Preparing for the worst, perhaps.

'Tell me, Mirren. Whatever it is, it will be okay.'

Rolle notices the veins in Nick's temple bulging. Anger, now replaced by sheer terror.

'Tell me, please, Mer,' Nick says a little more quietly this time, understanding suddenly that he might not want to hear what she is finally trying to admit.

'The CCTV,' Mirren gulps, her voice breaking with emotion. 'The mobile phone footage. That's what I couldn't tell you. I couldn't say it… the woman in the clip, with Alannah.'

Mirren looks up miserably at both of them, and it is obvious how painful it must be for her to get the words out. She lets her head drop forward onto her chest. Her eyes cast down.

'It isn't me.' She looks up desperately at Nick, tears brimming in her eyes.

'In the video, Nick, it isn't me at all.'

Her tears spill and flood her face. She uses the scruffy scrap of blanket to dab at her eyes. The scab has been pulled clear off her hand, soft exposed flesh glistens.

His heart thumps faster. He looks from Mirren to Nick and back again.

'It's Réa,' she whispers, her eyes on Rolle.

'The person in the footage with Alannah – it's Réa.'

31

Mirren

Usually when I drink, I picture my mother's face. I debate whether or not to tell that to my sister. She's lying on the sun lounger beside me on the Coral Beach Hotel balcony. It's nine p.m. I glance over and see she's dozing, chin down to her chest, eyelids flickering restlessly. I sip my wine – our third bottle – and watch a moth fly too close to the insect candle I've lit on our outdoor table.

I use the moment to reflect on all those years spent imagining my mother's death; testing how it might feel, probing it like a tongue might tease a sore tooth. I'd daydream about her funeral. About what I'd say. Would it bring relief, I used to wonder? An avalanche of regret? Pain?

In fact, the day I saw her slack, vacant face laid out in the bed at home after the undertaker's fluffing, all I saw was an old woman. And that made me even sadder. It was almost disappointing how unremarkable her ending turned out to be. In fact, my mother's death was a whole lot less complicated than all those strange daydreams I'd had over the years. Finality is simpler than people think. Watching someone die is profound. I tried to explain this to the parents of some of my patients before – about the strange peace that comes from seeing a person leave this world. It's not that they're gone, it's that nothing appears in any way different as they make that journey between being alive and being dead. Nothing, and yet such a huge something. That transition had always fascinated me. But for someone who brought trouble wherever she went, my mother's passing was the calm after a lifelong storm. Few understand what it is like to have a mother who doesn't mother. A relationship like this, stripped of nurture and guidance, is little more than a barren wasteland of female indifference. It isn't normal to compare the strength of someone's love for you against the weight of a glass bottle.

It always won.

My mother loved with a sting. Sitting in my childhood home a few weeks ago, the day I went to see her body, I was surprised that she looked even smaller dead. Her cheeks were sunken, the frown lines finally released in death. I held her icy hand in mine and tried to accept it all. The monster I'd made her out to be wasn't diminished, but it was sobering to realise that even monsters look pitiful in defeat. That type of pain lives a life all of its own. All I could do was watch, to observe, to distance myself. But like it or not, this person had carved me out, and I owed it to the world to do better for both of us. That's why I decided to try to love my daughters the same. To try to do better – to go against the grain of my resentment towards Alannah. My mother had been the way she was because of her own mother's rejection of her. That, Tara had tried to explain to me as I sobbed as a child in our bedroom after another slap across the face. You might think it would have made her do the opposite, to curl around her own children, but damage to our psyche so young is frighteningly unpredictable. The random swirls of our choices echo down generations.

My thoughts are dragged back to the balcony as the moth gets too close to the candle flame and spins once, before landing injured on the white plastic table by my wine. I flick it away and pour another glass. I didn't see my mother in the last four years of her life. I'd ignored the calls, the cards and letters, which started off neat and remorseful, and ended, spitefully slanted. She told me, one cold December day, that I had only myself to blame for the miscarriages, because I worked too hard. It was then I knew it was time to cut loose the empty vessel I'd been dragging behind me for far too long. A blessed disentanglement.

But it also meant that the link to Father was further removed. I sought him out in my mind like the *Tuatha de Danann* – legends of our childhood stories – sought out their mysterious islands, covered in fog and hidden to all but those who believed. I mostly found him though when I smelt the sea, its tangy allure brought back his gravelly laugh and easy affection. My mother's heart had failed her in life and its weakness brought her death. She was found in the bath the week I finally planned to visit, submerged in a scummy water grave. The timing is unfortunate, Nick said, shaking his head when we heard the news. He hugged me tight, understanding the flurry of my feelings. Guilt was her parting gift to me. Now she'd remain forever my unquiet ghost. That's why I didn't bring the girls to her funeral. That cold day, Nick, Tara and I sheltered together, our backs against the glare of old neighbours, like icy winds designed to chill. We were the children that 'up and left their poor mother alone,' they whispered. 'And she… a doctor.'

But nobody ever knows what really happens in any story. Not until the end. Besides, where were they when I was drowning alone in the endless pools of my mother's widowing? The loss of my father was never validated, never acknowledged. 'Be good for your poor mother,' was what grown-ups said to me after my father died, as if it was her loss alone.

'Don't cry, Mer,' Tara slurs beside me and tries to fold me into a hug. She almost falls off the sun lounger instead. I hadn't realised I had been sobbing. It's the second last night at the Coral Beach Hotel before we move to the apartment kindly provided by one of the volunteers. 'For as long as you need it,' the man from Amsterdam says, the one who'd helped me search the rocks for Alannah that first night. He was the one with me when I hid Alannah's necklace in my hand that day on the beach, keeping it close. It was something tangible I could hold onto – something precious of hers.

Tara and I started drinking hours ago while we waited for the detective to call me back. I look at my phone again and wonder what the hell Antonio Rolle is playing at. I've called him three times already in the past hour.

'How did you turn out so normal?' I ask suddenly, twisting to face my big sister. I wrap a purple pashmina around my shoulders. The cloudless nights come with a chill. Tara laughs hollowly and drains her glass. Her face glows slightly in the flickering candlelight.

'Don't kid yourself, Mer,' she says a little sadly. 'I'm divorced, I live alone with two dogs and have a part-time job in a library. I don't think I'm exactly an advertisement for a successful life.'

I think about how my sister couldn't afford the airfare to get here when I called sobbing the night Alannah went missing. 'I'll pay you back,' she'd promised, embarrassed perhaps to be so crude during an emergency. But Nick took care of all that – he looks after all our finances.

'I don't mean that. I mean you seem emotionally healthy, you're able to deal with stuff, you're tough.' I lean over and pat her awkwardly on her bare leg. 'We grew up in the same house,' I continue. 'How come I'm the one with all the issues?'

'I think everyone carries pain from their past,' she says, with the sage tone familiar to all younger sisters. Then she splashes another generous glug of rosé into her glass and refills mine. She's never mentioned my drinking, not even back then. Perhaps she thinks I need it right now. Or maybe she just needs a drinking partner. The irony is that she's always had a special bond with Alannah. Once more, I'm reminded that this isn't my loss alone.

'And look at you,' she says, spilling her wine as she swooshes her glass through the night air to máke her point.

'People probably look at you and think you have the perfect life. Successful doctor, handsome husband, two beautiful daughters…' She stops, reaches over and squeezes my hand.

We both sit there in silence for a moment.

'Poor Réa,' she says sadly, her head lolling slightly to the side. Easy tears spring up.

I glance back in at the room behind me, through the glass balcony doors, and see the shape of my older daughter curled into the double bed.

I'd climbed in beside her earlier after she'd finally admitted what really happened on the beach that day. I wiped her convulsing tears until she fell into a fitful sleep. I confronted her about the footage after the meeting with Nick and Detective Rolle – explained that I'd wanted to protect her, so I agreed it was me in the footage when I was at the police station.

'Why Réa? Why lie? This could have been really important,' I'd explained, trying not to let myself get angry with her.

'I couldn't tell anyone,' she'd cried, and I rocked her like I used to when she was a baby. Alannah had begged Réa to bring her to see the fish over beside the rocks, she told me, shaking as she spoke.

'I brought her to the rocks, and I left her there. It's all my fault. She just wanted to use her net. Maybe if I'd stayed, I could have saved her. She wouldn't have fallen in.'

'We don't know what happened, Réa,' I soothed, stroking her tear-soaked hair. 'Please don't cry, Roo.'

Réa was beside herself with regret, but I could see the relief in her eyes too. Unburdening is a helpful process, my therapist always said. For some things at least.

But I understand how guilt can erode.

'None of this is your fault, Réa. Do you understand?' I held my daughter's chin and looked fiercely into her eyes, so similar to my own. 'I'm her mother, I should have been watching her.'

I wasn't ready to tell her, or anyone else for that matter, about how I got Alannah's necklace. We all need things for ourselves – relics. We all have secrets we keep.

We lay face to face – me and the small version of myself, a mirror of shared grief and helplessness.

'Did you see anything at all, Réa? Did you notice anything when you were there with her?'

I didn't want to push her too much, but this was vital.

'It's all I've been thinking of. I'm running it over and over in my head. But no, apart from the boat, but I've told them that already.'

My heart skipped a beat when she said that. I sat up quickly.

'What boat, Réa? Did you tell Detective Rolle?'

'I said it to that other police guy,' she said. 'The main one, Logan. About the white-and-red boat that came into beach the other side of the rocks – into the little cove. I saw it from the rocks. He said best not to put it in my statement because I was too far from it to be able to describe it. But I wasn't.'

My face frightened her then and she'd started sobbing again, as I tried to find my mobile phone. I even tried calling Nick, but he didn't answer. I think we both felt a little closer after today – after the fright that Réa could have been caught up in all of this. The anxiety over finding our child had been distorted by anger. We stayed on at the cafe talking for hours after Detective Rolle left. 'I miss you,' he'd said sadly, and I let him reach for my hand.

'I'm sorry.'

Now we had to stick together, no matter what went before or what came after.

But suddenly, sitting on the balcony with Tara, I feel incredibly despondent. And pretty drunk. Finding Alannah seems harder every moment that passes. The thoughts of leaving this hotel without her are devastating. How could I pack that little suitcase up, fold in her starfish swimsuit and bury her purple flip-flops inside of it? It's like closing the lid to our old lives, zipping up her life into a darkened place. I press my clenched hand to my mouth, push it hard against my teeth, trying to stop the freefall of emotions that threaten to escape. We don't know how long we'll be here. Thinking beyond anything except the next hour is impossible.

–

'You are not a bad person, Mer,' Tara is saying to me now. 'You've just had some pretty shitty things happen to you.' Philosophising over whether I deserve such a kicking from the universe while tipsy with my sister is a waste of my energy. Even drunk I know this. Especially as my tiny daughter is out there somewhere under that velvety sky. Maybe hurt, maybe in pain, probably alone.

And while Tara continues talking, wine-wise, I lie back on the cold sun lounger and make a bargain with the stars that mock from above, twinkly with secrets they daren't tell. I beg the universe to absolve me from my sins. I count one hundred of them and wish for my lost thing.

I make a pact, an exchange. But I should know better. I hold no sway with this cruel realm.

And then the chirp of my phone with its exhaustingly cheerful ringtone cuts through the night. Nick's number flashes up. I'm happy and frightened simultaneously. But then remember he's probably just returning my call about the boat.

I slide the tab to green, squinting, my movements thicker and slower than they should be.

His voice jumps out from the speaker, horribly loud and bleak. He howls and I'm immediately completely alert. I scramble to my feet. Tara too. The pashmina crumples to the ground.

'Mirren…'

Nick wails in a way that I've never heard before. It leaks from the device in my hand, bleeding into the salt-soaked air. The bottom immediately falls out of my life.

'They've found a body, Mer.'

He is crying now, his voice gravelly with pain. Its vibration is everywhere, rippling through the world, ripping through me.

They'd found her.

'They are saying it could be Alannah,' he gasps, and then moans again. Tara has shot up onto her feet beside me. She's holding my shoulder, squeezing me back into this universe. 'Jesus, sweet Jesus, no, no, no…' I hear her whisper.

'My baby. It can't be my baby, please no. Please God no.' Nick sobs.

My eyes search the dirty black horizon – trying to find the chink that separates this world from the next. There's only black.

Grief separates, but it also binds. Would you swap one loss for the return of another?

I lost him so then I lost her.

32

The Timmins' boat was nine metres long and made from reinforced fibreglass. There was just enough space in the cabin for Bonnie and Earl to sit shoulder-to-shoulder, their preferred position, as they sat scanning the sea floor. The name *Rocky P* had been stencilled in yellow letters under one of the cabin's windows – named after a man whose body the elderly couple found off the coast of Tampa in 2008. His family had donated funds to help the Timmins buy a more sophisticated boat. It's an unusual vocation – trawling the sea floor with sonar equipment to find bodies. But environmental biologists, Bonnie and Earl, who met in the University of Georgia forty years ago, were happy to dedicate their lives to helping families bring loved ones home. A week ago, they'd heard about the plight of the Fitzpatrick family and had zipped down the coast on the *Rocky P* to help join the search for the missing child.

Their boat used external-scan sonar, a method used by the military or treasure hunters. Since they started their crusade to locate bodies of loved ones for nothing but travel costs ten years ago, thirty-seven precious treasures of a human kind, had been handed back to teary relatives standing on the edge of shores. Earl had been featured on a Canadian documentary series a few years ago. He'd had the film-makers tour the boat, pointing out the equipment and explaining patiently how it all worked.

Instead of light, it's sonar that emits pulses of sound, which travel easily through water, reflecting back off solid objects, rocks, sunken boats, trapped bodies, he'd pointed out. The images were displayed on a computer screen watched by the eagle eye of Bonnie. He'd pointed at his candy-floss-haired wife. He explained too how it was up to him to feed the electromechanical cable out into the waves, allowing the sonar device, a horseshoe-shaped hunk to tow behind the boat, along the bottom of the sea. You are literally digging for treasure, the producer had said, fascinated. Earl had nodded slowly. What they did was too extraordinary for any modesty.

Besides, if not them, then who?

Police, as well as search and rescue, usually spend three days looking for a body and then moving on – that's why many commercial operators get called in by families. But as anyone who'd lost someone this way knows, it's expensive, time consuming and usually fruitless.

The Timmins knew that in order to bring closure, to prevent people thinking they saw their missing relative on a crowded street somewhere, they needed to see the death – to experience things like bones or lightless eyes, no matter how excruciating that might be.

You needed to look death in the eye to really understand what it meant to say goodbye.

They'd been trawling for almost the entire day when Bonnie thought she spotted something on the sea floor about fifty kilometres north of Kite Island. They'd started off searching the ferry route taken towards the cape and on towards Miami.

'Something suspicious,' she called calmly to her husband, a grand-fatherly man, softly spoken, who wore a slightly battered Tampa Bay Rays baseball hat.

'I'll drop a GPS,' she said, busying her fingers with the dials. 'Do you want to do a ninety?'

'Yes, if you've seen something,' Earl called back to Bonnie, and he stopped guiding the cable any further.

Bonnie manoeuvred the boat so it was looming over the large grey object and they both examined the computer monitor carefully. The *Rocky P* bobbed steadily under their feet. It was a magnificent day, sparkling blue-white, too beautiful to find something dead.

Neither spoke for a few moments.

'Looks like a rock to me,' Earl finally said dismissively.

The number of false sightings in a day can be in the hundreds. Turns out there's a lot of objects at the bottom of the ocean that can look human shaped if you screw up your eyes a little.

That's what Bonnie did then; narrowed her eyes, pulled on the glasses that hung on a gold chain around her neck to get a better look.

'Hang on, see that shape?' Bonnie traced her fingers along the screen, frowning.

'Nudge it, Ned.'

Ned is the *Rocky P*'s resident diver. Bonnie and Earl call him The Man-Child behind his back. A thirty-two-year-old who acts like he's twenty-two, Ned, from the UK's East Midlands, is scraggy-haired and permanently bedraggled. He'd been 'interning' with the couple since he turned up with his guitar and a bag full of diving gear two years ago when they put out a volunteer call in Tampa's Craigslist. They agreed to pay him in food and accommodation – an arrangement that suited both parties perfectly. Although neither party would admit it, they'd grown used to each other and a friendship had formed. They enjoyed Ned's joie de vivre, and he relished their experience and guidance – something his own parents had never been able to offer him.

Now he lived on the *Rocky P* in hippie heaven while Bonnie and Earl, almost seventy and seventy-two, preferred the comforts of their small apartment, a ten-minute drive from where their boat was usually moored.

Ned was already geared up by the time he heard Bonnie's command on the radio. He noticed that Earl was walking slower than usual as he approached him at the back of the boat. It made him sad to think these days would someday end. Stopping abruptly was usually the signal that his services were needed. Under his diving mask, Ned's blond surfer hair was pinned down, long dehydrated tendrils soft against stubble. Earl helped load the tank onto his back and patted him on the shoulder, supportively – fatherly.

Ned knew the drill.

In fact, sometimes he wished his brain could forget all the things his eyes had seen.

Without a word, Ned tilted himself backward off the side of the boat with a small, neat splash. Once in the water, he descended, equalising the pressure in his ears, always taking a moment to notice that gloopy rush of serenity as he left one world and entered another.

Ned had been diving for five years, going from Club Med to Vacation Holiday resorts teaching rich families the technicalities of scuba diving. But it was when he discovered this part of the world that he knew he couldn't do anything else but this.

Here, all the seasons are under water, each with its own unique flora and fauna. He vowed to explore as much of this enchanting place as he could while he was alive and able. His parents called him a dreamer, but for Ned, there was nothing more real than the natural world he submerged himself into every day.

He watched the evening sunlight dance on the loamy sand below as he glided downwards towards the bulky mass. His mission was simple: identify and report back. As Ned's eyes adjusted to the murky twilight, his stomach flipped. It's a strange situation to be in, simultaneously hoping it was and wasn't the child they've been searching for. He let himself glide further down. He was nearly there. All he could hear was the blood in his own head, the husky rasp-slurp of his breathing apparatus as he fell lower and lower. Above, he saw the rectangle shadow of the boat's hull. A lone sailfish floated past unperturbed. Seagrass fanned out like human hair, swaying against the current, next to coral reef. It takes a century for an inch of coral reef to grow, he remembered reading somewhere, and once again felt the eerie spirituality of this otherworld.

He was ten metres away.

Nine metres.

When he was just five metres away, he bowed his head low, respectfully.

Ned picked out the unmistakable shape of a small human head. Ghostly fingers, almost translucent. Splayed, as if reaching out towards something.

He took a breath and closed his eyes. Only the fish might see his lips moving as he whispered a prayer. *Lie in forever peace beneath still waters. Rise with the tide. In oceans deep my faith will stand.* He'd never been religious until he started as a special kind of treasure hunter.

One metre.

He gently prodded the body with the long pole he'd brought down. Tiny fragments of sea life scattered in all directions. He couldn't do much more until they got the coastguard involved. Bonnie and Earl would mark the spot with a lone white buoy and then they'd all wait. Ned turned his face towards the surface of the water, looking beyond the blues, up to the sky and slowly, sadly bubbled his way back into the world above.

33

Mirren

The Past

On my first day of dissection hall, I was scared to even touch a bone. But after a few months of getting used to the dank, formaldehyde smell, I developed a tolerance for ugly things – the gnarled hands, the blue skin and frayed dead veins. I built up resistance, like I'd done all my life. Not because I was strong or special, but because my teaching curriculum was systematic. I discovered the discipline that kept me ordered. I eventually began my surgery posting under Dr Jonathan Kenny, a lecherous cardiac specialist who expected total adoration from all his students, but mostly the few females on the team. I was the only one who didn't pander to his wet-lipped leans. My first-year training was in the same hospital I knew Dr Lacey worked in. I spent the first few weeks holding my breath around hospital corners.

It was here I had my first encounter with death.

Bill had a history of arrhythmias that doctors feared would lead to a blood clot. He'd watched his wife of thirty-nine years die from pancreatic cancer the year before. Now, hospitals made Bill nervous, and he had nobody to hold his hand. He reminded me of my father with his work-calloused palms and broad, bent back. As we waited for the results of his latest tests, he told me about his grown-up son Kevin who was born with Down syndrome. No wonder Bill's heart hurt, I thought as I listened to its pathetic beat. Dr Kenny confirmed the worst a few hours later; Bill's heart was failing, and he didn't have long. For six weeks Bill was in and out of hospital. He always asked for me. 'The Galway lass,' he'd cough as he shuffled slowly into the ward. He'd sit in the corner of the ward, biting his lip, working on The Times crossword. I'd sit with

197

him sometimes, gently removing his hand from his face when he fiddled with his oxygen supply.

'Three across. State of equilibrium, seven letters.'

'Balance.'

I'd learnt the pathways of the heart from a book. But during this cardiology rotation, I'd seen those gleaming pink networks up close. They fascinated me – the elasticity of thin membranes that turned white the further you stretched them, the reliable bloodlines, snaking down their arterial rivers. I'd peered deep inside a human heart, my nose close enough to smell the meaty metallics that signify life. I imagined the bloody red mass of my father's heart beating slower and finally stopping. Once again, it seemed impossible to reconcile the certainties of anatomy with the messiness of what it means to be human.

And then Bill died.

I held his hand as he shuddered to a halt, his face the lightest watercolour blue – watered down.

That flicker between life and death – the exact moment the wick of a candle stutters and extinguishes – that is death. And it was quite beautiful in its own way. I wondered who would explain all this to his son Kevin. He'd never know that his father's last words had been about him. That was my first experience of a patient's death, but those that followed were rarely as peaceful. Nor was my inevitable encounter with Dr Emma Lacey. Hurrying down the back stairs of the hospital one day, I heard my name being called. Her caramel hair was pinned back, her peachy skin smooth with foundation. She smelt like coconuts and summer nights.

'How dare you,' *she spat, her voice shaking with the effort of containing the anger when she spotted me.* 'How dare you show up here after destroying my family. Are you fucking stalking me?'

I looked down at the floor, my fists clenched tight while the words bled out of her, vicious and unchecked. Because even though I knew there had been two of us in it, Jack and me, I'd betrayed her inexcusably. I lived in her house and seduced her husband and ran away from her children. But when she mentioned Jack and death in the same sentence, my apathy turned to horror.

'You killed him, Mirren. Do you understand?'

'No, wait, what?' I tried to speak; my knees shook. I pictured Jack with his kind, clever eyes, always a book in hand. Dr Lacey was crying now. Powerless over her emotions.

'Wait…' I repeated, horrified. Those poor children.

'He killed himself,' she said, her sobs loud against the echo of the tiled stairwell.

'Jack's dead?' I repeated, moronically. I held out my hand to steady myself against the wall, shock unbalancing me.

Emma looked smaller now, as if her rage had been the only thing sustaining her.

'I read his journal.'

But all I could think of was that Réa's dad was dead. That they'd never meet.

'I found out about the affair, and I left him,' Emma continued, winding her fingers around the string of her identification lanyard.

'I took the children from him.' Her voice broke then – and I saw she was angriest at herself.

'I told him to leave our home, to leave his children. Not that you deserve to know any of this.' She looked up at me again, hate in her eyes still, but it had diminished.

'He hanged himself in the garage three weeks later. He left a note saying that he couldn't live without us. That's it. Nothing more.'

Emma stepped forward. I thought she was going to strike me.

But she held up her hands in defeat.

'So, you see, Mirren. It's a real-life horror story that started with you. You fucked my husband, my children lost their father, and we all have to live with the trauma of what you did to us. Do you know what it's like to have everything taken from you?'

She turned to leave but swung around suddenly.

'I really loved you. Do you know that?' She shook her head sadly. 'I feel sorry for you, Mirren. You don't know what love is and that's why you'll never understand it.' Breathing heavily, Emma turned and walked up the stairs. I felt for the wall behind me, leaning against it as I processed exactly what she'd said. I slid to the ground, hugging my knees to my chest.

Jack was dead. And it was because of me.

She'd loved me.

I felt a pain low in my stomach, lodged tight. She didn't mention Réa. She mustn't know. Less than a week later, the lecherous Dr Kenny summoned me into his office. Placing his heavy hands on my shoulders he said he had concerns over my commitment to cardiology and that I didn't seem to be progressing as quickly as my fellow students. I was to be transferred.

I didn't bother shaking him off. I understood that this was my penance.

But being banished to the oncology department was one of the best things that happened to me. Despite the shadow of Dr Lacey that haunted me, I found a place for myself. I got used to the ugly things. If I couldn't fix things, I decided, I'd simply destroy them instead. It was just a matter of perspective.

A state of equilibrium, seven letters.

34

Rolle

A morgue is no place for the living, thinks Rolle, as he jogs up the steps of Calloway's only mortuary still in his dinner jacket. Alice didn't care he'd walked out on their meal. Of course she didn't, how could she? It had taken all his willpower to not look at his phone as they sat in the tiny bistro he'd chosen for their Valentine's date, feeling it vibrate in his pocket.

She'd finally admitted how lonely she'd been. How caught up she'd been in everything that had happened in Miami. Over creamy-sweet lasagne and red wine, Alice confided in him that Alannah's vanishing had triggered something in her. Especially after the Reid case. She'd felt compelled to help. Solving this might solve everything, she cried as she explained. Her tears were hidden behind the crevice of a dinner napkin as she tried to explain – dabbing them away in jerky motions, the words squeezing slowly out.

Rolle hadn't realised she'd been so caught up in his work. It was a reminder that here, Alice only had him. In Miami she'd always been the smartest person in the room, plenty of friends, the one with the loudest laugh. A history lecturer at Bayswater Community College, she'd taken a leave of absence for a year – to try to help him get over all that mess, he guessed. Their whole lives, she'd had a knack of calming him without him even realising it. His very own human worry stone. But he'd been so caught up in his own distress, he'd neglected hers. Sal Reid had worn them both down too. That case had taken so much from them.

In fact, their love story started before either Alice or Antonio were even born. Their mothers bonded at a pre-natal class as young, working parents-to-be trying to make their way in a strange new city. A photo of Tony and Alice as newborns lying cheek to cheek still sits on their hall table, the edges badly frayed, but intact if you look beneath the wooden frame. Family trips were spent together and although they were from different suburbs and went to different schools, the pair continued to stay close. He'd admired the way she stood up to the bullies at the park when her younger brother came under fire. She told him later that she always remembered the way he handled his mother's death, walking proudly at the funeral, his suit jacket far too big for his nine-year-old shoulders. He confided in her the words his mother had whispered to him as she lay in her final days: 'Have dignity for us both, Antonio. Hold you head high. Don't be afraid.' And then, crying, reaching for Antonio's hand and gripping it tightly. 'I will always be with you. I will always love you, Tony. Even when you can't see me, I promise I will always be there.'

He and Alice met again when they both moved to Miami – their fretful youth almost out of their systems, both trying to find a better life than their parents. He studied policing while Alice made her way teaching. Why history, he'd asked her one evening as they dangled their legs off Roosevelt Boardwalk. 'It connects us to a larger story,' Alice had replied, biting into her hotdog, thinking as she chewed. 'History shows us that who we are is so much more than just our personal life or even the experiences of our parents. We are connected to people and events across the globe and down through the generations. Plus,' she smiled, glancing at him, her dimples dancing, 'it's all about learning from the mistakes all those folks made back then. Trying to do better with hindsight.'

He decided then and there, sitting watching the sun bleed her last rays into the sea, that he'd like to start a shared history with his best friend. But that determination was hampered by intimidation. He'd never been the type to express how he truly felt. In the end it was she who took the first step, a year later at a mutual friend's wedding. Alice, beautiful in blue silk, had asked him to dance, laughing at his mortification as she twirled and jiggled, moving his hands expertly, this way and that, in a way that made it seem as if they were made to do this together. Up until they'd moved to Kite Island, they'd danced together regularly. Not that he'd be rushing to tell that to the boys at the station. But there was something about ballroom, about the swoop and bend of wrist against hip, the swift pivots, the ache of the music. But if he was honest with himself, it was the look in his wife's eyes as they spun, inches apart. It was the lean of her elbow on his shoulder as he held her against him, hooked together, matching time.

He was still remembering the way Alice's eyes shone as she danced when George walked into the restaurant and dropped the latest bombshell. Alice was in the middle of telling him how she needed his help when he spotted George walking in. Tracing the delicate tips of the peonies he'd gone to four florists to find, she told him that she felt it was time to finally address things, to lay it all out. But the intimacy of the moment was shattered by George's whispered interruption.

'I'm sorry, Alice,' Rolle had said white-faced, after George slunk off. A body had been found. Equally shocked, brushing away her tears, she'd urged him to go, that of course he had to. But his heart hurt because he knew that behind her pretty eyes, there was so much more that needed to be said.

–

Clinical smells waft around the low-ceilinged room. Beyond the mortuary's reception area, a windowless corridor leads to a large grey door which Rolle knows is all that lies between him and the wilted body that could very possibly be Alannah. Rolle had warned Nick and Mirren on the phone about the harrowing nature of what they were about to see. He already knew from the coastguard that the body, of what seemed to be a child, was greatly eroded by the effects of being submerged in the sea.

However, the depths that the body was located, as well as the wrapping it was encased inside, meant it would be possible to make an identification, just… and in the most horrific of circumstances.

The morgue in Calloway, a small unassuming building at the back of the only supermarket in town. The entrance door faced onto the large car park, which was currently empty. He'd arranged to meet Mirren and Nick outside. Lovell was, so far, uncontactable. Rolle had asked a deputy to go to his home on the far side of the island, where he lived in an Andalusian-style villa with his wife Jess.

It was 11:30 p.m. by the time the body was brought in. Usually, they would wait until the next morning for a drowning identification, but both the pathologist and all those involved in the search had no appetite to wait another minute before the poor child was named. In fact, delaying wasn't even discussed. Plus, the journalists wouldn't be buzzing around at this time of night, Rolle hoped.

He only realises how much he is shivering as he watches Nick and Mirren get out of the taxi. Mirren is supported by Nick as she steps out of the car, shaking so violently he doubts she will be able to walk the short distance from the car park into the reception area where he's standing. He starts out towards the door to help, but Candy beats him to it. The hotel PR, a seemingly constant presence, appears from around from the driver's door to hold Mirren's other arm. Mirren is wearing loose shorts and a T-shirt with *Bonjour* emblazoned across the front. She's tanned and only wearing flip-flops, her hair is pulled back into a messy high ponytail, making her look like a child herself.

The wobbly threesome exchange solemn greetings as they meet Rolle at the steps and walk in together. Mirren's sister is back at the Coral Beach Hotel. He later hears that Réa Fitzpatrick had to be given a sedative she was so hysterical after she heard the news. A morgue is no place for the living. Unless you have to identify your small child.

The assistant pathologist, a slight man with glasses and zero eye-contact, sits facing the couple in the reception room. In a monotonous voice he explains the technicalities of how things go. His ice-cold demeanour isn't helping the situation. Mirren is looking wildly around this way and that, searching for... he doesn't know what. Beyond here is a small room where they would be shown a photo and asked to make a formal identification, the man continues. Any further visitation would be determined after an autopsy. Did they understand, and could he get them anything? Some water perhaps?

Rolle glances sidelong at Mirren, who is hyperventilating, gulping in air, unable to let it out. She's trembling uncontrollably. Nick grips her hand tightly, stroking it anxiously, comforting himself simultaneously. He's crying, his tears falling openly, his grief too raw to be bashful.

Rolle looks immediately away as if burnt by the expression on their faces. What they're feeling in that moment is an intimate thing – a private devastation that he has no right to witness. He notices Candy staring at the floor too, rubbing Mirren's back, her other hand pressing down on Mirren's leg which is jigging up and down violently. She seems miles away. Everyone knows how this goes. The smiling child on the poster forever frozen in time.

He'd smelt booze on Mirren the moment she arrived. He was sure they all had. But to be honest, he's glad she has something to take the edge off. He wouldn't wish this on anyone. Rolle remembers saying something to Alice before, something that she'd called insensitive; he'd pointed out that at least they, as a childless couple, were avoiding the pain that comes with loving a child. It boils down to that poem, the Tennyson line about it being better to have loved and lost than never to have loved at all. Rolle wasn't so sure. He'd loved his mother and look what happened. Sitting in this tiny grief-strangled room, he wonders how you can ever balance the pain Mirren and Nick are feeling with the joy that comes from having a child?

How could it ever outweigh this miserable moment? But then again, maybe that's something he doesn't even know he's missing – something right in front of his eyes that he's too close to see.

Then suddenly, it's time.

35

Rolle

Rolle walks ahead of the couple, behind the assistant pathologist, who holds open the door into a smaller room. Someone has tried to make it look homely. There are pictures of local landscapes on the wall, including a beach scene, notes Rolle, grimly. There are thick dried flowers in a vase and the murky pastels splashed on heavy curtains. Mirren's legs have all but given up. She is being held up by Nick and as she trips, his arm puckers her T-shirt which rises. For some reason, it's that tiny exposure of her bare skin that threatens to break Rolle's heart. The vulnerability of it, the obliviousness of this poor mother. Rolle steps in to assist, discreetly tucking the material back down. She barely notices.

She feels tiny beside him, her head lolling towards Nick's chest like a ragdoll. Nick wipes his eyes on the top of Mirren's ponytail, and they wait in silence except for the sound of Mirren's intermittent guttural heaves.

Nick announces suddenly that he alone will identify the body to save Mirren further trauma, but she insists on staying.

'I need to see her. I need to know.'

A woman looks around the door. She's in her thirties, plain-looking, freckly, with a bun pulled back tightly at the nape of her neck. 'Nick, Mirren, I'm Eva, the grief counsellor here. I'm really so sorry we have to meet like this.'

She seems genuinely sad for them, thinks Rolle, grateful for the humanity they all so badly need right now. Most of the island has been on this journey with the Fitzpatricks, so why shouldn't they feel sorrow at the thoughts of a little girl being dragged up from her watery grave.

'My job this evening is to help make the process of identifying the deceased as gentle as possible,' Eva continues. 'I also want you to know that there is no rush. You can spend as long as possible on this. Does that sound okay?'

Eva gestures for them all to sit down. Rolle notices she has a white clipboard hugged towards her chest.

'Mirren and Nick, I have an image here that I will present to you face down. It will be a picture of the deceased's face surrounded by a blue sheet similar to those found in doctors' offices.' Her voice is kind, but Rolle can tell that she's also aware how powerless she is to take away the grief that's taking place in this one brief encounter. All she can do is to soften it, to prevent any re-traumatisation, to respect the solemnity and devastation of a moment that will haunt them always. Nick nods silently while Mirren tries to keep her breathing under control. She's saying something, her lips moving, but it doesn't seem to make any sense to Rolle. Perhaps she's praying.

Eva comes closer and puts her hand on Mirren's shoulder. Her nails are short and clean, she has a small gold bangle on one wrist.

'I want to make you aware that you will also see marks that are the result of the deceased being in the water.' She says it gently, her words deliberately slow to help the couple process what's ahead. 'It may not look like her at first.'

'It will be difficult to see, but I am going to be here with you the whole time and you can take as long as you need to see if this is your daughter or not.'

Eva places the clipboard down on the table between the Fitzpatricks.

'Take your time. Whenever you're ready,' she says softly.

Once again, Rolle feels as if he's observing something he shouldn't. He hopes his presence is, at least, somewhat reassuring. He suddenly misses Alice, and is flooded with grief that threatens to overwhelm, not just about Alannah – but about everything.

He forces the emotion downwards and focuses instead on the dehydrated bougainvillea in the corner of the room.

It's Nick who breaks down first.

Shaking, then sobbing, his head in his hands, he seems more vulnerable than Rolle has ever seen him.

There's no sign of the strong sullen character he'd met just over a week ago. Here is just the shell of him, drained by the heartbreak of the photo, face down, just inches from his bent face. Rolle sees Mirren, now seated, visibly gather what's probably the last of her strength. 'Come on,' she whispers fiercely to her husband, leaning her body across his back where he's bent forward in pain.

'Come on. It's for her, we have to do this for her, we have to, do you hear me, Nick?'

She pulls him to her tightly and they hang on to each other. The lump in Rolle's throat throbs as he brushes the tears quickly from his own eyes. Then he hears the tiny swoosh of paper as the image is turned quickly over and then the catch in Mirren's breath as she looks at the pitiful sight before her.

'Oh Jesus,' she breaths out.

'Oh Jesus Christ.' She's weeping now, her hands flat on the table supporting her body.

Then Nick's cry accompanies hers, as he opens his eyes and allows them to rest on the photo of the child's ravaged body.

It's barely human in its shape, twisted and distended almost beyond possibility. The blue sheet is crudely tucked around the girl's face and head so all that's visible of her features are the eyes, nose and mouth. At Rolle's glance from the other side of the chairs, he sees a long strand of yellow hair crinkled alongside a once childish face. He feels repulsed and then immediately ashamed. Mirren turns the photo face down again quickly and pushes her wrists into the sockets of her eyes. Nick's uncomfortable crying continues. The pain in this room is unimaginable.

Then Mirren speaks. Her voice sounds strangled, far away.

'It's not her, Nick. Is it?' she whispers. She's begging for him to agree.

Pleading.

Unsure.

'It isn't her. It's not her, is it Nick?'

She's rubbing his back, frantically.

'Is it her, Nick?'

And he shakes his head, haunted too, Rolle imagines, by the relief that this isn't Alannah.

It isn't their daughter. She isn't theirs at all.

This was someone else's baby, lying cold and fathomless beneath their fingertips.

36

Mirren

The Past

The first time I met Nick, he caught me. *I've always loved telling that story. The summer we met was the hottest in years. I was living in a small apartment with Réa near the Royal Canal in Dublin. The buzz of the traffic and the flow of people was so different from the silence where I grew up. There were swans on the canal that I pointed out to Réa as she wobbled on her green bicycle in front of me, turning back to make sure I was still watching. They were serene years. I spent all day studying and attending lectures while Réa played next door with my neighbour Bea and her kids. I threw myself into my medical studies.*

To celebrate my oncology posting, one night a few other trainees and I headed to the city's latest hotspot, a nightclub called Legs in one of the grimy basements in Georgian Dublin. I usually didn't have the stamina to work the hours I worked, take care of my daughter, and go out drinking all night. But this was a rare blowout. Réa was staying the night with Bea next door. 'Go nuts, Mer,' Tara had encouraged when I spoke to her on the phone. I cared about Tara and the pressure she was under looking after our mother back in Galway. But not enough to get involved. We all make choices, and we live with those decisions. I'd walked away and never planned on going back.

I smeared on red lipstick and attempted Dr Lacey's messy/sophisticated bun by piling my hair on top of my head. I glanced in the mirror – good enough. We spent the night, four exhausted junior doctors, laughing and dancing. When one of them started making clumsy passes, I shrugged him off and made my way to the bar. It was at least four people deep. I spotted a tall man near the front and caught his eye. His glasses made him look bookish, but he had an athletic physique.

'If you grab me a vodka and coke, I'll love you forever,' I mouthed, stretching up and over the throng of bodies to hand him the crumpled cash.

'Promise?' he called back, smiling.

I liked his mischievous grin and the ease with which he manoeuvred his way back through the crowd over to where I was waiting by the pillar.

'Thanks a million,' I shouted over the twangy thumps of East 17, my body jostling against his, our hands sticky with spilt spirits.

'What's your name?'

At that very moment, a surge of people rushed forward, and I lost my footing. I leaned back towards the pillar behind me but misjudged and started to fall backward. I wasn't used to wearing such high heels either. The tall man grabbed me and steadied me, ignoring my embarrassment.

'Don't worry, I've got you,' he said, smiling that smile of his. 'I'm Nick.'

'Did you just say whoopsie?' I asked, laughing, leaning back into his chest, letting myself be caught. And he did have me — in the most light-hearted, dizzying, delicious way. He held me then and he hadn't stopped holding me steady since that very first night. Over half-spilt vodka and flat Coke, he told me of his ambitions to make movies, and I told him about Réa and my work.

'A doctor, wow,' he'd said admiringly.

'Ish.' I'd laughed, enjoying for the first time, the rush of pride that made me giddy.

We talked for hours, swatting away those grinning friends of ours, making kissy sounds behind us and begging us to dance.

Then he walked me home along the canal. In the blurry dawn, chilly and fizzy, he kissed me and promised to call. He'd kept nearly every promise since.

—

That's why as we clung to each other that night in the morgue, I recalled that first steadying. I remembered how much I needed him in that moment.

And something else, something important – how much he seemed to need me too.

Just

    like

        before.

37

Rolle

Rolle pulls the car into the driveway of his rental house at lunch-time after another five a.m. start. He's beyond exhausted, and totally starving. He throws his keys onto the small hall table alongside all the framed pictures, unopened letters, a collection of coins, and looks at himself in the mirror. His hair needs a cut, and he definitely needs a shower. Damn, he'd murder a coffee.

He runs his hand over his eyes and sighs. Time to open that letter he's been avoiding. Although he's been expecting it for weeks, the words printed out in black and white on the court document still give him a jolt as he runs his eyes over it.

On March 18th at Miami District Court, he will finally face Sal Reid again. But this time he's the bad guy – the one who punched Reid's lights out while he was in police custody. 'Bad move, Tony,' his father would have said to him. 'The trick is to never get caught.'

He notices the Valentine's card he'd written to Alice open on the hall table. He smiles. Inside, in his neat handwriting, he'd put, 'God, I hate this holiday. But, I really love you, Ally. Here's to dancing into the next adventure, hopefully in Miami.'

He sighs, wondering when everything in his life got so hard. The shame of being asked to walk away from his work and to isolate himself here on Kite Island always makes Rolle's stomach lurch. He remembers his wife's face when he explained they'd have to leave their pretty home in Miami with their teal shutters and bright white porch. He told her they'd have to lie low elsewhere – all because he couldn't keep his shit together. She didn't deserve to be trapped in this purgatory, all because of him. He stuffs the legal letter crudely into his work bag and makes his way into their small kitchen. No need for Alice to get even more upset about this than she was already.

She's left his lunch in the oven – a baked potato, fishcakes and BBQ corn-on-the-cob. He eats it cold, standing up, pushing the thoughts of the court case away. He sticks on the TV news in the background. There's a small segment about the body found off Kite Island.

He sets down the plate quickly, as if he can hear better without something in his hands. How do the media get to hear about everything first? Fucking Lovell. Now what's he playing at? The glossy anchor tells them they'll have more as they get it.

Poor Mariah. Let down in death as well as in life. He thinks of those cruel bindings, the disregard someone had for her small body. Toxicology came back positive for opiates, but the cause of Mariah's death had been too difficult to establish due to the condition of the body. He shakes his head even thinking about it. Her body hadn't been in the water for too long, 'a week max,' the pathologist had said. The entomologist gave a better timeframe. He explained how the decomposition status meant Mariah had been dead for a much longer time. It was likely her body had been stored in a cold environment. Frozen, all this time. Rolle thinks of the freezer in the dark outhouse by the lighthouse shack and feels a wave of nausea. What were Mariah's final hours when she'd been taken at the bonfire with Tiffany? He figures that Kata or Red must have panicked and dumped her, once they realised the police would come knocking on their door. After the interview with Kata maybe? The boy seemed misguided yes, and impulsive, but Rolle still couldn't square the idea of him being a kid killer.

He didn't bother telling Glades about the weights, the bindings or all those layers of tape when he spoke to her. The idea of her child lying on the deepest darkest part of the ocean floor was desperate enough. He knew, as he looked at the mother's anguished face, that she wasn't here, that she didn't see him at all. She would be forever under those waves with her twelve-year-old child. Always just slightly out of reach.

'Did you find them?' were the only words Glades spoke afterwards. 'Please Detective, please find them, before they do this again.'

Thank God for Bonnie and Earl Timmins and their commitment to finding those lost at sea. He didn't know how they did it, but as they said goodbye and made their way off to another sad situation, it forced him to question his own role in all of this. How much of a difference is he even making? Because lately it sure as hell seemed like he was doing a lot of picking up of the pieces rather than keeping them from breaking.

But he'd seen cases like this before in Miami, girls drugged to be trafficked – and it didn't always go to plan. Networks like this usually targeted children like Mariah, those whose vanishing was put down to bad parenting, wayward personalities. 'Who lets their kid out that late at night, anyway?' he heard one of the other officers say spitefully. He may as well have said she was asking for it.

But Alannah. That was different. Rolle wonders if Kata and Red had acted on impulse. Or was there another reason why she might have been targeted? He knows some of those sickos put in requests for a certain height or hair colour, even paid extra, like these girls were on a goddamn menu or something.

He pushes the greasy corn-on-the-cob away with his fork, suddenly repulsed. This whole thing reminds him of his former work, the disposability of human lives like this – children's lives. How could anyone get used to seeing tiny bodies abused and then discarded in such a callous way? Finding out exactly the circumstances of Mariah's last few hours is a difficult but necessary part of Rolle's job now too. They need to find Lottie as well. She'll lead them to the brothers.

He scrapes the remainder of his dinner into the bin, praying Alice doesn't notice. He tries her phone but it's off again. This weekend they'll do something nice, just the two of them. He might take her to that seafood restaurant on the wharf – The Bucket and Spade – to finish their conversation. They could have garlic crab claws, maybe even a few beers just like old times, and laugh about their cheesy Valentine's cards. God, he misses that laugh. He looks around to see if she'd left a card out for him, but then his phone buzzes on the kitchen counter. He's surprised to see the name on the screen, Sam Harris.

'Hey Big Man, catch you at a good time?'

'Harris, you stalking me?' Rolle smiles as he lets the cat in the back door and removes its metallic bowl from the dishwasher. He hooks the phone under his chin to free his hands.

As they exchange greetings, he reaches up to the kitchen cupboard and takes out cat food. This was normally Alice's job – but by the frantic rubbing of cat around ankles, it didn't look like she'd been here for hours.

'Tony, I need to talk to you about something and it's pretty fucking huge.'

Rolle stops mid cat-food scoop and straightens up immediately.

Sam was the least dramatic person he knew.

'What's up, Sam?'

'I just heard that homicide picked up a couple of bodies up North Miami, at an old boatyard. Shot up pretty bad.'

'Go on,' Rolle sits heavily into the kitchen chair and pulls a notebook towards him.

'Looks like one may be that guy you had me look into.'

'Jesus, fuck.' Rolle breathes out, looking up at the ceiling as he slumps backward in the chair. Suddenly, he realises what Sam is saying. He sits up poker straight, praying he's wrong.

'The other body? Not the kid, is it? Don't tell me it's that kid, Sam, because I don't know if I can hear that right now.'

He runs his hands over his eyes, beyond exhausted. Sleep is still evading him at night.

'No, not a kid. Guy called Jorgen Montag. Part of a pretty big ring up here in Miami as it turns out. Drugs mainly, but they can pretty much get you anything to order. I hear they've a lot of high-profile clients. I spoke to a Billy Scaliata, you know, from Narcotics?'

Rolle knew him. Nice guy. Family man.

'He says Kite Island is the new route they've been using, only in the last year or so.'

'Okay. So now we know Kata's our trafficker. And Red.'

Rolle thinks suddenly of Glades pulling her robe tight around herself that night in the trailer. The sad shrine to her daughter. Her face at Marla's, etched in pain. Nobody to listen. Somebody should have listened.

'Deal gone wrong, do you think?' Rolle eyes the coffee machine longingly. 'But where's the girl then, Sam, bottom of the ocean too?'

'Afraid I can't help you with that.' Sam sighs.

A pause. Rolle knows his friend isn't done.

'Tony, there's something else. Fuck, I can't believe I've to say this.'

'Harris, spit it the hell out. You're not asking me to prom.'

'That Billy in Narc, we've known each other forever. Our kids play Little League together, you know…'

Harris sounds reluctant to expand and Rolle doesn't push.

'Anyway, he told me on the hush, that this case – the Red Roccio and Jorgen shooting – they're linking it to a UIA case here in Miami. At the precinct.'

'As in undercover internal affairs?' Rolle immediately stops doodling on the page.

'Yeah. It's got dirty as fuck down here. Worse since you left.'

Sam drops his voice.

'It seems the esteemed chief, Lynott Logan, and a few of his guys are being brought in to help with their enquiries, if you know what I mean. Nobody knows that, by the way, Tony.'

Sam hesitates. 'Turns out you pal Lovell's father is as crooked as they come. There are too many links to that cowboy Jorgen for it to be a coincidence. Plus, no cop makes enough to live out by Lake Seneca, not at any level.'

'So, the Head of Internal Affairs is being investigated by Internal Affairs?' Rolle tries to get his head around it. But it makes sense, in a way, that nobody had been watching the watchman.

'Think Lovell's involved?' The thought chills Rolle to the bone. But it might explain why he didn't tell anyone about Réa spotting the speedboat. And why he was so reluctant to link the two girls. No wonder he wanted to throw Mirren Fitzpatrick under the goddamn bus.

'Come on, Tony,' Sam continues. 'What do you think? Like Daddy, like son. Plus, Logan Senior has been supposedly off lying half dead in some hospital out West. Who do you think has had to step in to run the family business?'

Harris sounds uncharacteristically spooked.

'Listen, you heard nothing from nobody, okay. I'm too old to get dragged into this shit.'

'Of course, buddy. Thanks for the info.'

'Just hang tight, Tony, I'll see what else I can get. But watch him. He's a slippery fish.'

More like a shark, Rolle thinks.

Sam rings off and before Rolle has time to think anything through, he dials the desk at Miami, asks for homicide. Yolanda would give him the steer. They'd climbed the ranks together, Yolanda now worked murder. She'd always been straight with him. Only one of a handful of people from MPD that still kept in touch.

'No boat of that description found, bud,' she says, after the usual it's-been-too-long exchanges. And no package. She confirmed the bodies had all been male.

So, no Lottie. Either she was also dead somewhere, or she'd realised she was involved in some seriously deep shit and took off.

The daft cat was now on the kitchen table trying to eat his notebook. Where the hell was Alice? Last night they'd talked about looking up properties in Miami to rent until their renter's lease was up. We could even be home by summer, she'd insisted, but he could also hear the desperation in her voice.

Lovell's number flashes up. Rolle takes a breath, waits until the fifth ring to compose himself before picking up.

'Antonio?' Lovell's nasal tone always sounded like he was trying to get one up on him – private schoolboy syndrome, Antonio figured.

'We've found the kid's phone. It was handed into Candy this morning at the hotel anonymously. I wanted to let you know I'm taking Mirren in for formal questioning.'

'Any unusual activity on it?' Rolle asks. None of this makes sense.

If you are feeling out of your depth, bluff, his dad used to always say: fake it. He'd meant ducking and dummying during whatever judo or karate competition he was taking part in. But today, it was the only arsenal he had against his boss, who most likely had an entirely different agenda than finding the child.

'Nothing,' Lovell admits. 'But looks like it was online a few days after she died.'

'Jesus, Lovell,' Rolle hisses. 'Kid's just missing, not dead that we know of. Fuck.'

The level of his insensitivity was unbelievable.

'Well, if you hear hooves, think horses,' Lovell Logan shoots back. 'It's from the top, Rolle. They want the mother in. I know you fancy her and all…' he continues, laughing at his own joke and Rolle knows he's going to need a serious session in his home gym to bring his blood pressure down after this.

But he needs to buy time. To find Lottie. And whatever was on the boat.

'Listen, Logan, I've a strong lead that's just come in on the Alannah Fitzpatrick case, I'll fill you in, but I need you to hold off on this Mirren thing until I can untangle it.'

Rolle grimaces. He hates asking for anything. It weakened him, especially to this moron.

'I'm announcing Mirren Fitzpatrick as a suspect in her daughter's disappearance in the morning, body or no body,' Lovell says sharply. 'We found the kid's phone at the hotel, blood in the cove. The good doctor lied about walking her kid off on the beach. She has a history of neglecting her child, the medical knowledge of how to dispose of a body. She's responsible for her daughter's disappearance.'

Rolle baulks. Just how much had Mirren been keeping from him? Even now.

But he just needs to untangle this one last knot.

'I'm sure you just heard they found a few floaters over North Miami. One of them most likely one of those brothers.' Rolle bites down hard on his lower lip. 'We're going to search the port there for a body. I seriously advise you to hold off on the mother until we do,' he says firmly.

Rolle knew from Yolanda, off the record, that nothing relating to Alannah had been found in the boatyard where the bodies were discovered, but Lovell didn't know that. Not officially at least.

Rolle can hear him thinking, as he considers which scenario makes him look least incompetent. He'll have his own difficult choice: his own reputation or the wrath of Logan Senior.

'I mean, if you arrest the mother and then the kid is found caught in some gangland feud in Miami, it's going to look like a total mess,' Rolle continues.

Then, his dad's voice in the back of his mind: 'Bluff it, Sunshine. Then slam them in the gut.'

Logan hesitates.

'Fine,' he barks, annoyed. 'You have until Wednesday. But if you hear anything about that *Rainy Day* boat, call me immediately. And don't worry, you can have your five minutes in the cell with her. I hear you like a bit of alone time with those in custody.' Logan laughs nastily.

Rolle digs deep, refusing to react. How are they supposed to ever make the world a better place when such disgusting humans straddle both sides of the law. Maybe he's learning to control his emotions after all. More importantly, he knows the clock is ticking. And it isn't on their side. But until Harris gets back with more information, they're all treading water.

Rolle rings off.

He knows he must now do what he does best – investigate. But he'll have to go against orders, risk potentially getting in deeper trouble with the department. He thinks of Alice. He remembers the tiny glance she'd given back at their home as she closed the gates when they left Miami – a look he swore he never wanted to see again.

He sighs. We all have choices we must make – some harder than others. Well, he's tired of making them. Ultimately, we are who we are. And he knows exactly what that means.

Antonio Rolle walks to the coffee machine sitting on the kitchen counter. He relishes the crushing sound of the granules, watching as it rumbles to a steamy start. A hot trickle of tarry coffee drips into the waiting cup.

On the table, the cat licks its paws. Under it, on the notepad, his hangman doodle is just three moves away from certain death.

Rolle closes his eyes and downs the coffee in one.

38

Mirren

The brightness of the day mocks the cool heap of tiny bones, forever dark in that small pine box. I watch as it bobs and dips as it's carried towards the cemetery on the shaking shoulders of uncles and cousins. The small procession trails out of a modest church, just ten minutes from where Glades, Mariah and her little sister live in Ivory Bay. Mourners spill into its adjacent graveyard, the smell of freshly turned soil as sickening as the floral stickers adorning the side of the white coffin. Tiffany, crying loudly, wears pink to match the hue of her hair. Mariah's heartbroken cousin sings a goosebump solo of *Somewhere Over the Rainbow* – even more powerful without music. Her voice breaks on the final, haunting note, the silence punctuated only by a few strangled coughs from the back of the church.

I walk far behind. This isn't my tragedy. But it nearly was – and might be still.

Glades stumbles behind the procession, neighbours and friends supporting her on either side. She seems as wilted as the wildflowers she has crushed between her hands. I've seen it before, when I attended the funerals of my small patients back when I started out in oncology. Reaction to death or tragedy doesn't vary. Not really. I could tell Glades had experienced the shock and anger a long time ago, alone and forgotten behind the thin walls of her trailer. Now it's a sad acceptance that weighs her down. The inevitability that the outcome was always likely to be this tragic.

Today Glades will bury her twelve-year-old daughter, wrapped in her favourite pink hoodie, I heard somebody say, because it was impossible to put it on her broken body. Today Glades will look up at the sky and feel the suffering of two tragedies – the loss of Mariah, and the failure of the authorities to do anything about finding her. I wanted to send her something – a card, a bouquet, maybe. But it all seemed so fickle, so I sent nothing at all.

39

Rolle

Rolle watches the sad procession trip down the steps of the church towards the cemetery. He hears the scrape of a shovel in the distance, the repetition of dings as metal connects with rock. People clutch each other, dressed in their brightest clothes like Glades had suggested. But it's impossible to pretend this is any kind of celebration – no matter how flamboyant the T-shirts Mariah's classmates wear look against the light.

There were no cameras waiting outside the morgue the morning Glades emerged from the entrance alone – the day after the Fitzpatricks explained that that poor child wasn't their baby at all. She was supported only by the banister of the stone steps. Glades clung to it for a long time after seeing the image of her eldest daughter's face. The family liaison officer only got the message later that day. Somebody had forgotten to tell somebody else – the cracks in the system shredding the last ribbons of humanity of Glades' desperate situation. Rolle knew it had been Lovell's investigation, or lack of it, that had left Glades to cry alone on the steps of the police station all those months ago, begging them to find her child and then understanding that it didn't really matter, not to them anyway. All because she was dismissed by some of the officers as 'just some whore'. Their words, not his. That made Mariah even less significant in their minds – her worth diluted, her worth chopped and sliced so finely that it amounted to practically nothing at all. He bows his head as the coffin passes closest to him. Poor kid didn't have a chance.

Shading his face from the glaring sunlight, he sees Mirren jogging down the steps of the church, slipping on a pair of large sunglasses as she goes. But she doesn't have to worry, he knows there'll be no cameras here. There was little interest once the media realised the body wasn't little Alannah Fitzpatrick. There was a half-hearted attempt to suggest a serial killer but even the tabloids abandoned that notion within twenty-four hours. Rolle watches as Nick reaches for his wife's hand – the Fitzpatricks seem more solid, at least, he's happy to see. Then, as Mirren approaches Mariah's mother, Rolle watches Nick a moment. Nick Fitzpatrick makes his way through the patchy crowd towards the Coral Beach Hotel branded Jeep. Candy is there waiting for them, dramatic in black, even though the Fitzpatricks moved to a rental apartment. Probably just being nice, Rolle figures. Nick glances over his shoulder at that same moment, scanning the crowd, as if searching for someone. He catches Rolle's eye. Holds it. And for a fraction of a second there's something about his demeanour Rolle hasn't seen before. A restlessness, his body coiled as if ready for action, his face etched with an emotion he can't quite put his finger on. Then again, Rolle imagines, if it were him and his kid was out there lost somewhere, he'd probably be all over the place with panic and helplessness too, in whatever form that might take. Give the guy a break, he chides himself. Grief can take on surprising and unpredictable shapes. There are no rules for this. No way of ever knowing what's really going on in people's heads.

40

Mirren

Outside the church, Nick squeezes my hand and walks back to Candy's Jeep, which is waiting by the kerbside. He knows there's something I want to do. I wait for a small gap in the huddle around Glades. We face the dirty mound of the child's freshly dug grave together.

'I'm so sorry, Glades,' I stammer nervously, removing my sunglasses. I know that Glades knows who I am – everyone does now, so I spare the formalities of introducing myself.

'What a beautiful girl,' I gesture uselessly at the framed photograph of the girl that sits to one side of the grave, doe-eyed and grinning. She's broader than Alannah, I think, and then stop myself continuing any further comparison. That's just too much to bear, especially right now. Glades nods slightly, her eyes fixed to the ground. I feel the alcohol fuzz my senses, a slowness that dulls the too-vivid world around me. I usually welcome such a blur to my edges but now I wish I hadn't unscrewed the red bottle-top at all.

I squint a little against the brightness of the day.

'When my dad died, I remembered that energy can't be created nor destroyed. I liked the science of that – that no matter what, his energy was out there in the world somewhere.' I know I am possibly slurring, but I feel connected to both Glades and Mariah in some messed-up way and I want to do my best to relieve some of her pain.

'I think,' Glades says quietly, finally raising her eyes to mine. 'I think that I'd prefer to think of Mariah's energy at rest, at peace somewhere now. I'm not sure her death was peaceful, you see.' A tear drops from

229

her face onto the back of her hand and rolls down into the flowers that were thrown just moments ago.

'I just want her to be at peace now.' She turns her body towards me.

'Why are you here, Dr Fitzpatrick? You still have a chance to find your daughter. And a lot of people willing to help you from what I can see.'

She doesn't say that with any resentment. Her acceptance of the brutal sorting system we both know exists breaks my heart. This could so easily have been me.

'Your daughter might still be out there, with those fucking brothers,' Glades says, whispering as she swears, as if her daughter could hear.

'You have to get her, Doctor. Because this place is so messed up. They don't want to help. They don't care. You need to go find her yourself. I just wish I'd been brave enough.' She clutches my hand. Hers feel soft – doughy and damp.

'I wasn't there, you see.' Glades' face crumples and she leans on my shoulder for support. 'She was probably calling for me, and I wasn't there.' Her chest heaves and I don't know what to say to relieve any of her pain.

I narrow my eyes to absorb the words she's saying. And after a moment, she composes herself and leans closer. I slide my hand gently from hers.

'A friend of mine got hold of the girlfriend's details. She has family in Miami. I'll give them to you. This girl Lottie might be able to help find your kid. She might know something. Even if it means getting her back, you know... either way. Because the not knowing was the worst – not knowing if Mariah was alive or dead all that time. And I don't want that for you—' Her voice cracks. 'I wouldn't wish this on anyone.'

'I don't know, Glades.' I sigh. 'I just don't know what I'm going to do. They want to blame me for all of it. I'm afraid they won't find her at all.'

I realise that despite how different we are, Glades is only one of a handful of people in the world who understands what it is like to be a mother in this situation. The judgement, the blame, the rush to drag me down. One wrong glance, a dry eye, a mistake from the past – the system is designed to demonise the angel. We were both supposed to keep our daughters away from harm. And look what we did. The scrutiny is the punishment.

'This is your only shot,' Glades insists, as we stand shoulder to shoulder by the small grave. 'And don't go looking to the cops for help. Useless fuckin' assholes.' She spits out this last part loudly, defiantly, over her shoulder.

She turns to face me again. 'Give me your phone.'

I slide my phone from my pocket and wait while she pulls out her own. Her screen is cracked in places, and I notice her nail varnish is chipped. I remember my mother at my father's funeral. How I'd helped her shave her legs that morning. There's no right way to deal with grief.

Glades makes me add the address and phone number into my own phone. 'Lottie Oaks,' I read, rolling the new piece of information around in my head. Mourners linger, waiting to pay their respects to the grieving mother. She leans into me close, a gesture so intimate that I can smell her perfume. I hiccup awkwardly and try to disguise it as something else, but she doesn't seem to notice.

'Kata is a runner over and back to Miami. Drugs mainly,' she says. 'They come in from elsewhere and he takes them over to the city from Milton Point by boat. Get it? There are a few pervs that want girls too. When Red, his brother came over, he upped the game. Now they do whatever they get asked for and get paid serious cash.'

She looks at me quickly as I take a step backward, recoiling at hearing my worst fear spoken out loud so bluntly.

'Sorry.' She shrugs, but I've understood this could be a possibility ever since Rolle suggested it that first day on the beach. I exhale and remind myself of my plan. Simply to get her back. Anything that comes after, we'll deal with then. I just have to get her back.

'Don't expect the police to help you, Doctor. Go on and find the girlfriend. Put your foot on her neck and find out where they took your Alannah.' Glades' eyes glint. 'If it were me, that's what I'd do. I'd find that little bitch and get her to bring you to wherever they took her.'

An elderly woman approaches. Glades wraps her shawl carefully around her generous frame and leans forward to whisper fiercely in my ear one final time.

'Just go yourself. Fuck the rest. Find her, Mirren. Or you'll end up standing here like me.'

She turns to receive her friend's embrace. I stand looking at the photo of Mariah's smile for a few moments longer. Glades disappears into the outstretched arms of well-wishers gathered by the empty hearse.

Alone by the grave, I look back at Mariah's portrait and my eyes blur a little. I see Alannah's face instead and shake my head to get rid of the vision. This can't be me. Glades is right, I can't let this be me.

I hurry towards the car, almost falling in my haste. I could do with a drink, but another part of me is screaming to sober up, to stay sharp. I think about what Nick said to me last night. It wasn't an argument exactly. More of an explanation.

'I knew I was elbowing in on a tight relationship when I first saw you both together.' He gestured to Réa, lying on the bed at the apartment with her headphones on. 'But I thought that someday you'd both let me in. God knows, I tried. Then when Alannah came, I was suddenly the most important person in the world to her. I loved that.' He stopped. 'I love that still.'

He cleared his throat, but the emotion it triggered was obvious.

'Can you understand that when you constantly get pushed away, told to stay behind certain walls, that it gets lonely?'

He had turned to me then and took both my hands in his. 'Mirren, you are unreachable. Do you know that?'

I didn't know what to say.

'It doesn't stop me loving you,' he'd said sadly. 'But I can't love you enough for both of us. I said I was leaving because I wanted you to care. I wanted to push you so far that you would smash down walls to keep me.'

He bent his head, brushed his hand across his face.

'You smashed the glass in my hand instead.' A small smile then, gallows humour.

But I was still so angry.

'Nick, the reason I went to that bar was because of what you said. That's the reason I took my eyes off Alannah. And now you are telling me it was all some fucking game?'

It's only in books or movies that one conversation forgives all. Reality is a lot more nuanced. Life is just a series of confusing perspectives we keep juggling to try to align.

'You blamed me,' I reminded him. 'How can I forget that? How can I forgive that?' But my fury had no flame. Neither of us had much left to give. All I knew was that I loved and needed him, and he said he did too. We needed each other. This tragedy had brought us closer. And despite his quiet confession about our finances that followed, I didn't tell him that I'd already known. I didn't tell him I'd already been planning around all of that.

-

As I make my way across the cemetery towards the car, I remember the statement given by Glades on a small news segment last night. Something she said had stayed with me. 'Nothing can bring Mariah back,' she'd said to the reporter, twisting her hands. 'But we can find those responsible for her death.'

Something *can* bring Alannah back. I'm sure of it. It's me and it's Nick. We built this life together, and it's our responsibility to make sure it doesn't crumble. Not any further, at least.

I look down at the contact details Glades has given me on the screen of my phone and then over to the waiting Jeep.

It's idling under the trees. Nick gets out and holds the door open.

He smiles a small version of his very Nick smile. Suddenly I see the boy I met all those years ago at the nightclub in Dublin. I hear our first exchange from across the bar.

'I'll love you forever,' I'd shouted at him.

And his boyish voice grinning back, 'Do you promise?'

Our home consists of the four of us – it consists of all the mistakes that came before and since. I decide I'm going to stand our crooked house up again myself. No matter what. I won't lose them too.

I take a breath and walk towards him. I can't bear to find another child in the water.

We are going to find Alannah ourselves.

I promise.

41

Mirren

The Past

On the children's oncology ward, I quickly forgot about Emma Lacey. There simply wasn't time to prioritise anything other than saving the small, wide-eyed children that watched me as I swept into their cubicles to prod. Their parents made up for their child's wordless stares, unfolding lists of careful questions, pleading with me to do 'whatever it took' to save their baby. As a mother, I understood. I'd do anything for Réa, with her faraway look and sharp imagination. By then, she'd already started school, a small, state school a five-minute walk away from our home where she'd bring home pages of beautifully drawn pictures. Her teachers often described her as withdrawn. I explained that it took her a while to warm to new people. She'd clung to me for weeks at the school gates, refusing to leave my side. We each were all we had in the world for so long.

Then along came Nick.

On our first date he took me for dinner on a riverboat on the canal. We threw bits of bread into the water to feed the ducks, despite our grumpy waiter's protests. We drank red wine until our lips were blue and went dancing in another basement jazz club, two streets from my apartment. I expected him to wait a few days before calling, if at all – a lifetime of expecting the worst was a habit hard to shake. But he'd messaged me the next morning to ask me to come watch a movie with him that night. Nobody had ever been so forward with their feelings. I'd had to fight to be loved all my life and here was this handsome man who couldn't stop telling me how lucky he felt. He worked as an assistant in a film production company and lived a short bus ride from us in a small two-bed terrace in the suburbs. Despite my long working hours and commitment to

Réa, we managed to squeeze in time together. After five months dragging myself home for the babysitter, he suggested we stay over with him for a weekend. Réa's tantrums threatened to derail things, but this was my time now. One year almost to the day that we'd kissed by the canal, we moved into his house together. I knew it would be hard for Réa to get used to spending so much time with Nick, especially when I was at work, but our new minder was a jolly Polish lady who lived nearby and who doted over her.

Life with Nick was as close to perfect as I'd dared to imagine. When I told him the story about Jack and Emma Lacey, he'd wrapped me in his arms and called Jack a fool for letting me go. 'My one and only,' he whispered into my neck as he pulled me to him when I came home from work. But Réa's outbursts were getting worse. 'Nick shouts at me,' she said to me one day when I told her we were going away for the weekend. Nick looked baffled and then hurt when I gently mentioned it to him that evening. I put it down to jealousy. When Réa started saying Nick was hurting her, I knew I'd have to confront them both. She was only a child, but already she could see the power her words could bring. Over the following weeks, I spent extra time with her, reminding her of my love, reassuring her that it would always be her and me, that nothing could come between our love.

When I spotted the bruising to her arms, I'll admit I re-evaluated things. That gave me a shock.

But when I gently brought it up at bedtime one night, she told me in a small voice that she'd made it all up and hurt herself. 'Change is hard,' I told her, tucking her in, my heart beating frantically. 'But it doesn't mean it's wrong. Please never hurt yourself again, Roo.'

'You love him more than me,' she stated quietly, and I hugged her and told her nothing and nobody in the world would ever replace her.

At night Nick and I planned our move from Dublin to Galway. I wanted to be close to where I grew up – the boggy heart of Connemara. Despite my mottled childhood, the truth is that I longed for its contorted coastline, punctuated by sandy beaches, patchy fields and crumbling stone walls. I dreamt of the bruise-coloured lakes and the lonely expanse of the wild marshy bogs.

I wanted to go home, and I wanted to bring Réa and Nick with me. But as we planned our future, I also worked hard on the future for my tiny patients.

Breaking

Then baby Arthur came along, and everything changed.

–

At three years old, Arthur still had his cherubic baby face – smooth skin and powder blue eyes. You wouldn't have guessed he had leukaemia.

Not initially anyway. His blond curls flopped across his eyes as he waddled over to me and handed me a drooled-over dinosaur when we first met. He was blissfully unaware of his mother's tear-soaked face. His father, a gentle Lithuanian man, had to leave the hospital room, immediately overcome as I gave them their son's devastating prognosis. The next time I saw Arthur I played snap with him for an hour. His eyes seemed wider now, or perhaps it was the loss of those angelic curls. I found myself marvelling over his dimpled hands and lopsided grin. What if Nick and I could have one of these I thought, for the very first time. And the seed was sown. As we hunted for our future home, I harboured the concept of a baby of our own.

Arthur was the catalyst. He made me fall in love with the idea of him, as he doled out sloppy kisses. On the children's ward, there was a special corridor where the floor had stickers that resembled a car racetrack. The nurses had even lined 2A with miniature chequered flags.

Whenever a child finished chemo, or got the all clear, instead of a bell, they'd jump into one of the small toy cars, and the nurses and doctors would wave flags and cheer as they crossed the finish line. It was a wonderfully, dumb idea. Dumb because I saw the faces of the parents and children who never got to drive down 2A. Their journeys ended a different way – no flag-waving involved. My star patient Arthur wanted nothing more than to cruise down 2A. We promised him he'd finish the race, that he'd pass the finish line. But the longer I worked in oncology, the more cynical I became. I saw how positivity didn't always get you there. I dreaded those words: battling cancer – like it was something you'd failed at if you succumbed. But I rallied for the parents, for their hopeful faces, for their 'my child will be the one that beats this' mantra. All the while, Arthur grew up and in. He lost his baby face and his eyes hollowed out. He stopped asking to zoom down 2A. He stopped giving hugs. He developed mucositis after reacting badly to chemotherapy – that meant litres of blood seeping through his gut lining. I'd destroyed everything I could for him – all the good parts too. The last time I saw him I told him the story of the Children of Lir, one of my father's favourites. Now Réa's too. I told him about the swans flying away and living forever in the stars.

'Didn't they get lost?' he asked in his raspy voice, so weak he struggled to turn his small head. 'Didn't they miss their mummies?'

Out of the corner of my eye, I watched his mother double over in silent devastation, clutching her stomach – her baby's first home.

I took a page from my notebook and folded it into an origami swan. He gazed up at me, pale and exhausted.

'Weren't they afraid?' he asked quietly. By now, Arthur was almost four.

'They weren't afraid,' I whispered back, my fingers smoothing down the crinkles of the paper into smooth sharp edges. 'Because they knew their mums and dads would spend forever trying to get back to them. And they could always see them from up there in the sky.'

This seemed to placate him – the vision of gliding through the blue, watching from above.

His funeral, a week later, was the saddest I'd ever attended.

The nurses from the hospital made a racetrack on the church aisle. They wheeled his coffin over it – his own heartbreaking finish line. From the back of the service, I didn't take my eyes off the backs of his parents' heads. If I looked beyond them, I'd have broken down completely. I was never a religious person, but when the songs played, it was hard not to hope that Arthur had gone somewhere special, somewhere good.

I went home and whispered to Nick that I was ready to have his baby. Then more things aligned. The perfect role came up in the Center of Excellence – a specialist oncology unit on the Mayo border. We found the tumbledown cottage on Galway Bay a few weeks later. It was wild and raw, lopsided. Ours.

And as I stood by our magnificent sunken cottage with its wildflower carpet and yellow gorse, I realised that for the first time I was in exactly the right place at the right time. And although I couldn't save children like Arthur, not all the time, I'd discovered I found a purpose in trying. By trying to mend bodies, I'd fixed myself in parts. Mostly.

I looked at Réa clambering over the high grasses exploring the cottage site. There was plenty of work to do, but we had time, a glorious amount of time to build and fix and repurpose. We'd spend a lifetime whittling and reshaping until it was good enough for us.

Then Nick was lifting Réa up onto his shoulders, pointing at the sea and I saw what they saw; graceful white herons sweeping down into the glistening foam beneath, ducking, then rising from the waves, soaring up. From here they could almost be swans.

I closed my eyes and pictured my lone paper swan, crumpled and proud resting on the edge of a white coffin, in a small church suffocating with sadness.

42

Rolle

'No way,' Rolle says, when Mirren tells him her plan. 'Not happening.'

They'd arranged to meet on Wilkes Beach. The place where this had all started. It's a stunning day, bright in all the right places. A few sunbathers stretch out lazily, sunning themselves, as if a small child never went missing here at all. Now, instead of searching for Alannah, the police are hunting for her mother. Or will be soon at least.

'Lovell's in the process of obtaining the paperwork for your arrest,' Rolle told her when she called earlier begging him for his help. 'Mirren, I'm sorry. You are out of time. I shouldn't even be talking to you about this. Besides, it's out of my hands now.'

Since Mariah's body had been found the week before, there was renewed pressure to return Kite Island to the paradise resort reputation it had always enjoyed. International investors had already earmarked Calloway for an expansive regentrification. New apartments were popping up all the time, and the transport minister had recently announced a multi-million-dollar investment for its port to improve facilities and welcome even more tourists. It was all about growth and it was working – before the child's disappearance at least. In other words, Alannah Fitzpatrick's vanishing wasn't just tragic – there were fears that it was going to be very bad for business across Kite Island.

But Rolle agreed to meet Mirren. To hear her out.

He sees her slim figure walking quickly down the steps of the boardwalk. She perches on the stone wall overlooking the sea beside him and crosses and uncrosses her legs nervously. He watches her watching the children build sandcastles for a moment, wondering if she notices the parents standing closer to them than they might have been before. Her tragedy is their warning. Her dark hair is tucked up untidily beneath a white baseball cap. He imagines she's tired of constantly being photographed – of her sad face being reduced to nothing but hysterical news content.

'Thanks for meeting me.' She glances at him quickly. Then back to the beach.

They both sit looking out to sea as she floats her plan.

'No way,' he says, immediately uncomfortable with what she's suggesting. 'You shouldn't leave Kite. And I sure as hell can't take you.'

He sees her hands are shaking, but her speech seems clear.

'I've stopped drinking,' she says quietly. 'And I found that girl Lottie.'

Antonio spins around to look at her.

'Where is she?' he asks sharply.

'I'm not telling you unless you agree to help me. To take me with you. I think she has Alannah, but I can't do it alone.'

For the first time since he saw Alannah's small frame walking along on the CCTV, he feels a tiny jolt of positivity.

What if the child is still alive somewhere? What if he can save her?

Mirren explains how she'd left endless messages with Lottie's mother, pleading with her to please get in touch.

'I got the answering machine. So, I kept calling. I left messages that Lottie might have some idea where my daughter could be.' She turns to him as she talks, her words tumbling out in haste.

'I begged her, as a mother. I said my child should be at home with her family – that she was just a little girl, and she needed me. That she was all alone in this world.'

Mirren's voice breaks. She takes a moment to compose herself.

'The tenth time I called, I just sobbed. You'd do the same for your daughter, I cried.'

Mirren looks at him. She seems so certain that this is the right call.

'Lottie's mother eventually got back to me. She left a message saying the only place Lottie might have gone is her father's cabin. She told me she thinks Lottie is in danger, and not to give the address to anyone. Not even the police.' Mirren shrugs at him ruefully. 'But I guess you're different.'

Rolle pulls his phone out, looks at it and frowns. 'I have to take this,' he mutters and gets up to walk away.

A voice on the end of the phone tells him that the DNA in the freezer belonged to Mariah. It was all the proof they needed that Red and Kata were involved. And now, Red is dead.

He closes his eyes after he hangs up and listens for a moment to the twangy sounds of a day at the beach: foreign accents, a baby crying in the distance, the hush-rush of the ocean, the clink of plates from a nearby restaurant. The smell of fried fish and espresso fill the air. He pictures Alice twirling somewhere. He feels so desperately sad – torn. For the first time in a long time, Rolle wishes he could pick up the phone to his own father who always seemed to know the right thing to do. He wishes he could explain to Alice how all of this makes him feel.

He walks slowly back to Mirren. There's something she needs to know, but it isn't about Mariah.

'Kata's brother was found dead,' he tells her. His body blocks the sun. She squints up at him.

'And Lottie?' she stammers.

He shrugs.

'I've a friend in Miami. He's keeping me up to date. There's so much more to this, Mirren. It's much more dangerous than you think.'

He turns his head nervously, scans the boardwalk.

'I'm sorry, Mirren.'

And he really is. Sorry he was powerless to do anything at all.

She jumps up, clutching at him as she begs, and he feels worse.

'Is she okay?' Mirren raises her voice. 'Tell me.' And he doesn't know if she means Lottie or Alannah, but he sees the desperation in her eyes. He understands – Lottie is her last glimmer of hope. They both know that. The Fitzpatricks couldn't stay in Kite indefinitely. This is the only strand left to pull before they end up at home in Ireland, searching the face of every child that passes them on the street, trying to make it fit their daughter's.

'Tell me.' She grabs at his shirt roughly and pushes him away at the same time, hammering at his chest. She lashes out at him, but he knows she's fighting the whole world, and it seems to be collapsing around her.

'Please help me,' she begs again, tears rolling down her cheeks. Antonio grabs her wrists and pulls her to him. He lets her sob into his chest, her head resting against the scratch of his shirt. 'Shhhh,' he's saying. Like a father to a child. His arms holding her up.

'Shhh, Mirren. It's okay. It will all be okay.'

So many damn promises.

'But you need to tell me where Lottie is. I can't help you if I don't know what we are dealing with here.'

She starts to slide to the ground, completely spent. Antonio pulls her up, refusing to let her fall. He sits her on the wall. Fixes the cap that has tipped backward off her head. He leans close to her face, suddenly deciding.

He thinks of the little girl at Sal Reid's trafficking house wrapped in a threadbare blanket. He thinks of Mariah's ghostly fingers. *Fuck, how could he not?*

'Fine. I'll take you there. But you have to tell me where Lottie is,' he says, knowing he'll also have to call in a few favours from Sam.

'Osprey Island,' she whispers so quietly he almost doesn't hear her.

Rolle straightens up and immediately reaches for his cell. Google maps confirms that Osprey Island is an hour from here. He thinks he knows it – a much larger island, deep in the Everglades.

He pictures the thick, soupy reeds, the dark overhang of its most forested parts, the winding river arteries. He suddenly realises there's no better place to hide someone the entire world seems to be searching for.

43

We depart the next morning just after six a.m. in a small boat hastily arranged with a smiley young skipper who doesn't ask questions. Nick and Réa remain behind in case there are any developments. Nick tried to insist on going but I refused to give in. I lost her. I would bring her home. Besides, Lottie might react better to a mother. And Réa needs him. Nick hugs me and tells me to bring our girl home. He feels thinner under his creased polo shirt, and I don't want to let go. Réa presses a folded piece of paper into my hand as I leave and tells me not to open it until later. It's the drawing of her sister, I presume. Her eyes brim with tears as I pull her towards me. My little Roo. Despite everything, we all know that this day, this voyage, is likely to bring us answers. Either way.

I wave back at Nick as the boat chugs out of the port, away from Kite, the orangey sunlight transforming him into a shadow that gets longer and longer as we sail towards the horizon. Then I turn to face the direction we are headed. Two of Rolle's men are coming along too. I refused to hand over to Rolle the address Lottie's mum had given me until we got much closer. There was no way I was letting him take off without me.

It's almost two weeks since my daughter went missing.

'I'm coming for you,' I whisper, salty tears mixing with salty air.

Osprey Island is the largest of the thousands of tiny islands off the Florida coast. The diamond-shaped landmass is 30 km from Naples, west of Miami. They call it the gateway to the Everglades and as they navigate the boat closer, it becomes apparent why. Flanked by nearly

100 miles of islands, bays and estuaries, access to the address I've been given isn't going to be easy. Up ahead, the soft blue turquoise of the ocean gives way to a harsher landscape, acres of saw-grass marshes and mangrove forests thicken the water. The skipper manoeuvres skilfully – but we are no day-trippers. Lottie's dad's cabin is located towards the more remote northern side, dominated by hammocks of hardwood and soggy wetlands. Remote is an understatement. As we grow closer, the air reminds me of the boggy peatland from home, dirty damp air and something else too. Something I can't quite put my finger on.

I wonder if Lottie will be there at all. And more importantly, would she know where Alannah is? Perhaps she would even have her there? The thoughts of my daughter potentially being within grasp overwhelm. All I want to do is let the swirl of alcohol hit the back of my throat, to let all the pain ebb away, but I made a vow. I want to remain focused until I find Alannah, whichever way that may be.

Today is the day I'll find her, I decide. I expand the thought into a mantra. *I will find her today. I will find my daughter today.* No matter what.

I unscrew the top of the water bottle and hear the quick hiss as the bubbles race up from the bottom. I drink deeply. Then, still watching the horizon, I see Detective Rolle point out another boat to the skipper. We manoeuvre towards it and two men jump onboard.

We are forty-five minutes away, I hear someone say.

Rolle smiles encouragingly as he introduces the pair, guys from his old team in Miami. Once again, I'm overcome with gratitude for his sincerity and strength of mind. It's impossible not to feel safe when I'm with him. The men are called Harris and Becks. Harris is squat with a military style haircut. He grins at us both and leans against the edge of the boat, squinting as Rolle fills them in. Becks is a skinny white guy with mean-looking eyes. As they talk quietly, I watch the landscape change from smooth deep blues to lumpy mottled greys. They mention Lovell Logan in low whispers. Since the first time I met him, as I sat on the beach that first grey morning, I felt Lovell's indifference to our tragedy. With Antonio, I immediately felt his empathy, I felt his urgency to find Alannah. But with Lovell, it always seemed to be about box ticking, delays and bad decisions: focusing on me and Nick for a start. The night he took me into the station to show me the footage on his phone, I saw something in his eyes – something ugly. I'd seen it before; a familiar ruthlessness, the need to get ahead no matter what. I wasn't sure what he was playing at, but the fact that he was hounding me instead of finding those brothers made me hate him.

'How can we be sure Kata and Red didn't just do to Alannah what they did to Mariah?' I ask Rolle quietly as the boat changes tempo. The two men are talking among themselves, Harris points in the distance while Becks swigs from his water bottle.

'We can't, Mirren,' Rolle says, shaking his head a little. 'Anything could have happened to Alannah, but this is the only solid lead we have so we are going with it. Plus, they are planning to arrest you, so we've very few options left.'

I shiver at the thought and then remember my mantra. *I will find Alannah today.*

I finally give them the exact address of Lottie's father's cabin and Harris enters it into his phone.

Rolle zooms in on the satellite picture. 'It's set back on a narrow estuary with mangroves surrounding. I don't think we've any choice but to wade in from the boat. Any objections?'

I'd swim there from here if I thought I'd find Alannah. Suddenly I wish Réa could be here when we find her – to hold both my daughters at the same time again.

My stomach knots as we approach the shoreline, navigating lumpy reeds until we come to the third estuary. We're so close.

'Ten minutes out,' Harris calls, smiling at me encouragingly. I've seen the way he and Rolle interact – a camaraderie I find touching. It's clear they're close. That they've been through a lot together.

'Good guy.' He inclines his head towards Rolle. 'If anyone will find her, it'll be him.'

It's a statement designed to reassure, but the idea that everything comes down to this moment is almost unbearable. And having to stay on the boat as agreed has rendered me helpless.

Then the water thickens, the marshy grasses cling to the bottom of the boat like long tangled hair fanned out in the bath. I think of my mother and shiver. I finally realise what the air smells of too; the tarred underbelly of my father's boat – the one he used to take me on to fish. I clench and unclench my fists, feeling nothing but empty air, the possibility of finding Alannah simultaneously thrilling and sickening.

'Five minutes,' Rolle calls, as the channel narrows.

He's up front with the skipper waving at me, telling me to stay quiet please, as we drift, engineless, towards the dark looming overhang.

It sucks us into its shadowy tunnel, the surrounds thick with clawing mangrove, the air heavy with humidity, silence, hope.

44

Rolle

The cabin is a two-storey house on stilts, in a clearing among the mangroves. The spindly elevation leaves space underneath to moor boats. On the raised deck that surrounds, a wooden swing chair overlooks the deceptively still water. In any other scenario, it could be an inviting sanctuary. But today its isolation, here in the gloom, is a disturbing reminder that somewhere close, a small child could be being held against their will.

The skipper hangs back, slightly out of view of the cabin, the grey-green foliage concealing the boat's position. There's one boat moored in the shadows beneath the cabin – a red-and-white speedboat. A blue tarpaulin covers the back.

Rainy Day.

Thank Christ.

It's immediately clear they'll have to go on foot from here. With no idea if Lottie is alone or not, Rolle knows they are blind to how many people could be inside. It wasn't like Rolle could call for back up either, not here. He's out on a limb and they have one chance to get this right. He glances over at Mirren, wringing her hands, tortured by the unpredictability of it all. Though he's a realist about Alannah's safe return, he knows he needs something to keep him motivated. Seeing Mirren's small hopeful frame, he takes a mental snapshot as she crouches low on the boat. She's straining her eyes, no doubt to get a look at anything that might signal Alannah's presence, her whole body tense with anticipation.

A vibration in his pocket suddenly distracts. He lifts out his cell and glances at the screen – Alice. He'll have plenty of time later for his wife. He's just so close to making everything right. He slips it into the waterproof case and hauls on his backpack.

With a small nod to Mirren, Rolle slips over the edge of the boat followed by Becks and Harris. They wade waist deep into the watery forest. Rolle and Becks head around the back. Harris will slip under the cabin from the water and try to access the house from the stairs beneath, close to where the boat gently bobs.

Waiting until nightfall isn't an option, but the overhang is dark enough to conceal the team as they pick their way across the tough terrain. Rolle's feet squelch in the inky pools between trees and grass. It's difficult to get a foothold, and a few times he slips forward, grasping at gnarled roots to steady himself. Sweat drenches his clothes, the mosquitoes buzz in his eyes. How much longer, he wonders, pulling his foot free from the mud once more. The phone vibrates again in his zipped pocket. He stops to pull it out, squinting to see the caller ID – Alice again. He'll have to ring her back. He squeezes the side button of the phone, switching it to off. He, Sam and Becks will work off the radios from here.

After half an hour of battling the swampy undergrowth, the side of the cabin rises before them. He stops a moment and listens for movement, for noise, anything, but the only sound is the squelchy hum of the forest. Rolle indicates to Harris to slip underneath the cabin while he and Becks hoist themselves up over the side of the raised wooden deck. A light snaps on in one of the rooms. Rolle hesitates for a fraction of a second and then drops neatly over the other side of the barrier, crouching low under the window.

The drone of a speedboat cuts sharply through the day. At the same time, Sam Harris speaks quietly into his ear, 'Boat approaching.' Rolle's heart hammers in his chest. He closes his eyes and remembers his training. He pictures himself surrounded by nothing but white – bright white everywhere. No distractions, 100 per cent focus. Images of the Sal Reid operation threaten to flood, but he banishes them all, and slows his breathing. He'd been too late then. He wouldn't let that happen again. 'Standby,' he commands softly into the radio, thankful they had the foresight to conceal their boat. Rolle presses himself tight against the weathered porch. The boat manoeuvres underneath the cabin leaving a trail of foamy bubbles across the water. He hears voices, at least two separate male voices.

'Boss?' he hears Harris murmur via the radio.

'Hold,' he repeats, frantically running scenarios in his head. The men from the boat enter the cabin directly from the boat port, via the lower stairs. Rolle is just forming the bones of an idea when a crash vibrates through the thin wooden walls.

A female screams.

On Rolle's command, they smash through the door. Despite the lamp light inside the cabin, it's almost as dark as outside, the same musty bitterness to the air. Immediately the force of a tackle sends Rolle flying back against the stair rail. An excruciating pain shoots across his left shoulder and Rolle knows that his collarbone has snapped in two. A weak spot from throwing too many heavy bodies over his shoulder in competitive martial arts. He sees Harris on his feet running in from another room. Shots are fired. A wiry man with a scruffy ponytail pushes past Rolle, up the stairs.

The girl.

Clutching his injured shoulder, Rolle staggers quickly to his feet. Trying to hold his arm steady, he takes off after the man. There's no sign of his gun.

Upstairs there's a small corridor with three closed doors. Rolle stops abruptly and listens, breathing heavily. Somewhere in the house he can hear a girl crying.

They are so close.

Wiping the sweat from his brow with his sleeve, Rolle eases the first door open. He tries to ignore the pain radiating across the top half of his body. There's an unmade bunk bed with a yellow teddy sitting patiently by the pillow. Rolle spots the iron ladder for the bunk propped up against the wall and grabs it. The next room down is a small, white-tiled bathroom with barely enough room for a toilet and a sink. As he turns, there's suddenly a flicker of movement in the mirror's reflection, and the man with the ponytail lunges at him from behind. Rolle tries to use the ladder to defend himself, but the angle is all wrong and his shoulder won't do what it should. He tries to twist his body, pushing backward against the bathroom tiles, trying to knock the man off his feet, but the bathroom is too small to get any momentum. The squeeze around his throat tightens, and Rolle's vision blurs. The hold is familiar – one they've done countless times in training. But he's never had to escape chokehold with a broken collarbone. He forces himself to think, knowing he doesn't have long. Dying with his head beside a toilet was never part of the plan. Rolle lifts his right foot to the porcelain sink. Using it as leverage, he coils his body forward and with one practised flick of his body, he jolts backward, headbutting the man with the back of his skull. The man cries out, slumps to the ground, clutching his face, giving Rolle the chance to get up and run.

Wheezing heavily, he makes his way downstairs. Harris is crouched over their buddy Becks. A crimson stain curls around him. Harris has both hands pressed into a wound on Becks' leg. He glances at Rolle, a grim expression on his face, but there isn't time to assess. They don't stop until they find the child.

Another high-pitched scream comes from below the house. Rolle staggers towards the narrow wooden stairs that lead down into the basement boathouse.

Could it be the kid?

He races down, three at a time, noting the blood smears on the banisters as he goes. Pain thrums across his entire body. Whoever's down there is hurt, and wounded animals are even more dangerous, he remembers, cursing himself for losing his gun in the frenzy of the chase.

Under the cabin, the shadows are long. Reflections on the surface of the dark water disorientate. The boats lug uncomfortably, rising and falling with a slunk-gunk against the narrow wooden pathway running the length of the jetty. Rolle sees their own boat, stationary, a short distance away in front of the cabin. Mirren must have heard the gunshots and forced the skipper to come in.

Then he spots her, soaking wet, climbing out from the water up onto the jetty and running towards the smaller boat. Her clothes are stuck to her body, her hair slick against her head. He realises that Mirren must have jumped from their boat, in her hurry to get to whatever she's seen. He grimaces in pain, his head swimming as he tries to put all the pieces together.

Rolle sees a tiny movement on the red-and-white boat – the turn of a blonde head. He sees something else too, something in the shadows on the other side. A third person. The glint of a raised barrel.

'No,' he shouts, his throat on fire. 'Wait.'

Lovell Logan steps out from the shadows. He's almost unrecognisable – his hair is dishevelled and he's not wearing glasses.

From somewhere nearby comes the sound of frightened sobs. Mirren's frozen halfway along the jetty. She stares at Lovell in disbelief as he talks quickly, his words tripping over each other.

'Detective Rolle, the people's fucking hero,' he spits, frothy saliva forming on both corners of his mouth.

He laughs suddenly as he steps closer to them, a horrible sound. 'GPS led me right here. Think I'd let that junkie Red take what's mine?'

Rolle attempts to put himself between the blonde girl on the boat and Lovell.

'It doesn't have to be like this,' he says. Delay tactics. Keep them talking. Lovell continues to wave the gun towards the boat, a mania to his movements. He is angrier than Rolle's ever seen him – a vicious unleashing. Maybe partly because he realises that he's made a mess of the one job his father had asked him to do.

'Bleeding heart Antonio Rolle,' Lovell smirks, no sign of the nasal whine anymore. No need to sound like a goddamn lord when you are as dirty as the worst of them, Rolle thinks, disgusted.

'Always so fucking predictable. Who do you think arranged those cameras at Reid's cell? We knew you'd lose your shit, and we needed you out of there.'

He's waving the gun, venom making him careless. There's little time to absorb the magnitude of what he's saying.

On the other side, Rolle sees Mirren creeping towards the direction of the soft weeping. In her haste, she trips on one of the ropes mooring the boat. The sound makes Lovell swing around.

Rolle seizes the moment. He runs hard at him, all the determination of the past few months squeezed into that moment – he shouts Mirren's name at the same time, but he can't get there in time. He's not close enough.

Panicked, Logan swivels his gun towards the boat. Towards the now hysterical crying.

The gunshot, when it comes, is unimaginably loud in the confines of the small wooden area under the cabin. Lovell immediately clutches his stomach, staggering a few steps back from the impact. Shock registers on his face as he looks from the boat, back to the wound that's now seeping blood quickly over his fingers, turning them red. Antonio scrambles towards the gun that's lying on the wood where Lovell dropped it, but Lovell is closer. Grasping it shakily in one hand, Lovell turns to the boat where the shot came from, and he fires twice. Carelessly.

But Rolle is upon him. He slams into Logan with his good shoulder, knocking him into the water. Rolle hears the crack as his boss's head hits the side of the wooden jetty before the splash. At the same time, he sees Mirren clamber onto the small boat, slipping and falling in her haste. She's screaming Alannah's name as she reaches for the blonde girl. Mirren pulls the small limp body towards her, holding her close. Her cheek and shoulder turn crimson – the imprint of a final desperate hug. Rolle staggers over to her. A Glock semi-automatic lies on the floor of the boat. Mirren's eyes are wide with shock and fear. She's pushing back the girl's blood-soaked hair, murmuring frantically, lips to temple. But she seems so far away. Everything is edging on black, the pain ripping all reason away. Rolle is completely spent, but he lowers himself down into the *Rainy Day*, his weight making everything shift slightly as his feet hit the deck. Rivulets of red run along the bottom of it, iron and salt water mixing into a putrid paste. It's then he sees the girl in Mirren's arms isn't a child at all. She's a girl with long sandy-coloured hair. She's moaning softly.

Lottie.

The stench of blood and fear overpowers. Rolle watches as Mirren sways back and forth, rocking the girl as she cries out Alannah's name – a pitiful wail that cuts right through him. 'I'm sorry,' she's crying. 'I'm sorry Lana.'

'It isn't her,' he shouts at Mirren, but his voice is a croak. She looks at him, in confusion and heartbreak, and continues to cradle the girl. But then she looks down again, peeling the hair back to reveal Lottie's face. Finally understanding.

Despite the shooting pain in his shoulder, Rolle kicks off the tarpaulin at the back of the boat and rips the well-wrapped bags underneath with a knife from his backpack. It's powder. And lots of it. This is what they were loading and unloading from Wilkes Beach that day.

He remembers Becks bleeding out upstairs, pulls out his phone and turns it back on.

Immediately it vibrates in his hand.

It's Alice.

Suddenly he needs to hear her voice more than anything else in the whole world. He needs her to tell him that he hasn't failed once more.

But her words, when they finally unfurl, leave him paralysed with fear. His face drains when he registers what his wife is trying to tell him. He stands motionless for a moment, listening. Trying to understand.

Then Antonio Rolle slumps to his knees, he drops his phone into the base of the boat – its silver glint instantly dulled by the river of fresh blood that swallows it up.

45

Alice

11 days earlier

The secret cove is sectioned off by giant boulders from where the Coral Beach Hotel sits – all shimmery glass and sharp edges. I found it when I first arrived on the island after I followed the little dirt track through the palms and undergrowth that led me here. While Antonio works, I drive here to stare at the frothy waves and think about everything that was taken from us, wondering if we can ever get back to the way things were.

But today is different.

Today there's a boat bobbing far too close to the shore.

It roars to life as I ease the Ford closer to wet sand, drawing white, angry bubbles in the surf as it goes.

The wind's stronger than usual too – it makes the sand grains race along the length of my normally silent beach. The gust dimples the surface of the ocean, muddling the straight line of the horizon – so different to the horizon in Miami, the backdrop for so many of my and Antonio's happiest moments. I picture those evenings after my work at the university when we'd meet at sunset, sip cold beers, our arms touching, our warmth bleeding into each other. Antonio would spend hours talking about his work – a therapy of sorts, but a passion too. The importance of helping others, of never again feeling like that helpless boy that sat by his mother's bed watching her die.

The sequins are what first catch my eye.

They glint in the light as the wind whips the waves, churning everything in their great frothy circles. For a second, I see movement on the top of the rocks, near the Coral Beach Hotel side – a flicker of something. But it's probably just seabirds, observing the greedy waves crashing below. The late afternoon sun bounces off the water. I decide it must be playing tricks on my eyes, as I let myself remember how the rot of trauma slowly began seeping deeper into our lives the further Antonio buried himself in his work. He closed himself off. To me and to the world. Sal Reid may have been the catalyst, but what happened in that cell in Miami was a manifestation of years of difficult cases. Tony saw that as his failure. But, by not being able to help him, I'd failed too.

I squint through the windscreen. Today something just isn't right.

The rough coral sand invades my sneakers as I make my way towards the water. There's no one here but me.

I squint to get a better look at the rainbow colours in the surf, catching my eye. It's then I see what seems to be a body being dragged out.

Instinctively, I race into the water. Waves spit and slap at my face as they claw the sequined form out further. I look back at the beach in desperation, as the current pulls me towards the rocks.

Arms outstretched, I reach towards the person, my eyes blurring, all the blues disorientating. My fingers grasp at heavy material, and I hold on tight.

It's a little girl.

A child.

Her hair fans around her, rippled like silk ribbons. Her head flops to one side. I try to turn back, but we are being dragged closer to the rocks. We have no chance against those slimy boulders. I swim against the insistent current, propelling one arm forward and scooping the water back behind me, while the other pulls the little girl alongside. There's a viciousness to the water I have never experienced before.

Eventually at the shore, I collapse to my knees, breathing heavily. The child's sundress sparkles as she lies in the shallows. Waves lap around us, like tiny hands trying to drag us back in. Her face is frighteningly pale but I scoop her lifeless body up like a baby and walk towards the car, my legs buckling underneath me. I get a better look at her. Arms bent back and her face skywards, it's as if she's sacrificing herself in some way, to some hidden force. I remember Tony describing this feeling – after he raided the house with the little girls during the Sal Reid case. I remember how he said he'd collapsed afterwards, his legs unable to take him any further after the shock of what he'd discovered. He wasn't able to save those children – but maybe I could save this one.

At the SUV, I lie her gently on the sand, my teeth chattering uncontrollably from the shock. A cut to her head bleeds heavily onto the sand – a bright red puddle. I drape my beach towel crudely around her and start to pump her chest. Open the airway, turn my head, listen, pump, wait, blow. Like we'd been taught in school.

But nothing happens.

I try again, wiping away the smear of blood that has turned her face a sickening pink. Then fear gives way to frustration. Months of pent-up emotion spill onto the beach, just like the blood that now gushes steadily beneath the girl's head. I ignore the zigzag of exposed flesh covering one side of her cheek as I bend and blow.

Then, a tiny gasp, almost indecipherable.

She takes a breath and I turn her head to let a thin string of mucus trickle from her parted lips. My phone shakes in my hand as I try to dial. The phone battery is far too low. I fumble to call Antonio's number, praying he'll pick up. It rings out.

'Fuck,' I scream into the abyss, the wind whipping my hair across my own face. With clumsy fingers, I punch in the emergency services digits. It rings twice and someone picks up. I can barely speak, my freezing lips struggle to form words. 'Beach,' is all I can manage.

'Madam,' the woman on the end of the phone says with frustrating detachment. 'Madam, which service do you require?'

Stammering, I try to explain again, but the screen goes blank.

My stomach flips in panic.

It would take at least half an hour to drive to the hospital.

Then a blood-curdling scream comes from behind the rocks – from the other side. I jump up, searching for whatever it was that made that horrible sound. But the black rocks loom before me, too high, blocking access to the Wilkes Beach side. The seagulls screech noisily overhead. Maybe it wasn't a scream at all.

The child moans softly behind me and I know I can't stay here. Hoisting her up against my chest, I manage to lift her into the back seat of the SUV. Then I'm speeding back up the grassy embankment, the wheels spinning in the sand as I press hard on the accelerator.

The child starts to vomit, her head lolling against the beach towel on the leather seat, smearing blood. Unable to get rid of the liquid coming up from her lungs, she gurgles disturbingly. That's when I understand that she will not survive another fifteen minutes like this.

Think, Alice, think.

My heart hammers as I try to decide what the right thing to do is, knowing whatever decision I make now could be the reason the child lives or dies.

I remember Tracey Behan's house, just a few minutes from here. It's one of a few other beachfront properties I manage as short-term lets. I always have all the keys of all my houses and apartments on my keyring. I need to sit the child up – to call for help. I think of the first aid kit there, the warmth. I weigh up the decision, aware of the magnitude of what's at stake.

My foot presses down harder on the accelerator, veering slightly off the road, over the lines at the side of the road, kicking up dust and small pebbles in my haste. *Please child, please live.*

The taste of coppery blood is on my lips. Her blood.

A sharp left turn. Down a small, bumpy avenue with a grassy line at the centre of it, a two-bedroom house greets – hanging baskets burst with frangipanis that sway obliviously by the front door. The sun has begun to lower, staining the sky a dusky orange.

I disarm the urgent beeps before dragging the little girl out of the car. It's only later I realise I should have let it ring out – an alert for others to come, perhaps. But the brain has a funny way of reacting to trauma. We all do different things given the same moment. Her sodden clothes fall heavily to the floor as I wrap the girl in clean sheets, tucking them in around her like she's my own child. She doesn't stir. She's still shivering but breathing more regularly as I wrap thick gauze around her head wound, from a first aid kit under the sink. I apply good pressure to stem the flow. I criss-cross plasters over the jagged wound on her face, trying to ignore how serious the injury looks.

An hour later, I allow myself to breathe once more. The child is sleeping – her gentle breaths a welcome relief from the earlier gasps and gurgles. I alternate the hot water bottle around her body for a while, allowing my own muscles to relax slightly.

By then, darkness has curled around the beach house and there's nobody for miles. I pull the second sofa over to where she lies and rest for a moment, my eyes never leaving her face. I imagine this is how parents watch their children sleeping – a mesmerisation of sorts. Her long eyelashes, like the tips of paintbrushes, flutter against her pale skin. Her blonde hair has dried sea-salt stiff, blood encrusted in places. I push it gently off her face. Her nails are painted pink, chipped and scuffed – and her tiny fingers are still blue tinged from the cold. I rub them, massaging in my own warmth. She's safe here for now.

Then night arrives, the room takes on new shadows. My own eyes grow heavy with the rhythm of her raspy breaths, and I fall into a deep sleep next to my little foundling.

46

Alice

10 days earlier

The light is brighter than usual by the time I open my eyes.

Immediately shocked that it's morning, I jump up and check the child is still breathing. Her colour seems good, though blood from her wound has stained the pillow beneath her head.

It's time to get help.

Antonio mainly sleeps in the basement these days and leaves at dawn. He probably hasn't even noticed I'm not home. He notices very little about me these days, I think sadly.

I flick on the TV to get the time, startled to see it is 12:50 p.m. I have been with the girl for nearly twenty hours.

Then, panic.

Breaking news reports across every local channel: a child has been reported missing. Her parents are guests at the Coral Beach Hotel. I look at the girl beside me. She's called Alannah.

I whisper it. An unfamiliar name. *Al-an-nah*. She's Irish. She's somebody's child.

Pacing the room, dread weighs me down. I need to let someone know that she's safe. That she's here. I don't want to disturb her, but I need Antonio. I need him to fix this, to explain that I did the right thing.

Then, a thought that warms the chill of the moment.

Now he can be the one that finds her. He can save her.

I think of all the cameras and realise this is exactly what it will take for him to finally do what he needs to do. An undoing of the past, perhaps? Redemption. I look at her sleeping face and understand why this is happening. She will be okay for another few hours. I lock the door and drive the short distance home. By the time I pull into the driveway of our rental, the radio news is reporting that her mother was in a bar at the time her child vanished.

What kind of mother does that anyway?

Antonio isn't home. Of course, he isn't, it's the middle of the day. I need him to physically see her and bring her back safely. He needs to be the one that rescues her. With trembling fingers, I charge my phone and grab some food – tomato soup, juice and bananas. I throw some yogurt into the bag and run upstairs for dry T-shirts and more towels, plasters, an icepack. I throw the bag into the Ford and try his number again.

Come on, Antonio. Answer.

I speed back to Tracey's house, driving too fast over the bumpy track, frightened suddenly about how I might find the girl. But she's sleeping still, and I'm not sure if I should wake her or not. I offer her tiny spoons of soup and she stirs a little, but I don't think she knows where she is. I keep the news turned off; I imagine for a little bit that she's mine.

'Mummy,' she groans sometimes. Reaching out.

'Shhh,' I whisper, stroking her little face. 'I'm here. You are safe with me.'

I didn't take her. I saved her.

To save us, Antonio.

—

Then too much time passes and my good deed warps. Now instead of being a hero, I'm going to get Antonio in trouble. I sleep alongside the child, disorientated. Days blur as I care for her. Convincing myself that fixing her will fix us.

Home late again. Sorry Ally. Promise I'll make it up to you x.

I read his text and realise I've already lost him. Suddenly, the thrilling rescue looks like something else – something grotesque; a childless woman stealing a baby from the waves, keeping her from the world. Suddenly, it is something I can no longer control.

I recognise the mother in Calloway when I go to the pharmacy.

I watch her wandering around carrying leaflets, swaying like seagrass, an aimless lean into nothing. Knowing Alannah is safe with me, I allow myself to believe that this is a punishment of sorts. Doesn't she realise the mistake she made? For not loving her child enough to keep her safe. For going to a bar while she wandered off.

The more the media hysteria grows, the more the days begin to blur.

'Are you okay Alice?' Tony keeps asking with worried eyes, when I finally do go home. But this is too big now, too big to say aloud that I'd made everything so much worse for him. As soon as she's fully better, Antonio can rescue her, he can finally have his moment. I picture the cheering crowds, the image of Rolle cradling the child as he delivers her safely back to those she belongs to. It spurs me on, that warped hope that what I am doing is right. As if any good can ever come from such things.

Our little cocoon starts to feel like something else entirely. Something very wrong. I know Alannah needs proper medical help. She's confused. We are both disorientated.

'Mummy,' she whispers often, her little hands waving in agitation. In a perverse way, I feel like I'm protecting her from something. That as long as she's with me, she'll be safe. At dinner in the restaurant, I decide to tell Antonio. To admit what I'd set in motion. But he's distracted. He's so consumed with the case that he barely listens to me.

Then a body is found, and he's gone again. He's with that mother, saving her instead. In fact, he's so busy saving her that he doesn't notice that I'm drowning – that I've been drowning since Miami. I put the Valentine's peonies in a vase at Tracey's house and watch them slowly wilt.

After more days pass, the child won't keep water down. Her breathing grows even more shallow. She's getting worse.

Shortly after, the seizures start.

I hold her small body as she fits, her eyes rolling into the back of her head. I know then I have to end whatever this has become. I'm numb with fear, about how it all looks – how one thing can so quickly become another.

When her body eventually sags, I call my husband's phone over and over, panicking. He finally picks up. It's eleven a.m.

'Alice,' he breathes, as he hears my voice. 'Alice.' He sounds very far away.

'I have the child, Antonio,' I say immediately, clutching the phone to my ear, my voice strangling in my throat. I try to steady my trembling words.

'Alannah. I tried to save her.' I sob. 'Now she won't wake up.'

That's when everything comes crashing down.

47

Mirren

My father swore he saw a mermaid out at sea on the day I was born. 'I walked in after a clatter of a day,' he'd recount, his accent rumbling and melodic, 'and there you were, draped across your mother's chest, a more slippery, red-faced creature I never did see.'

The name Mirren comes from the legend of *Li Ban* – a woman whose entire family drowned. She transformed into a half-human, half-salmon and was eventually caught in a fisherman's net. My mother said it was lucky my father hadn't seen an eel on his way home that day. Now, speeding along on the boat towards Miami General Hospital, towards my daughter who may or may not be alive, I watch the blues blur and understand how *Li Ban* must have felt; trapped underwater while life flowed in distorted ripples above her.

I look up at the other blue, the mirrored sky above. Detective Rolle explained that the air ambulance would transport Alannah the short distance from Kite to the specialist head injury unit in Miami. I search upwards, but the sky is vast and I'm just a small white trail down below.

I pull at the man's oversized shirt I'm swaddled in. I picture the blood-soaked clothes I left behind in a soggy s-shape on the floor the bedroom of that spindly cabin just a few hours ago. Detective Rolle took them from the wardrobe and wrapped me in them, after I'd frantically searched the house for Alannah. By then I was shivering violently, unable to speak, but he guided me through to the house, his own hands shaking, and helped me to change.

Then he disappeared to speak into somebody's phone, Harris pacing beside him, murmuring supportively as Rolle ran a hand over his jaw.

It wasn't just Lottie's blood that had soaked me. Becks was in a bad way when we got back up into the house after the shooting. I adjusted the rough tourniquet that Harris had fashioned and switched to work-mode. I was Dr Fitzpatrick again then. There were other men at the house – some too far gone to help. Then there was Logan. I picture the grim hump of his back, floating, face down in the water under the house, arms outstretched. Then Rolle trying and failing to retrieve Logan's body, as slippery in death as he'd been in life.

Then, completely spent, I sat on the swing chair on the deck of the cabin and howled into the swamp, my daughter's gold chain that I found on the beach the day she disappeared glinting around my own neck. Birds scattered in alarm at the sound of my voice. I surrendered to the fact that Alannah was probably never coming home. Then the swing chair shifted, and Rolle was beside me, running his hands through his hair, creating finger streaks in the blue-black of the strands.

When he spoke, everything shifted once more. He told me what Alice had said. Dropping his head into his hands, he told me quietly what had happened, his words muffled and raw. And I leaned my head on the curved bulk of his shoulder – the uninjured one. Unable to speak, I sobbed in despair on the swing with someone else's blood crusted underneath my fingernails. Rolle, sick with sorrow, didn't move either. And we sat there like that for a very long time. Saying nothing. Alannah was so close to me in that moment, that I could almost hear her little voice calling out.

-

As the police boat gets closer to Miami, I allow myself to think about Alice.

Antonio's wife had saved my daughter, but she might have killed her too. I realise something else; while I was on one side of the rocks, searching for Alannah, Alice must have been on the other, finding her, leading her away. Separated only by the wall of black boulders between us, like a confusing fairground hall of mirrors. A distortion. Or as Rolle had put it, a good intention turned sour. Now, not knowing whether to thank her or hate her was beyond my emotional capabilities.

Just as the boat changes tempo and as we arrive in Miami, I remember something else too. Something even more important.

48

Rolle

Rolle watches Mirren crouch down by the side of the police boat, her dark hair obscuring her face as she bends to examine something clutched in her hands. By then the gears have shifted and the waves churn impatiently under the bow. Buildings loom in the distance – they are almost at Miami. But Rolle's mind is still back in the cabin in Osprey, re-living those last few horrible moments.

After firing the gun at Lovell, Lottie fell backward into the *Rainy Day*, blood from the bullet that caught her ear spread across her face. She'd been lucky. He hadn't demanded answers until she'd been loaded onto the rescue boat on a stretcher. By then, she'd nothing to lose by telling the truth.

Kata and Red looked after the drugs once they arrived into Kite from Mexico, she'd told him, flatly. Florida was considered an easier alternative for smugglers that had upped security on the Mexico/Texan border in recent months. Then usually they'd transport whatever they could – methamphetamine, fentanyl, cocaine – into Miami. More recently they'd been using the cove beside Wilkes Beach. The only information they had was that someone was being paid to look the other way on the Miami side. But none of them realised it was cops paying cops. Not until that night at the boatyard. She'd broken down at the mention of Kata, pleading with Rolle for her own answers. But as far as Rolle knew, the chef's body hadn't yet been found.

And Mariah, Rolle pressed her. What about Mariah Whitaker?

'I used to babysit her,' Lottie had sobbed, still clearly in shock, her face pale, a crude triage bandage covering one side of her head. 'Her and her friend. But all I did was introduce them to Red the night of the bonfire. He's the one who drugged them and decided he could get good cash for them over in Miami.'

The girl seemed relieved to finally unburden herself, Rolle imagined. But what did she think would happen?

He helped lift her stretcher into the waiting boat. She was almost a kid herself – just another one caught up with the consequences of bad choices that seem right at the time. 'Kata had no part of it,' she was keen to emphasise, as a paramedic tucked silver blankets around her. 'He'd only agreed to transport drugs – nothing more. They argued and one girl ran off. The other wouldn't wake up.' Lottie starts to cry. 'They panicked and hid her body, but when the Irish kid went missing, the police came around, so they had to dump her body. Out in the water.'

He pictures poor Mariah's face and closes his eyes. The cruelty of mistakes that break hearts.

–

As the police boat enters Port Miami, the waves churn a little differently. A sense of foreboding descends on Rolle so suddenly that he clings to the polished rail to steady himself. The sun shines obstinately overhead.

Back before cancer ripped Rolle's mother from him, she was the only one who could chase this feeling away. She was the one who reassured him at night that the raincoat thrown awkwardly over the back of the door was just a coat. Nothing more. She'd bend towards him, rearranging the sheets tightly, adjusting the gold cross he always wore around his neck and whisper that everything would be okay. 'There is no such thing as monsters, Antonio,' she'd say, kissing his forehead, smelling faintly of apples. Then she'd leave the door open a crack to let the light in for him.

Back then, his fears were twisted serpents with scales that gleamed like fish-bellies, and ferocious teeth – grotesque creatures that lurked beneath the bed or behind wardrobes. A few years later Rolle learnt about new fears, ones that involved scary-looking tubes and days holding the mixing bowl up to his mother's desperate retches. He'd fall asleep to muffled weeping and increasingly wretched coughs in their thin-walled home, wishing the coat on the door would come to life and swallow him whole. This new creeping monster, the one that began stealing his mother's smile was worse. An invisible scourge no light could possibly tame.

Shaking his head slightly, Rolle thinks of Alice's pitiful sobs in his ear as she told him about the terrible thing she'd done – her words a reminder of just how far they'd drifted. He thought back to all the signs he should have picked up on. His detective skills no match for this emotional blind spot.

'Please don't hate me, Tony. I'm so sorry. I thought I was helping,' she'd wept, her voice frightened and frightening, before he let the phone fall from his fingers in shock. But he couldn't abandon Alice – no matter what she'd done. Besides, he understood that this was all *his* fault. He'd uprooted them, he'd been blind to her unravelling.

We live in a world characterised by duality. Light and dark, good and evil – two sides of the same coin. One impossible without the other. Alice's actions weren't malevolent, he knew that. But he also knew how they'd be twisted by the goddamn media and the rest of the world. There has to be a villain in every story. And they'd make her the monster; he knew they would. Alice's fragility was his priority now, once the poor child survives, of course.

Glancing at perfect blue above, Antonio silently begs the universe to keep Alannah alive. He vows to make things right with his wife. He imagines reaching for her hand, walking through their front door again. He imagines going home.

But Logan's twisted face keeps snapping into his mind, the way he'd sunk slowly down into that gloopy water – one thing pretending to be another. There are some people you just can't save from themselves, no matter how hard you try.

–

At the other end of the boat, Mirren's leaning over the edge watching the sky, one hand over her face, shading it from the harshest light. He imagines what it must be like for her, knowing her daughter has finally been found. The fickle media would already be rowing back on all the aspersions cast on the ice-cold Dr Fitzpatrick. That thought helped ease some pain in the mess he knew lay ahead.

But he'd deal with all of that later. Right now, his head aches as badly as his shoulder. The boat bumps softly against the wooden barrier as they dock, a soft treeline just visible past the humped harbour terminal. Ropes are thrown to be secured. Then Rolle remembers something else Alice said to him. It wasn't long after the Sal Reid case, when some of his deepest regrets were raked up again, like debris deposited untidily on an already-sloped shore.

'There's no shame in not having saved your mother, Antonio,' she'd whispered, her cheek against his, as they swayed sadly one evening in the kitchen when they first arrived in Kite. It was a slower dance than they were used to. 'You need to make peace with that. You can't save everyone.'

Rolle takes a deep breath and remembers how he'd centre himself before a karate tournament – focus on visualisation, on everything turning out all right, even if it never really had. *Can't let the darkness win, son*, his dad would say.

Alannah will be okay, Rolle tells himself, as he steps onto land. And he'd fix the mistake Alice had made.

He'd leave the door open a crack. He'd let the light in.

49

Mirren

Miami General is a pyramid-shaped building surrounded by perfectly pruned palms. Its pristine exterior is framed by manicured lawns both sides of the reception area. Inside is similarly neat and ordered. Walk there, don't go here, no dogs, sanitise your hands. In a place where sick humans and their messy emotions abound, it's all about controlling what you can control.

Nick is the first person I see when we walk through the sliding glass doors. He stands looking for me, searching the faces of the visitors and patients circulating under the spikey modern lights.

For a moment, a few seconds before he notices me, I take in his face. Even unshaven and with dark circles pooling under his eyes, he's attractive. The sleeves of his white shirt are rolled up untidily, and his legs are strong and tanned. Police officers stand close, waiting for Detective Rolle.

Nick and I lock eyes, and I can't help the tide of tears. We walk towards each other. I run the last few steps and slam into his chest. Nick holds me tight, my face buried in his neck. He smells like himself, like trees and toothpaste. Then Réa comes behind us and wraps her arms around us both. Against the angled lines of the shiny hospital building, we are an anomaly – a curve of sobbing humans, curled tight.

'She came round for a few minutes.' Nick clutches my hand, not letting go, even when we eventually step back to get our bearings. As if he'll lose me too if he's not careful.

'But she's weak. They're running tests. We don't know anything else yet.'

I look at Réa, who eyes me uncertainly – it is too much for all of us to imagine that Alannah is alive, that she is really here. The idea of touching her, of holding her, is still impossible to believe. Réa reaches for my other hand. I'm not sure if it's for me or for her, but either way I'm grateful for its warmth against my icy fingers. I squeeze back tightly. It will be okay, my grip reassures. *We will be okay, you and I.*

Nick leads the way, up the escalator, towards the first-floor wards, but first I glance back at Rolle who is deep in a mobile phone conversation, his voice low, sadness etched across his eyes.

I know Rolle is suffering. His work is only beginning: an investigation into what Lottie knew, Lovell and his father's corruption to untangle, and a trip back to Kite Island to speak to Alice – to try to understand.

We all have our secrets, some deeper than others.

I catch his eye as he paces the reflective floors of the lobby, gesturing while he talks, waving away medical staff who hover around to try and treat his injury. His strength is somehow diminished by the slump of his shoulders. I remember this is the hospital where he told me his mother died.

This is the end of something, we both know that.

Thank you, I mouth slowly from across the other side of the lobby as the escalator whirs and rises. I remain facing him.

He watches me ascend, and answers with the gentle nod I've grown to know over the last few weeks. A half-smile in acknowledgement, but his brow is creased, those almond eyes troubled.

Being the hero doesn't always mean winning. In fact, maybe it never does. But Antonio Rolle believed in me when nobody did, not even my own husband.

Antonio Rolle didn't find Alannah, but he never gave up on me. For that I would always be grateful. He resumes his pacing, one hand raking back his hair. He glances at me one last time, gives a small bow too.

Or maybe I imagined that part.

I turn away.

Not everyone gets their happy ending – even if they deserve it. But I'll take mine.

The mechanics of the stairs snag and judder, then drag onwards. I leave one level behind and move towards the next.

Towards Alannah.

50

Mirren

We huddle at the nurses' station, waiting for the doctor they paged to arrive.

'It's important you speak to him before you see your daughter,' the nurse explains. 'To update you about how she's doing.'

I glance at the clock behind her and sway, suddenly feeling the effects of the last twenty-four hours.

Nick puts his hand out to steady me. 'Woah, you okay? Sit down, Mirren.'

'I need to see Alannah.' My voice is louder than I plan.

'As I've said, Professor Hussain won't be long,' the nurse repeats, leaning over us to take a clipboard from a man in blue scrubs. More people line up behind us.

Suddenly all my suppressed anger rises from deep within.

'Bring me to my daughter. I need to see her.' I'm almost spitting at the wide-eyed nurse, but I can't take any more obstacles. I must see her, to reassure her that nothing that came before matters. I want to cleanse the past, like the way my father washed away the fish guts that clung to the insides of his boat, sloshing buckets of salt water roughly against its edges. Nick puts his arm around my shoulder and tries to lead me away, but I shake him off and move back towards the front desk, pointing my finger at the nurse.

'Tell me where my child is.' I'm just inches from the woman's face when I drop my voice. 'Right now.'

'Dr Fitzpatrick?' An authoritative voice cuts through the stand-off and a smiling man of Middle Eastern descent steps forward with his hand outstretched in greeting. He's about Réa's height and is wearing a grey suit. He pushes his glasses further up his nose with his forefinger.

'Is she okay?' I ask, as he leads us into a small side room and gestures for us to sit down. The formality is suffocating.

'Just tell us, please,' I implore, my hands out, palms up. What is it that they won't tell us?

'Alannah is sedated after having undergone some tests, but we are hopeful she'll wake up soon. I'd like to tell you what we know so far about her condition if I may?' He looks from Nick to Réa and then back to me. There's a box of tissues on the table. How many hearts have been broken in this room? I want to ask. But the truth is that it's a horrifyingly familiar backdrop. The difference is that I'm usually the other side of the desk. How many hearts had *I* broken in rooms just like this? More importantly, why had I never kept count?

Réa stands as Nick reaches over across the divide between the two chairs to hold my hand, but I shake it roughly off. I need to hear everything, without any distractions. Nick asks permission to record the conversation and Réa gazes out of the window, as if to escape this too-small room. Like a bird trapped in a cage.

'Alannah was dehydrated and undernourished when she was found.' The doctor begins. 'We have reason to believe that she may have an acquired brain injury – which would explain some of the seizures she's been experiencing. It's likely it happened when she hit her head on the rocks as she fell into the water, as described by the witness who found her.'

'Jesus Christ,' I whisper. Réa reaches both hands up to the sides of her head, rubbing the flat of her palms against her temples, as if trying to massage the vision away. Nick sits quietly, perfectly still.

'Until we get the test results and obviously run some more, we won't know the extent of it,' Dr Hussain continues. 'From a pessimistic outlook, we may be talking about speech difficulties, problems moving... personality changes.'

Nick breathes in sharply. But I know how this goes. I've seen the flicker of that light behind patient's eyes, exactly like he's describing. I've seen that clouded confusion diminish a person before my own eyes.

Not always. But sometimes. Enough times.

'However,' Dr Hussain looks up from his notes, sensing our dismay, 'there are indications, already in Alannah's case, that it could be quite mild. She's responding well, considering all she's been through. We will know more as soon as she wakes, and over the following weeks, but the paediatric brain is still developing. That's on her side.'

'She recognised me.' Nick speaks for the first time. 'When I was with her in the air ambulance, she called me Daddy.'

His voice breaks and he turns away for a moment to contain his emotions.

Dr Hussain nods encouragingly. 'And that's a very positive sign, Mr Fitzpatrick. But while we wait for neuroimaging results, I'll warn you that often in cases like this, we find post-traumatic amnesia – she may not remember everything that happened immediately after the injury. Her memories may be fragmented. We are also looking for intracranial injuries like bruising or blood on the brain. Those things take time to appear, if at all.'

'So, it is unlikely she'll remember what happened?' I ask, and Dr Hussain nods.

'Will she recover?' Réa speaks for the first time. I look down at my hands. This line of questioning is far too devastating to absorb. This is her sister she's talking about.

'The severity of the traumatic brain injury isn't always apparent, especially so soon after the incident. But I'm hopeful that Alannah will still be the same little girl, eventually. Already her hearing and sight seem intact. There are also excellent rehabilitation facilities in Ireland that can help her recover anything she may have lost. We can put you in touch with those in due course. If needed,' he adds.

'Lost?' Nick repeats. We're all so surprised that she's here, that we've not considered the problems that may surface later.

'Like I said, Mr Fitzpatrick, we'll know more in the coming days. Now shall we go see her?'

–

Walking through the hospital, the clinical smells bring me back to the morgue, the moment when I looked at the picture of poor Mariah. Nick tightens his grip around my hand as Dr Hussain pauses in front of a room, the last on the right. I push open the door, bracing myself for what lies behind it.

The room is in semi-darkness, save for the pale light from a standing lamp in the corner. The specialised bed takes up almost the entire room. An army of monitors stand guard both sides of the bed.

Then I see her.

Tubes slither around her little body as if they're pinning her down. I follow the trail of one line downwards until it reaches the small hump huddled under the blue hospital sheets. Alannah.

Reaching towards the shape of my daughter, I stroke her face – the face I've dreamt about, the face I know off by heart. I clasp her hand to my lips, kiss it softly and whisper an apology into her lifeless fingers. I'm sorry I wished you away, I whisper, my lips on her skin. Her head is wrapped in white gauze, a small sprig of blonde hair peeking out above it like the top of a pineapple. Her cheek nearest Nick is the injured one, and I can't yet see the injury they told us was there. She is thin and frail but here with us again.

Finally, things could be right.

Nick goes around the side of the bed and takes Alannah's other hand. Sedation has left her pale and peaceful. Réa stands at the foot of her bed. She breaks down at the sight of her little sister, pushing tears away with the back of her hand. We stay like this for a while. Each lost in our own thoughts, weighing up all the joy and pain that brought us to this moment, interrupted only by the steady beep from the machines.

My overriding hope is that she doesn't remember a thing. She shouldn't ever know what happened to her. She can't ever know.

Alannah's eyes dance in her sleep, the delicate skin of her eyelids moving as she dreams, in whatever twilight she now inhabits. I think back to my dream on the beach – when I tried to grasp her hand and failed. I grip her little fingers more tightly now, noticing the chipped pink nail varnish I'd painted on for the hotel show she was supposed to take part in.

I rub a circuit over her hand, her thumb first, around the back of her hand, a gentle squeeze. I do this over and over until she finally stirs. Her eyelids flutter open – just like they did as a baby. She turns her head slowly towards me and tries to speak. Nick stands up and leans close to her face.

It's then I see how bad the injury across her face is. A distortion of her smooth flesh criss-crossing her left cheek. Réa comes around my side of the bed, hesitantly.

'Alannah,' I say gently, trying to slow my own heartbeat. 'Do you know where you are?'

There's a moment when she looks at me – her eyes clouded with something I don't recognise. I grip the side of the bed tightly. It almost makes me take a step backward.

But then I see it. I see that it's her.

'Mummy,' she croaks and coughs a little, grimacing in pain. She looks at Réa and her eyes immediately soften.

I breathe out a lifetime of sadness. I let everything I've felt over the past days, over the past eight years, over the past forty something years, slip from my shoulders, into a puddle of pain, and guilt, onto the hospital floor. I let it wash over me, trying to imagine it absolving me from everything that came before.

Nothing else matters. Except right now, here in this room. I imagine what we might look like, four heads bent together, hope coiled tightly around our shoulders, the quiver of anticipation about the next chapter. About what happens now.

We sit there, Nick, Alannah, Réa and I, in the half-light, holding hands. And although nobody knows exactly what comes next, we hold on tightly, our bodies curled towards each another, as day slowly turns into night.

Epilogue

Great Ormond Street Hospital for Children, London

One month later

The girl's skinny legs shake as she tries to raise her arms over her head. She's doing well, thinks Nurse Kate. She'll be here for another two weeks, trying to rebuild her strength and to repair some of the damaged nerve pathways that continue to slow her down. Alannah's hair hasn't yet grown back where they'd shaved it. Trying to even it out, the child's mother had cut her long golden strands, leaving her looking pathetically sweet.

Kate was there when Alannah and her mother looked at the facial injury together in the mirror, when the gauze was finally changed. Alannah had touched it gently, the scar that ran the length from her left ear to her cheek, across her eye. 'I look different,' she'd said, her voice wobbly. The wound was too jagged to stitch, the doctors had agreed, but skin grafts could be a possibility down the line. Kate was distracted by Dr Fitzpatrick's horrified face.

Kate's Irish too. She's grown close to the family during the time since they arrived from the media circus in America. She spends a lot of time with Alannah, singing her favourite songs, mainly in Gaeilge to her. They make the child giggle, even though Kate knows they mostly end sorrowfully.

Tá cailín álainn, a dtug mé grá dhi
Sí 's deis' is áille, ná bláth 's ná rós
Gan í ar láimh liom, is cloíte atá mé

Ó a chailín álainn, 's tú fáth mo bhróin
There's a beautiful girl to whom I gave my love
She is kinder and lovelier than a flower or rose
Without her hand in mine, I'm weak
O beautiful girl, you're the cause of my grief

Kate's family in Tipperary couldn't believe she was nursing the famous child from the television. *What's the mother like?* was the first question her own mother asked, dropping her tone conspiratorially. The truth was that Dr Fitzpatrick was understandably anxious, always asking questions about when Alannah's outbursts would subside. Kate had done her best to explain, but she'd seen that look on people's faces – the realisation that an injury like this can change a person. Accepting the change in Alannah, that wasn't going to be straightforward, even if her mother was a doctor.

She'd been outside Alannah's room, the other day, when she heard the husband and wife speaking in low voices and peered in. 'I'm trying,' Mirren Fitzpatrick was saying, tears coursing down her cheeks. And Nick back to her, reproaching: 'Jesus, Mirren. She needs you now more than ever.' Alannah had been at a physio session at the time.

The sister never says much either. Kate knows this is the kind of tragedy that could erode even the closest of families. But Réa Fitzpatrick spends her days looking out angrily from underneath her thick black fringe. Everyone is on edge. Especially because of the nightmares. Most nights, Alannah wakes up screaming, imagining she is in the water again. Kate wonders sometimes if the time Alannah spent in that woman's house had traumatised her. The psychologist spoke to the family – about learning to live with change, about redefining expectations and managing stress. Sometimes she'd speak to the family without Alannah present. Funny how you become part of the furniture when you're a nurse – silently floating through the room caring and fixing, and nobody notices. The psychologist said once that she wasn't sure if Alannah didn't remember, quite common with such injuries, or if the shock of the experience had been suppressed because it was too much for to handle. She gifted Alannah a small pink notebook as 'homework' and asked her to draw anything that she could remember – anything at all.

All Alannah knew was that she'd had an accident. Nothing more. They kept her away from the news, as everyone waited to see what she'd remember in her own time.

Kate, however, was glued to the networks. She learnt that Alannah had been treated well by that lady – the detective's wife who found her. But maybe if she got help sooner, she wouldn't have such health challenges. Withholding treatment and blocking an investigation would make up part of the case against that woman, Alice. Kate had seen the footage of her being led into the police station, a coat over her head, her husband running ahead of her, up the steps, pushing the cameras roughly out of the way, his face haunted by stress. Mirren had watched the news beside Kate, grim-faced and silent.

How did she react? Kate's mother wondered during her weekly phone call to Tipperary. *When she saw the footage?*

It looked to Kate like utter terror, but she'd told her mother not to be so judgemental.

After that, the Fitzpatrick family had issued a statement asking for leniency, pointing out that Alice Rolle had saved their daughter's life. The complexities of what came next shouldn't discount that, it said. Kate wasn't the only one who was surprised at their graciousness. Social media had gone into overdrive with all kinds of wild theories about what had really gone on during that holiday.

–

On the day before the Fitzpatricks were to return to Ireland, Alannah had her worst nightmare yet. Kate held her hand as she thrashed and screamed. Normally Dr Fitzpatrick did the nights, holding her daughter's hand.

Sometimes whispering, always weeping.

That night the screaming was much louder, the child far more disorientated. When she finally woke, Kate was stroking her head. 'I was on the beach,' Alannah told her. Wide-eyed, Kate held her breath. Alannah had never mentioned the incident before.

'I was looking for Mummy. I couldn't see her. She wasn't at the bar.' The child's words were tumbling out, crashing against one another, the puckered flesh on one side of her face lit up by the light from the street. Kate felt uneasy somehow.

'Réa brought me to the rocks, I was catching fish with my net.'

It was as if she was remembering everything at once.

'The fish were so fast; I couldn't reach. I was too high.' Alannah started crying loudly then, thrashing against the frame of the bed, her hands balled into fists.

'I climbed to the tallest rock—' She stopped then, her chest heaving as she remembered, and then fell back onto the pillow, gasping for air.

But it was what happened next that gave Kate goosebumps.

The child sat bolt upright and started screaming, a series of short, piercing shouts that came together as one straight line of horror. 'No, no, no,' she screams. 'Stop. Please no!'

Kate spotted the notebook beside the bed and thrust it at her. 'Draw it, Alannah. Get it out of your head.'

An hour later, Kate peeked in at the child. Both parents had arrived. She was sedated, her misshapen hair stuck up behind her. It reminded Kate of when she'd lopped all her Barbie dolls' hair off as a kid. 'You've destroyed them,' her mother had scolded. But she was only trying to make them better. The next morning Alannah had reverted to her distant stare. Laura, Kate's shift replacement arrived early to give her a bath ahead of her discharge. But as Kate left, she spotted the pink notebook tucked in under the locker by her bed.

Impulsively she reached for it and, glancing over her shoulder, opened the first page.

What had the child been so afraid of?

There's a pencil drawing of a girl standing on the beach. The cartoon sunshine has two eyes and a big smile drawn on its surface. Kate smiles too. There is an arrow pointing to the girl with the name A-L-A-N-N-A-H scrawled in spidery handwriting. She turns the page. Another drawing. The small girl-shape is standing on top of a pile of black circles – rocks, with a small fishing net. Kate hears a sound behind her and instinctively drops the notebook. But it's only the kitchen staff rolling past with the breakfast trays. She picks it up, flicks the next page over, her mouth dry.

On the next page, the same stick figure of the little girl is drawn, this time falling into the water on the other side of the rocks. A drawing of a taller person catching the little girl in an oversized net held in both hands – scooping her out of the sea. There's a bright rainbow overhead. That must be the detective's wife scooping her up.

Then Kate notices a jagged tear line dissects the notebook between both pages – as if something has been ripped out. As if there's another part to this story.

And it's gone.

Kate's heart beats too fast. Maybe that's all Alannah remembers, she considers. After all, the doctors had explained that most brain injuries mean the victim doesn't remember everything. But… she runs her fingers over the central spine of the notebook. There are tiny tear lines where it looks like more pages have been torn out in the middle.

Something isn't right.

Kate walks around to the bin on the other side of the bed. Empty.

She hears a small creak as the door opens. Dr Fitzpatrick walks in quietly.

Kate jumps involuntarily, knowing straight away that her body language is ridiculous. 'Hi,' she squeaks, suddenly mortified by her embarrassing conspiracy theories.

'Is everything okay, Kate?' Mirren smiles.

For such a tiny person, her sharp features command attention. She's wearing cream trousers, the crease perfectly ironed, and a long, burgundy cardigan. Her hair is blow-dried into a dark halo, and with her eyeliner, she looks like a completely different person to the delicate creature on the news Kate had watched with her family at home. Is it just her imagination or does Dr Fitzpatrick's face change when she sees what Kate is clutching in her hands? A small ripple of something crosses over it and then, just as quickly, passes. Her serene smile returns. Kate gently rests the notebook back onto the bed and smooths the sheets self-consciously. 'I've just finished my shift, so I wanted to say goodbye. Laura's giving Alannah her bath.' She squeezes past Dr Fitzpatrick, noticing a strong smell of brandy.

'Thanks for everything, Kate,' Dr Fitzpatrick says, blinking slowly, her eyes slightly unfocused. Kate hasn't seen her like this before. So detached.

Once out of the room, she glances back at the mother.

With the sun coming from the window behind her, the woman's eyes look almost black for a moment, blank and unreadable. Then the light changes, a cloud over the sun perhaps, and Dr Fitzpatrick's face comes back into focus.

It *has* been a long shift. Her mother would call it the long stare – so exhausted that your mind plays tricks. 'Bye Kate,' Mirren calls softly and although she was always complaining about being too hot on the ward, Kate shivers.

Mirren

I shut the door behind the nurse and pat the pocket of my cardigan gently. The pages torn out from the notebook crinkle against soft wool. You see, the truth is never straightforward. And none of the pieces ever fit perfectly together.

Alannah never returned from that beach that day.

The moment she fell from the rocks and into the sea, she was swallowed up, lost to me. Like I'd always known. Sometimes I look at the little girl in the hospital bed and wonder who she is, who she ever was? I picture the zig-zag ridges of her skin that refused to knit back together – a disconnect.

I spent my life losing things. Well, this time I refuse to let it be taken from me.

You see, I know who pushed her.

I know who stood there paralysed after it happened, a moment of jealousy, an impulse. I figured it out that day on the police boat to Miami. I looked down at the blood on my hands, blood that wasn't my own, and I remembered something important. Something I'd been given. Unfolding the pencil sketch she'd done for me, I stared at all the grey squiggles that make up a person. Those eyes, so similar to mine, stared back at me from the page and I realised the drawing wasn't of Alannah at all.

It was Réa. She'd drawn it as I slept that day at the hospital on Kite Island. A self-portrait, half in shadow, the page edges rough, the white parts smudged. On the back, she'd written her own version of an explanation.

Maybe I'd always known she'd been involved once I found Alannah's phone at the bottom of her bag in the hotel room. I think of the nail marks that appeared on baby Alannah's arms a few weeks after she came to us. White fingermarks against the pink of her flesh. Réa had always been so resentful, so jealous of the love she refused to share.

And now I had to choose.

I considered telling the authorities the truth. I spent nights running it through in my head, the most torturous of thoughts. But I can't risk them taking Réa from me. I can't risk losing her too. She's the only thing that's truly ever been mine.

None of this comes easy, by the way.

But I can't deny who I am anymore. Because even though my father scrubbed his boats incessantly, he perpetually stank of fish.

The little nightingale from the bedtime story I used to tell Réa understood the sacrifices we are forced to make for love. Because after the little bird spent the night singing with a thorn in her heart, the rose finally took shape. A rose with bloodied petals.

Louder and louder grew her song. Bitter, bitter was the pain and wilder, wilder grew her song. Then fainter, fainter still.

The beautiful rose pierces the little nightingale's heart, her wings grow quiet, and the light fades from her eyes.

Don't look at me like that. There are some sacrifices you must make, even when it breaks your heart.

I tap on the bathroom door, a little unsteady now, I'll admit. A nurse is combing out the wispy remains of Alannah's once golden hair. The child looks up at me, smiles crookedly. For a moment I think of my mother, her hair fanned out, fear still etched in her dead, watery eyes.

'I'll take over from here.'

The child says nothing – still in a faraway land I cannot reach. I realise now that this is the scar I've always carried. The one simply too jagged to ever heal.

The nurse leaves and I close the bathroom door.

Only I hear the soft metallic click, as I lock it gently behind me.

She looks at me in the mirror with eyes that look like none of us.

I have two daughters – only one of them shares my face.

I turn to face the girl.

Acknowledgements

I loved writing this book. I'm so proud of it. But it wouldn't have been possible without the hard work and dedication of some brilliant people. It's a pleasure to express my heartfelt thanks to all those who supported me along the way. Their names should be up there on the front cover too.

I'm especially grateful to everyone at Canelo for their expertise and guidance in bringing this story to life. A special thank you to Louise Cullen for such incredibly insightful editorial steering and Siân Heap for her detective's eye for detail.

To Madeleine Milburn, my utterly brilliant agent and all the dream team at MM – especially Liv Maidman and Rachel Yeoh who have championed this book tirelessly from its very first inception.

Sincere thanks also to Glenn Meade, industry stalwart and my very generous mentor who continues to motivate and inspire me with his very sage advice on thriller writing.

To my cousin Michael O'Connell of the South Carolina Police Department for walking me through all the elements of the US crime processes. Any errors are, of course, mine. A big confident and dramatic thank you to Eva Coffey for her generous time which I enjoy so much.

To my siblings Tracey, Barry, Paul and Annika Cassidy and all my extended family. I'm so grateful for their continuous cheerleading, for this book and always. To my sister Annika, for all the creative collaboration and willingness to brainstorm any time of the day or night.

To my mother-in-law, the late, great Anna Mulvee, for her endless kindness and unwavering belief in me. She continues to inspire me every day. To Patrick Mulvee, my favourite father-in-law, for insisting on celebrating all the early successes, and for the countless gelato jaunts.

To my own parents, Noel and Ann Cassidy, who didn't just show me the world but told me I could go get it too.

To the great community of writers that never fails to lift me up. Especially Andrea Mara and Linda O'Sullivan for all their encouragement (and croissants). Thanks to Ashley Audrain and Kathryn Croft for their kind support as I navigated the initially daunting world of publishing.

Thank you to my fabulous girlfriends for always spurring me on and for understanding my tendency to daydream. To the school mums who support me in more ways than they'll ever truly know.

Finally, and above all, to my personal dream team:

To the best children world; Eva, Bobby and Isabella. Thank you for inspiring me. From the hand-drawn book cover suggestions to the alternative (HUGELY creative) ending ideas, you have been so incredibly patient and sweet while Mummy wrote pretty much everywhere we went. This is all for you.

To my husband Karl. Thank you for reading every single word and for being so unfailing kind and wise with each draft. Thank you for all the cups of tea, the excuses for bubbles (another chapter done!), our shared sunrises and the reassurance, in your very Karl way, that of course I could do it.

And that I'd smash it.